It's Hard Being the Same

****

ERIC "TURK" CURTIS

First Printing: 2016

ISBN 978-0-9978293-9-6

Published by Ricky Gaines

Cover Design: F. Ruiz

Assistant Editor: Ricky Gaines

Senior Editor: A. Parra

Capital Gaines LLC
4023 Kennett Pike #2082
Wilmington, DE 19807
Email: capitallgainesllc@gmail.com
Phone: 415-857-5433
Website: www.capgainesllc.com

Acknowledgements

First I'd like to say thanks to Marilyn E. Curtis, my amazing mother, who after 20 years never gave up on me, and always encourages me to keep striving to do more. To the late Jeffrey Little, he showed me no matter where you are there's always a story to tell. To the other two members of *Uncaged Stories*, Rahsaan 'NJ' Thomas, Julian 'Luke' Padgett, I thank you both for opening my eyes and for me to get over my stubbornness. To Zoe Mullery, each week you come to San Quentin and share with us your knowledge of writing. You taught me that it's okay to think outside my comfort zone and I was asked to do that with my short stories.

Eric 'Turk' Curtis

Dedication

This novel is dedicated to big dreamers, to real hustlers, and to the usefulness of transferable skills...

To my Capital Gaines LLC Team... Thank you very much for having the courage, faith, confidence and fortitude to rock-steady with me on this movement.

Extra special credit goes to the first lady of the Capital Gaines Team - because you are without a doubt, the heart and soul of this enterprise. Thank you very much for being yourself - which is Big Hearted, God-fearing, and Loyal.

To the author, "Turk", Congratulations Bruh'! I told you that we were gonna' do the damn-thang'! You've created an excellent work of fiction, and it's been a pleasure to publish. This is not the first, and it won't be the last "L.A. TO THE BAY" connection. Hopefully though, next time we won't have so many damn obstacles to overcome. LOL.

To our readers everywhere, thank you and I hope you enjoy.

Cheers to longevity, healthy living, and even bigger dreams.

Ricky Gaines \ Slick-G \ Publisher

It's Hard Being the Same

****

ERIC "TURK" CURTIS

Chapter 1

CANDY

"Candy will you wake up, we're gonna' be late," Sandy said.

"Damn Sandy, I'm up already, and all that yelling isn't gonna' make me move any faster," I said, slowly beginning to move.

"You know this is our last day of school forever, now you need to get yo' butt up."

"Man, you act like you got something planned," I said.

"You can best believe I got something planned, and it's called you and I getting paid in a major way. But right now you need to get up so we can get this graduation over with. Candy, you know mama is gonna' be up in here doin' all that yellin' if you don t hurry up."

"Don't you see me movin'? Damn, just because we're twins don't mean I have to move every time you move," I said, becoming annoyed by Sandy's harassment.

"Yo' butt seemed to move just fine last night when you was taking them niggaz' money on that pool table. You worked them outta' every dime they had," Sandy said, bluntly.

"That was different. I was in my element last night. You put some titties in somebody's face and there is no way they can concentrate." We both laughed.

As you can see Sandy and I are identical twins. We're eighteen going on twenty-five. We have shoulder length hair, skin that looks like caramel, almond shaped eyes, and both of us pretty much have the bodies that would make any straight woman do a double take. Although our mom, Promise, tries to make sure we have everything we need and most of what we want, the two of us still find ways to hustle, and last night was no different. Sandy had on a cut to fit Royal Blue mini skirt and matching heels. With us being over six feet tall, it looked like her legs went on forever. I wore an off white leather skirt and matching jacket, high heels and just a cream color bra under my jacket. Since I wasn't planning on letting anyone get too close to me I wasn't trippin'.

Being born and raised in Compton California, things were not always easy, and again, mama did what she could to make sure we were alright. Jamel, our dad did his part when he could. They separated when we were young, but Sandy and I loved them both the same. Jamel was, and I guess you can say still is, a Compton Crip. But he couldn't leave the streets alone. Mama said what was even worse, was that he couldn't leave those other women alone. But I must say he really came through eight months ago on our eighteenth birthday. When we awoke that morning there were two brand new Volkswagen Jettas outside for us.

With Jamel being one of Compton's biggest hustlers, I have no doubt he hit some kind of lick to get them. I never really been able to talk to him about his street life, but Sandy would ask him any and everything. Sometimes she got the answer she wanted, other times he would tell her something like, "Baby girl, if you put people up on game there's two thangs that can happen. Niggaz will find a way to mess up yo' shit or they will tell the police on you, and believe me, you never want them people in yo' business."

So last night we took my car because Sandy could care less about driving. She would rather kick back, smoke a joint to get her head right and play dee-jay. It was early Friday night and we were on our way to Long Beach. The Vault 360 is supposed to be the hottest club out there right now.

"Sis, this new Sade is really nice," Sandy said, turning up the car stereo.

"I know. Now you gonna' let me hit that or what?" I said.

"Girl you know yo' butt don't be smoking like that."

"Yeah I know, but every once in a while I will, and besides, that smells good as hell," I said, reaching for it.

"You know sis, sometimes you really amaze me. Here!" Sandy said, passing me the joint.

As we reached the club, it was just turning eight o'clock and there were more people in the parking lot than there was inside the club itself. Being that Long Beach was just like Compton, one big ass ghetto, niggaz was out there trying to shine. There were a few high end cars, but the rest were strictly hood cars and trucks. Black and Yellow Bird, both Kelly Park Boyz' had their drop top low riders out.

"Candy you know I love the way Black's "64" be lookin', his shit is hella' clean...You see the black with peanut butter insides...sitting on 13" hundred spokes...Ooo' Girl, he's shittin' on fools," Sandy said, smiling and in complete admiration of both Black and his 1964 Chevy Impala low rider.

"Girl, that fool need to take some notes from his boy Yellow and update that shit with some dubs or deuces," I said, while hitting the joint.

Sandy may act like she don't, but she's had it bad for Black Bird since our first year of high school.

"You know what sis, I just might buy me one of those after we hit this lick," said Sandy.

"There you go again. Shit, for the last two weeks all you've been talkin' about this so-called lick. What is it, and when are you going to tell me about it?"

"Soon, I promise. Hey, why don't you pull over there so I can say "hi", to Black?"

"Oh hell nah, you see all these niggaz in this parking lot?" I said.

"Yeah so, what's that got to do with anything?" said Sandy

"Sis you know I love you, but I didn't get dressed like this to do no parkin' lot pimpin'. Besides, I'm hungry as hell. So let's go to T.G.I.F.'s, and get something to eat. We'll talk there, and by the time we're done we should be ready to get our groove on in the club," I said.

"I'm with that, and since moms didn't cook tonight, I might as well let you buy me something to eat," Sandy said.

"Oh wait, there's Toni," I said. She was sitting on her fly ass

Camry.

"Who is that she talking to?" said Sandy.

"I don't know, but you know if he ain't no crip, she wouldn't have any words for him," I said, as I pulled up and let my window down.

"What's up baby boy? You sure are lookin' right. What's your name?" I asked, knowing Toni was already up on game because the three of us were almost inseparable.

"They call me Voodoo, what's yours?" he said.

"Candy. Is that your lady?"

"Nah, but I'm tryin' to make it that way," he said.

"Damn bitch", Toni said, "you just gonna' get at him right in front of me like that?"

"Look at him though, he's so fine. Where you from Voodoo?" I said, smiling.

"Due Rock Crip, why, you plan on coming to pay me a visit?"

'I don't know, I might," I replied.

"Well why don't you get out and holla at us for a sec?" Voodoo asked.

"Nigga if you saw all the ass that would get outta' this car you might fuck around and call the police," I said.

"Bitch, I don't believe this shit, you gonna' disrespect me like that? Now if I was to hit yo' ass with some hot 380 slugs you'd think I was wrong," Toni said. All the while Sandy was over there on the passenger's side laughing hysterically, barley able to control herself.

"Shit, now y'all hold up, ain't nobody doin' no shootin', and if they do, it's gonna' be me. Y'all two is fine and all that, but I'mma' gangsta, and that bull shit game y'all tryin' to run ain't shit. But I'll tell you what, let me knock back a couple of "X" pills or some "Molly's" and I'll blow all three of y'all backs out," Voodoo said.

"Layla," Sandy said, "I know you not gonna' let this thug ass nigga come around my nephew? His ass probably got more bullet holes then 2Pac did. Then you talkin' about fuckin' somebody, nigga please, it ain't that much fuckin' in a damn orgy. Layla, lock up yo' shit and come on we're going to get something to eat."

"Layla, I thought you said your name was Toni?" said Voodoo.

"It is, but a select few get to call me Layla," Toni said.

"Shit, how many names do you have?" Voodoo asked her.

"Enough, and if you're lucky, the next time you see me, I might tell you the rest," Toni said.

"Shit that sounds good, and you can best believe I wanna' see yo' sexy self again."

"Well right now I'm going with my sisters and then I'm sure we're coming back here, so tonight might be your lucky night."

She hit the alarm on her Camry and blew Voodoo a kiss. All he could do was say damn as he watched the Black and Samoan beauty jump in the car. Toni is not as tall as we are, but in every other aspect she was just as pretty as us, if not more so. Her extra-long curly hair usually got guys' attention first, and we won't even talk about her body yet. She's just a natural born beauty…but ghetto'ed out the game. The three of us spoiled the hell outta' her son Daishawn, he's so cute.

Watching Voodoo take off, Toni asked, "Candy, when are you gonna' stop playing that bull shit game of yours? You know that shit don't work," Toni said, sounding kinda' pissed.

"Fuck that," I told her, "you see how sexy that nigga was?"

"Yeah, and if he can ride and change my gears like he did that Suzuki 1000, I know it's gonna' be all good."

"Check this out," Sandy said, "I bet his ass is broke as hell."

"I don't know," Toni said, "I can smell money a mile away."

"Well that's good," Sandy told Toni, "cause I'mma' need yo' smart ass to do just that."

"What?" Toni asked.

"To find this money that I know is out there," Sandy said.

"What?" Toni asked again.

"To find this money that I know is out there," Sandy said, repeating herself.

"What the hell are you talkin' about Sandy?" Tony asked, sounding confused.

"Toni, don't pay her ass no attention, for the last two weeks she's been talkin' about hitting some lick," I say, to Toni.

"Yeah, and I plan on doing just that. Toni, you're the smartest person we know," Sandy insisted, "hell, you could make a computer have an orgasm if you wanted to. We're gonna' need yo' skills to keep us outta' prison." It was true, even though Toni was straight ghetto, she was M.I.T. College material. She has a 4.0 G.P.A., and hates any and everything to do with school. But she insisted on learning all she could. She said, "Hell, if I gotta' be in that bitch every day, I'mma' learn something while I'm there." And learn she did. I think it came from her dad. With him being incarcerated all these years, he's always putting her up on game. He was always telling her, 'Just because you're from Compton, mostly everybody around you will be all street, some kind of hustler. That means we mimic our surroundings, so in some way you're gonna' be all street too, a hustler. But if you get an education and combine that with what you learn from the streets, no one will be able to get over on you.'

He also told her, 'Baby girl, I notice two things from your letters. You love gangstaz and you have an uncanny ability to learn. Wherever you choose to go in life, use that. And if you ever find yourself throwing rocks at the penitentiary-like I did, just make sure it's big ones and you know what you're doing.'

"Sandy, I don't know what type of shit you got going on inside that head of yours, but I ain't tryin' to go to prison for nobody. I'm still tryin' to find a way to get my pop's outta' there," Toni said.

"Well if that slow driving-ass nigga over there would hurry up and get us to Friday's, I'll tell y'all about it while we eat," Sandy said.

"Shut up nigga, you always talkin' shit," I said.

"Toni, you know how I feel about yo Pops," Sandy continued, "and I ain't trying to put you on the inside of them walls with him. But if we pull this off, we're each lookin' at four or five million dollars."

"Bitch, are you crazy?" Toni half screamed, pulling herself towards the front seat, "four or five million. Fool we couldn't get that kind of cash if we robbed a dozen banks."

"Sandy, I'm not robbing no banks," I said, looking at her

sideways.

"Candy did you hear me say anything about robbing any banks?"

"That's the problem, you ain't said shit!" I replied.

"Damn," Toni said, "do you know what I could do with that kind of cash? It will be in cash, right?"

"Yeah."

"I'm really starting to like the sound of this." Toni's phone rang as we pulled into the parking lot. "Hello."

"What's up Boo?" said Shawn, Toni's baby father.

"Nothing, me and the twins just pulled into Friday's. Someone was hungry as usual."

"Shut up nigga, I haven't eaten since this morning," I told her.

"Where's my baby?" said Toni.

"Right here, that's why I called, he kept asking for you, I think he misses you. Me too."

"Nigga please, yo' ass wasn't missing me when you was fuckin' that chick from Carson," replied Toni.

"How many times do I have to apologize for that?" Shawn said.

"It doesn't matter, that's yo' woman now. And besides, we're still cool, I still got love for you. After all, you gave me my beautiful son."

"Mommy!"

"I hear him in the background, put him on."

"Hi mommy."

"Hi baby."

"Hi Daishawn," Sandy and I yelled. At one and a half, Daishawn's words pretty much consisted of momma and daddy, the rest was gibberish. Lookin' just like Shawn, it was hard not to love them both.

Toni said, "what is it baby?"

"Com' 'ome."

"In the morning baby, I'll be there in the morning to pick you up. I love you, put daddy back on the phone."

"What's up fatty?"

"Nigga please, I know you didn't just call me fat?"

"What else would you call that ass?"

"I call it you not getting none."

"Damn, it's like that?"

"Yep!"

"Look, I have to go. We're about to order our food, then we're going back to the club to get our dance on. Kiss Daishawn for me and I'll be there around eight or nine to pick him up."

"What about me?"

"What?"

"I don't get a kiss?"

"Ah shut up nigga, bye!"

"Since Sandy said I was payin' for dinner, I'm tellin' you now, whatever y'all order, it better not cost more than ten dollars."

"Damn Candy, yo' ass is cheap as hell," Toni said.

"I was just playin', and besides, I got enough cash right now to choke yo' ass half to death," I said.

"Yeah, well I've seen people choke on quarters before," Toni shot back.

"Ha ha, very funny. Anyway I'm not trippin', 'cause I plan on takin' every dime some fool got in his pocket tonight."

"That's what I'm talkin' about," Sandy said.

"Candy, I just want three things, some Baby Back Ribs, a salad and a big ass 7 Up," Toni said.

"That sounds good," Sandy said. "I'll have the same. I don't need that much, I still plan on having some fun tonight and getting my freak on."

"Sis, I sure hope you're talkin' about dancing?" I said, as we all laughed. "Anyway, I think I'll have some Red Snapper and fries."

"Where the hell is a waiter? Now that I'm here I'm hungry too," said Toni.

"Alright, while we wait let's hear about this plan of yours," I said.

"Damn nigga, you hear about a lil' money and yo' panties get wet," Sandy joked.

"Shit, for the kind of money you talkin' about moms might wanna' get in on this, and you know she goes to church every chance she gets."

It's Hard Being the Same

"I can imagine all the things I can do for Daishawn, the best education possible, and you know I can't forget about my pops," said Toni.

"We'll order and then we'll talk," Sandy said.

After we ordered, I told the waitress that she was pretty.

"What did you just say?"

"I said she was pretty, why, you gotta' problem with that?" I replied.

"No, I just never heard you say something like that before," replied Toni. "You know I'm always seeing you pushin' up on all them dudes, I just thought...Hell what's up with you and Yellow Bird? The way you be talkin' about how he loves lickin' on yo' pussy, I just thought he was all that?" Toni added.

"He do what he does and I ain't complainin'. And before Sandy opens here big ass mouth, no I'm not gay. I just thought she was pretty that's all."

"Yeah right! I'm tellin' you now, I catch you lickin' on some chick's pussy, I'mma' tell Daddy," Sandy said.

"Don't worry, you won't," I said, as I nodded and smiled, at the Mexican female waitress. In return she responds with a pretty smile and a nodded and gave me a slight wink.

Chapter 2

SANDY

As we ate I began to lay out my plan for them, but before I could really get started Toni interrupted me. "Sandy I already told you. I'm not going to prison for shit, so you better make this good."

"Oh it's good alright, and as long as you don't go hitting the wrong keys on your computer we should be alright."

"Should be, what kind of talk is that? I'm with Layla, I'm not going to jail," Candy said.

"Look, if we stick to the script, we'll be rich as fuck and be able to push through Compton like we own that bitch, feel me?"

"Until you tell us what's up, the only thing I'm feelin' is this fish." She got a high five from Toni.

"Check this out, we're going hit the DEA. The Drug Enforcement Agency."

"What? Oh hell nah! Are you crazy?" Toni cried, "Candy this fool done lost her mind."

"I agree. Sandy that Chocolate Thai you smoked earlier really messed you up in the head. You want us to rob the DEA?"

"I told you this is not a bank so you're not going to need any guns."

"Well whatever you wanna' call it," Toni said, "I'm doing it with my 380, you know I never go anywhere without it."

"I told you, we're not going to need any guns, now will y'all hear me out please? All over this country, each time the DEA makes a major drug bust, the cash and drugs are kept for evidence while whoever got busted goes through their trials or whatever."

"So you want us to rob a federal court house after a major drug bust?" Candy asked.

"Hell nah fool! And if you say robbery one more time I'mma' hit yo' ass with one of these rib bones."

"So what then?" Candy asked.

"I've been watching this show called Border Patrol."

"Border Patrol, what's that?" Candy inquired.

"It's where they show people trying to smuggle shit into this country," Toni answered.

"Right. You should see all the drugs they find in a single day," I said.

"That's the Border Patrol, what does the DEA have to do with anything?" Candy asked.

"Well in one of the episodes they showed how they store all this shit, then they burn it somewhere just over the border."

"Well I'll be damned if I go to a Mexican prison," Toni said.

"Toni what the hell is wrong with you? Yo' ass is not going to prison, I told you that. Shit you got a better chance of goin' to jail fuckin' with them crip's you love so much."

"She got a point their girl," said Candy.

"Ah shut up Candy, yo' ass like them just like I do."

"Sandy, this fish is good, but can I have one of your ribs?"

"Damn girl, they got a whole kitchen full of this stuff, just order you some."

"Quit being so tight and give me one, damn!" Candy pleaded.

"Here", Toni said, "you can have the rest of mine. We need to hurry up, 'cause by ten thirty I plan to be on a dance floor."

"Anyway, I know the DEA does the same thing, but they like to hold onto shit until it's time to burn it. How long that takes? I don't know. But what I do know is - they have warehouses out there, none-descriptive buildings full of seized drugs, cash and lord knows what else. I'll tell you what too, I want it."

"That sounds good and all that, but how are you going to find it?" Toni asked.

"Not me, YOU! For once you're going to put that elaborate ass computer of yours to good use."

"Okay, how is that?" Toni asked.

"First we need to locate somewhere where they store whatever they've seized, and I'm thinking somewhere in San Diego, close to the border."

"Why there?" Candy asked.

"Watching these shows, a lot of the times shit will make it across and into this country, but still get caught up in San Diego. Now all big head here has to do is find out where they keep everything."

"And how am I supposed to do that?" Toni asked.

"Shit put yo' hacking skills to work." It was true, Toni had hacked into a few bank computers when times got a lil' hard for her mom's. Never anything major where someone would really notice, and so far the few times she did it, she only took what was needed for them to pay some bills.

"Toni, all you have to do is find us a location and get into their inventory records. We need to know how many people work the night shift. We need to know about the alarm system and what will happen if you turn it off."

"Their inventory should tell us how much money is in there, right?" she asked.

"Right."

"So do you think you can get us this information?"

"Shit, this is sounding better and better, and for that kind of money, if I can't find it on my computer, hell I'll walk up to the front desk of that nearest office and just ask them where they keep the shit."
The three of us laughed as we finish off the rest of our meals.

"So what do you think Candy?"

"It sounds good and everything, but you just expect us to break into some building and then just walk out with a load of cash?"

"Basically, yeah!"

"Okay, let me ask y'all this, have either of you ever broken into a building before?" Candy asked.

"No," Toni said, "but my dad once told me, the most important thing to know about breaking into a building is, they can't put an alarm on anything that doesn't open."

"And you said that to say what?" I asked.

"As long as we don't open any doors we should be alright. I don't know, that's what he said."

"Well we will just have to check it out, if and when we find the building. But I'm telling y'all, they showed so much money, stacks and stacks of it, just sitting there."

"And you want us to go get it?" Candy asked.

"Why not? Aren't you sick of being poor?"

"Yeah, but I can think of something worse than being poor."

"Like what?"

"I know," Toni said, "she's gonna' say like going to jail."

"You damn right I was," Candy insisted.

"Okay, I feel you, so I say we get all the information we can, check everything out, and depending on how things look, we'll decide from there."

"I know I could find out what we need to know. So right after graduation tomorrow I'll get started. Now let's get outta' here so I can get my freak on," Toni said.

"Unlike Sandy, I know you're not talking about dancing."

"Fuck you bitch, so what if I like to get my sexy on. At least I wasn't talking about fuckin' that Mexican chick over there."

"No I wasn't!" Candy yelled.

"Yeah right," Toni told her, as we went to pay for our meals.

"Damn, this shit is expensive. Can one of y'all loan me twenty dollars?" Candy asked.

"Damn girl, why you always playin' broke? A lil' while ago you had enough money to choke me to death," Toni said.

"I'm a lil' short because I bought something for baby Daishawn this morning. It's so cute, wait until you see it."

"Alright here." After Toni handed over the money and Candy paid the bill, she said, "You know I lied, right?"

"You know I hate yo' ass sometimes. I will get my dub back, even if I have to use me "380" to do it," Toni said.

"Yeah, yeah, I love you too sis," Candy said, sarcastically.

CANDY

Like fifteen minutes later, I pulled into the parking lot of the "Vault" for the second time that night. There were very few people still outside. "See I told you if we wait a couple of hours this place would be live and on the inside."

"Okay," Toni said, "let's park this bucket of bolts and go in."

"Bucket, I bet yo' ass don't be saying that shit after we hit this lick and I'm pushing around Compton in a fat ass Benz."

"Yeah and yo' black ass is gonna' go to jail for real."

"Fuck all that, right now both y'all is still broke, and I got one thing on my mind," Sandy said.

"Yeah, what's that?"

"You see that over there?"

"Yeah, so?" Toni said.

"That means Black is still there, and I definitely want to get close to him tonight."

"Yeah, yeah, whatever."

"I'll tell you what," Toni said, "how much money you got on you right now?"

"Why? I'm not paying for yo' ass to get in."

"Nah that's not it. I bet you a c-note right now, when we get inside that nigga got his hand on some chick's ass."

"Shit I'll take that bet too," I told her.

"You bitches ain't shit," Sandy said.

"We know!" Toni and I said in unison, as we laughed.

There were only a few people waiting in line. When we reached the door, the bouncer said, "Since I think you three are the prettiest ladies to come through here tonight, this one is on me."

"Well we sure do thank you," I told him.

"Not a problem. What is your name sweetness?"

"Toni."

"Well beautiful, when the doors close for the night, maybe I'll come buy you a drink."

"You call me beautiful one more time, you might have action," Toni replied.

"You ladies enjoy your evening, and hopefully I'll see you later."

As we entered the club Sandy said, "I sure hope you don't be pushin' up on nobody's woman tonight."

"Who you talking too?"

"Why you are the one that answered? You knew I was talkin' to yo' ass."

"Be careful girl," Toni said. "You know how she likes to pull bitches hair out."

"She wouldn't dare," Sandy said.

"Keep fuckin' with me and see. And just for talkin' shit, I just might find me some pussy to play with," I said, sarcastically.

"Oooh, I knew it, you have been fuckin' with women," Toni said.

"No I have not."

"Whatever Candy," Toni insisted.

"Hey do y'all smell that?" Sandy asked.

"What?" Toni said.

"Weed. I'm about to find something to hit, then I might let something hit me, later y'all." And she was off. The club was all that. The atmosphere would almost make you forget we're right in the middle of the ghetto. Instead of their Sunday best, everyone had on their ghetto best.

"Toni, since we are officially done with school tomorrow, will you toast a glass of wine with me?"

"Yeah, as long as yo' ass don't start thinking I'm sexy."

"Man shut up and come on."

"Can I help you two beauties?"

"Damn girl, we must be looking extra good tonight, niggaz keep throwing around that beautiful shit like dice."

"Shit am I wrong?" he asked.

"Not all all."

"So what can I get you ladies?"

"Two white wines," I told him, then he turned to go get our drinks. "He's kinda' cute, ain't he?"

"He's cool," Toni replied.

"Here you go ladies, that'll be ten dollars."

"No, here you go," I said, handing him a twenty.

"Look, I have two questions for you."

"What's that?" I asked.

"What's your name and do you taste as good as you look?"

"Girl I know this nigga didn't just say he wants to eat yo' pussy?"

"Will you shut up and let me work? My name is just like something very sweet. What's yours?"

"Money Mike, and I own half this club."

"You look pretty young for something like that."

"Like my name, I'm all about them ends. Now you gonna' tell me your name or what?"

"Shit, if you start lickin' on me, my name will hit you like a bolt of lightning."

"Girl will you stop it? Mike she doesn't mean that shit."

"I might, I might not."

"Okay Candy, you're giving me a sweet tooth."

"See I knew you would get it."

"Yeah I got it, but are you going to answer my second question?"

"All I can say is, if yo' game is tighter than everyone else in here, you might be able to find out how I taste."

"Shit my name is Money for a reason. How many other niggaz' in here do you think own a business at twenty four?"

"You got a point their baby boy, but if you about yo' money like you say, you better get back to work 'cause you got a lot of people waiting on you." All he could do was laugh as we walked off.

"Let's find a table", Toni said, "I need to let my food settle. Candy you know Yellow Bird has been watching you since we got here?"

"Yeah I know, I peeped him out already," I said.

"So what's up with the two of y'all?"

"I don't know, I got love for him, but all that shit he's movin', the gang bangin', I know that shit is gonna' catch up with his ass, and I don't wanna' be there when them hot shells or the cops come," I said.

"He's doing it like that?" Toni asked.

"From what Sandy said, Black is movin' at least fifteen bricks a week, and you know where one goes the other one goes. So Yellow Bird has to be doing the same," I said.

"Damn girl, I didn't know they was movin' shit like that. Why them niggaz' will only ride around in them Low Riders is beyond me," Toni said.

"Girl first and foremost them niggaz' are die hard Crips, and even though we've been around that shit all our life, it scares me. I don't know how you do it," I said.

"Like you said, we've been around it all our lives, are you scared to be with me?" Toni asked.

"No," I said.

"And that's how I feel hangin' out with niggaz' like Black and Yellow Bird," Toni said.

"But you're so smart, you can do and go anywhere you want," I said.

"So can you and Sandy. But Compton is all we know right now, and I love my city. So with that being said, I love you and Sandy, congratulation to finishing high school, and let's hope like hell this shit

Sandy wants us to do works out. Now drink your wine so I can go put this mini skirt to work," Toni said.

The music was all that, but at a moderate level where people didn't have to shout to be heard. We spotted Sandy on the dance floor between two dudes. It looked like she was working them instead of the other way around.

"Will you look at her ass?" I said, pointing at Sandy on the dance floor getting her freak-on.

"Girl that ain't nothing." Toni downed the last of her wine and headed towards the trio. She immediately started doing shit that surprised them all. Toni looked like she was trying to use one of the dudes as a stripper pole.

"I love this song, and Jay-Z makes me wanna' get my freak on," Toni said.

Before you knew it, almost two hours had passed and the four of them practically had sex out on the floor. But Toni had other things to take care of so she made her move.

SANDY & BLACK

I knew I was doin' way too much. I also knew Black has been watching me pretty much the whole time. When one of the guys I was dancing with came up waving my panties in the air, Black had enough.

I wasn't much for dancing so I let Sandy do her thang, but oh boy was trying to take it to another level. "Hey Yellow, you heated?" I said.

"Do fat people stay hungry?" Yellow replied.

"Alright, watch my back while I go get Sandy's freaky ass," I said.

"Man will you let her do her thang, she's having fun. You see all these fly ass bitches up in here?" Yellow said.

"Yeah, but ain't none of them got ass and legs like Sandy."

"Shit, her and Candy are identical. You couldn't tell them apart if they were dressed the same," Yellow said.

"Nigga you know what I mean. Just watch my back," I said.

I had been keeping one eye on Black too. Although he wasn't my man, he sure thought my pussy belonged to him. So when I saw Yellow Bird pat his side where I knew he kept his gun, and Black stood up, I broke wide to the ladies' room.

Chapter 3

BLACK & SANDY

This nigga think she's slick. I peeped her move and I followed her. She made her way to the ladies' room, so I waited a few minutes then went in after her. There was two other women inside at the mirror putting on lipstick. But my presence made them gather their things and leave. I guess they exited, sensing something was about to happen.

"What's up sexy?" I said.

"Hi, what's up with you Black?" Sandy replied.

"I saw you out there doing yo' thang, and right now I'm about to do mine. Come here." As she came to me I unzipped my Levi's 'cause my dick had swelled to an unbelievable size.

"Nah nah nigga, what you gonna' do with that big ass shit?" Sandy said.

But she already knew the deal. Her pussy was already half ass wet from when that nigga snatched her panties off. "Jump up here on the counter and just enjoy the ride." Sandy was fine from head to toe, even her pussy was pretty. It looked like a rose that was about to open.

"I swear Black, you mess up my skirt and I'mma' hit you dead in yo' pockets."

"Don't' worry, I got you." I opened her legs a lil' wider and when I slid my dick inside of her, her eyes got wide like she took a hit of crack rock, and immediately started moaning. "Baby girl, you know with you moaning like that, I'm going to want to fuck you until the sun comes up."

"Speaking of cumming, I want you to cum with me," Sandy said, grinding on my dick erotically.

"That's what I'm trying to do." In and out of her I went, hittin' her real good.

She threw one of her legs over my shoulder and held the other one with her left hand. I really liked the way things were turning out. With her legs up like they were I could hear how wet her pussy was as I banged away at it.

To me his dick was so good, I thought, if this shit could only vibrate I would lose my fucking mind.

I wanted to pull her titties out so I could suck on them, but I knew we had already done too much. "You like that shit, don't you?" I said, kissing her on her neck.

But before I could answer or even cum, he pushed inside of me as hard and as far as he could go, held it there for a second, then pulled out.

Surprising her, I dipped down and gave her pussy the lightest kiss I could, then moved over to the sink and washed my still throbbing dick. I dried myself off, fixed my clothes and started to bounce.

"Where the hell you think you're going?" She half yelled.

"If you want the rest, you gotta' meet me at the Comfort Inn or something," I said.

"You know we got graduation tomorrow."

"Well I guess you gotta' be satisfied then. And if I see another nigga come up in here, I'mma' send the homie up in here to dust his ass off. Oh and one more thing, get yo' hands away from yo' pussy."

"You's a cold nigga Black. Sometimes I can't stand yo' ass."

"Yeah, I love you too," I said, as I walked out the ladies room like nothing ever happened.

Damn that was a first. Then he was gone. I don't believe this nigga just left me like that. My pussy was still hot as hell, and I can't even finish myself 'cause I know somebody is gonna' walk in here any minute now. I said fuck it, let me clean myself up and get outta' here. I was just happy he didn't say anything about that dude taking my panties off. I still can't figure out how he did that shit. If he got any more tricks like that, I might have to check him out later.

As I left the bathroom, still frustrated, but under control, I went to the bar first. When I reached the bar Mike asked if I would like another White wine. "No thank you, but I would like a shot of Hennessy on the rocks."

"Coming right up," Mike, the bartender said. By his puzzled look I could tell that he noticed something was different.

"Hey, why did you change clothes?" he asked.

I wanted to play it off, but I really needed a drink, so I told him about my twin.

"I didn't, that was my sister."

"Damn, there's two of y'all? This is truly an amazing world," Mike said, still staring intently as if in a daze.

"Thanks for the compliment."

"Here's your drink, that'll be eight dollars," Mike said.

"Here you go," I said, handing him a ten.

"Thank you. Enjoy the rest of your evening, and please do me a favor, tell your sister Candy to come spend some quality time with me," Mike said, with a smile.

"You got that coming, but it's up to her to come back you know."

"I feel you, and thanks anyway," he said.

After leaving the bar I found Candy shooting pool. Since she only had a bra on under her jacket, which only had three buttons, all the guys were getting an eye full as she took her shots. As I came up she handed me two thousand dollars. "What's this for?" I asked her.

"Just hold it, I'm about to hit these niggaz' for another thousand right now," Candy said, confidently.

"Man you let this chick beat you like that?" her opponent's homie said, who was watching the pool game from the sideline.

"You see how fine she is? Shit, I can't even concentrate," her opponent said, with a look of defeat on his face.

"Well, you better do something, 'cause it's two of them now," the guy on the sideline said, pointing in my direction.

Everyone laughed. "Eight ball right corner pocket, and that's game baby boy," Candy said.

"Nice shot sis."

"Thanks. I knew we were going to need some equipment for our venture coming up, so I figure I'd come in here and work these boyz'. Where's my bodyguard?" Candy said.

"Who you talkin' about?" I asked.

"Toni, I want her and her 380 around if these niggaz' try to trip," she said.

"Fool shut up, ain't nobody thinkin' about you. Come on let's go check on her ass."

"You boyz' sure you don't wanna' play again?" Candy asked. No one wanted to lose any more money, so we left, shaking our asses and laughing together.

"What's up y'all?" Toni said, just coming into the pool hall.

"We were just coming to look for you," I said.

"Yeah right," Toni said, sarcastically.

"We were," Candy said. Then she turned to me and said, "And before I forget, give me my money Sandy."

"Here, you act like I was tryin' to keep that shit."

"Nah, I would never think such a thing. Hey, you know I saw y'all out on the dance floor, that shit look like a four-way orgy." All we could do was smile.

"I was surprised that Black let that shit go down," Candy said.

"He's not my man," I said.

"Shit, all that freaky shit she was doing out there, I know Black Bird is the one that won in the end," Toni said, shoving me playfully.

"What's she talkin' about Sandy?" Candy asked.

"Let's just say I'm glad no one had to go to the bathroom about fifteen minutes ago," I said.

"Sandy, no you didn't," Candy yelled.

"No sis, I didn't," I said.

"Liar! When the nigga took yo' panties off, I knew it was on," Toni said.

"Damn Toni, you been watching me like that?" I said.

"I had to keep an eye on everybody," Toni said.

"And why is that?" Candy asked.

"Cause I've picked like ten people pockets. Why you think I'm the only bitch walking around with this big ass purse?" Toni replied.

"Girl you sick. Look, it's 12:45, I think it's time for us to get outta' here," Candy said.

"Shit, I'm the only one that didn't get any money tonight?" Sandy said.

"No", said Toni, "but you did get yo' sexy on."

"You know that's right! But that's not good enough, I want both, come on." As we left the pool hall, I told Candy, "Hey, you know oh boy wanted you to come spend some time with him."

"Well right now he has his hands full," Candy said, pointing at the bartender engaged in conversations with three women.

I lead them through the crowd. It was like I was following my own scent, which led me back to Black.

"What's up-bigger that you need to be," I said, motioning towards Black's manhood with a grin on my face.

"What's up, you changed yo' mind?" Black asked.

"Nah, but I do need to talk to you for a sec," I said.

"What's up Candy? Hey Toni," Yellow Bird said.

"Don't talk to me, I'm mad at you. I've been in this bitch for hours and this is the first you've notice or even acknowledged me," Candy said with an attitude.

"When have you known me to sweat some chick?" Yellow Bird said, nonchalantly.

"I'm not just some chick," Candy said.

"Yeah you right, so I'll tell you what, give Sandy yo' car keys and you come with me for the night. I'll freak yo' ass so good you'll think you had an outter' body experience," Yellow Bird said.

"Shit", Toni said, "that sounds good to me."

"Nah-Nah Toni, 'cause if I was fuckin with you, I might have to throw some hot ass slugs at that nigga Shawn. I don't need no baby daddy drama," Yellow Bird said, shakin' his head from side to side.

"Anyway, he was talkin' to me Toni, so I got this. Sorry baby boy, NO-CAN-DO-YOU," Candy said, with a devilish grin.

"Sandy, come sit here and talk to me," Black said.

"Ah hell nah nigga, I'm not getting anywhere near that shit. Don't laugh, it's not funny Black. Besides, this will only take a second," I said.

"What's up love?" Black said, skinning and grinning at me, with all of his pearly whites showing.

"That's twice nigga," I said, "don't let it happen again."

"What you talkin' about?" asked Black, acting like he was puzzled by the comment.

"Nothing! Forget it," I said, trying to switch the subject of the conversation. "Check this out, and don't say no, 'cause I know you got it. Don't ask a lot of questions either 'cause I can't explain it right now, but know this, I'll double you up when I complete my mission."

"Sandy, what the hell you talkin' about?" asked Black again, this time seriously baffled by the comments.

"I need to barrow a "G" for a lil' while," I said.

"Shit, as good as you were earlier, here go two 'G's' lil'mama," he said, reaching into his pocket and handing me two-thousand dollars.

"Candy, you need some money?" Yellow Bird asked.

"Nah I'm cool, I just worked them fools in the pool hall. And besides, just because we were born at the same time, don't mean we bleed at the same time."

"TMI lil' mama. I don't need to hear about all that shit," Yellow Bird said, wit' a grimacing look on his face.

I know we set out to get cash from dudes like we usually did, but when Candy and Toni told me they were hustling for the lick I needed to do something. I knew Black kept a large knot on him at all times, but I didn't think he would break bread like he did. Pops always told us to use our heads to get what we wanted and not our bodies, but this is one time my body served me well. I've never asked Black for money before, the only time I ever asked him for anything, it was to drive his Low Rider. He knew I'd been dying to drive it too, so reluctantly he agreed. "Look," he said, "you can go down Greenleaf, turn right on Long Beach Blvd., turn right on Alandra, right onto the Drive and come down Caldwell until you get back here." I knew why he said it like that. Although this was his hood and everybody knew his car, niggaz' will still shoot you dead for some 13" Dayton's. I enjoyed myself on the short trip, and you can best believe I tried to run the batteries down hitting every switch he had.

The shit was more fun than when he did it. I was tempted to go again, but I pulled up to the house and laid the whole car down. "Look y'all, it's coming up on 1:30 a.m. and we have a big day tomorrow. Black, thanks for the loan and I'll get this back to you," I said.

"Remember, you said double," Black Bird said.

"Yeah I remember, but I said two for the one. You gave up the other "G" for that bomb'ass pussy I gave you earlier. Now do you remember?"

"Shit, you can give me one more hour and you can keep that lil' shit."

"Oh no my brotha', you had all the time in the world, but you left me fiendin', now you want some more… Not!"

"You two cock-hounds have a good night," Toni said, and we headed home.

CANDY

The next morning came on way too soon. It was so hard to get started. Sandy was yelling and before long Promise was in our room doing the same thing. "Candy, if you don't get up and get moving you're going to miss your own graduation. And what I tell you two about drinking?"

"Mom, me and Layla had one glass of wine as a toast," I said.

"I don't care, you are not grown and should not be drinking alcohol. Sandy, what are you laughing at? I know if she had a glass, you most likely had a whole bottle of something. Is that why you didn't drive last night?"

"Mom, do I look like I have a hangover?" Sandy said.

"Girl do not get smart with me this morning. Now y'all hurry up and get ready so you can come eat. Was Taylor their last night?" Mom asked. Taylor is Black's real name.

"Yeah he was there, why?" Sandy asked.

"Then yo' butt probably had something worse than alcohol."

"Mom please!" Sandy shrieked.

"Mama, all I know is, I lost sight of her two or three times, and when I didn't see her, I didn't see him," I said laughing.

"Mom, she's lying and she know it," Sandy said.

"Anyway, y'all come on and eat, I made you guys a nice breakfast. You guys are getting grown and I know I won't be cooking for you much longer. Now hurry up, and don't forget to make up your beds."

"Mom, you can still cook for me any time, no matter how grown I am," I said.

"Girl shut yo' hungry ass up," Sandy said.

"Sandy you better watch your mouth in this house. Now for the last time, hurry up and come downstairs," Mom said.

"Candy, what do you think it's gonna' be like if we get this money?"

"I don't know, but I hope it doesn't change us. We've been close a long time and money like that always seem to change people."

"I feel you, just promise we'll look out for mom."

"Sandy you know she got that comin', but you know she's gonna' trip hard if we come up in here with the kind of money you talkin' about."

"Yeah I know, so we're gonna' have to find somewhere to put it."

"And where might that be?" I asked.

"I have no idea, you're the smart one around here," Sandy said.

"What about the bank?" I asked.

"Fool, we can't just walk in and deposit four or five million in a bank, yo' ass sure will go to jail," Sandy said.

"No, we'll get some safety deposit boxes," I said.

"Damn, why didn't I think of that?" Sandy said.

"Because I'm the smart one, remember?" We finished getting dressed, cleaned our room, and headed down to breakfast. At the bottom of the stairs Sandy hugged me and said, "If you keep thinking like this we're gonna' be rich as hell girl."

As we came into the kitchen Promise told us to sit down. "This looks good mom," I told her.

"It should be, I've been in here cooking since six this morning."

"Why did you make so much?"

"Two reasons actually, one, it's not every day my girls graduate from school. And second, I was hoping your father would be here to share this day with you."

"I'm sure he will be at the ceremony", Sandy said, "you know Pops be making all kind of moves."

"Yeah, that's why he is always letting you girls down or in some kind of trouble," Mom said.

"Mom, you know he loves us, and at least he's not in prison with Big Ten," Sandy said.

"You know mom, Sandy has a point."

"I know, I just wish he'd leave them streets alone. Candy, will you see who is at the door?" As I opened the front door, to my surprise, Yellow Bird was standing there holding a dozen yellow roses.

"Good morning beautiful, these are for you."

"Oh thank you, they look and smell wonderful."

"Yeah, much like you do. I'm glad you like them."

"Candy, who's at the door?"

"It's Keith mom, he brought me flowers."

"Well tell him to come in."

"Good morning everybody," He said, trying to project his voice into the open doorway.

"Candy, sorry I can't stay, me and the homie Black got some moves to make this morning."

"Whose Escalade is that?" I asked looking over his shoulder.

"It's mine, why you want it?"

"Ah shut up nigga. I just never seen it before, you always in that low rider, I thought that was all you had."

"Come on now, you know trying to make moves in that shit would attract too much attention."

"So where you headed?"

"We have a few traps to check, then tomorrow we're going to Bakersfield, then out to Sacramento."

"Alright, you be careful and I'll see you when you get back."

"Alright, K's up."

"Nigga don't be hittin' me with that gang shit."

"Sorry about that, force of habit."

And he was gone. When I got back to the kitchen I said, "Look Mom."

"Ooh baby that was so nice of him, and they're beautiful. Give them here so I can put them in some cold water."

"Thank you. You know I can't believe he did that."

"The question is, what did you do to make him bring you flowers?" Mom asked pointedly.

"Yeah Candy, I'd like to know that myself," Sandy said, as she looked at me with an eyebrow raised.

"Why don't you be quiet and eat Sandy, dang? It sounds like you're jealous. Mom, why couldn't he just think it was a nice thing to do?"

"I guess. Y'all almost done eating? We need to get going."

After we got our caps and gowns we headed for the door. As Sandy and I stepped out onto the porch a white limousine pulled up to the house. The man that stepped out was every bit of 6 feet-four inches tall, and black as the night before. His head was clean shaven and he wore a dove grey three-piece suit.

"Jamel, what are you doing? And what's with the limo?" Promise asked.

"I know you didn't think I would miss my girls' graduation, did you?" He asked.

"Ooh daddy", Sandy said, "this Cadillac is clean as hell."

"You like that?"

"Yep! I just thought we would see you at the ceremony."

"Hi daddy, thank you so much for coming, now Sandy and I can show you both off at the same time."

"You girls know anytime I do something for y'all I try to go all out."

"Yeah," Promise said, "cause we all know it ain't that often you do." Mom was still hurt from their broken relationship, but she appreciated the effort that Dad put forth in relation to Sandy and I.

"But like I said, when I come through, it's in a major way," Jamel said, smiling and hugging Sandy.

"Anyway, where's Toni? I thought she would be here," he said.

"Not too sure, I know she had to pick up Daishawn from his dad, you want me to call her? I know she would love the limo," I said.

"We don't have the time, it's already after nine o'clock."

"Promise, time is all we have. Besides, these things never start on time. Hell, our graduation didn't start until noon," Pop's said to mom's.

"Sandy, go make sure the house is locked up, we need to be leaving," mom said.

Chapter 4

CANDY

The day seemed to go by in one big blur. The ceremony was over by twelve noon. We caught up with Toni, her mom Stacy had Daishawn and by 12:30 we had taken so many pictures we could have made our own personal Year Book. By a quarter to one the limousine pulled out of Dominiquez High School and jumped on the 91 freeway and headed to Lake Wood for lunch.

"Promise, is there anywhere special you would like to go for lunch?" Jamel asked.

"You know I could easily have cooked us all lunch."

"Look, this is a special day and I wanted to do something nice for my three ladies."

"Mom, he's trying to throw some money around and I say we let him," I said.

"I know that's right," Sandy said.

"Okay, but just where did you get all this money anyway?" mom questioned.

"I knew this day was comin' so I've been saving."

"Jamel, you couldn't save the hair on your head, so stop lying." That got a laugh out of me and Toni.

"Oh it's like that?"

"You know I was just playin', you used to like my sense of humor. Now driver, please take us to the Panda Express." Everyone laughed some more.

Once lunch was over we headed back towards Compton. Jamel handed us both a white envelop that contained a thousand dollars each. We were both surprised by this gesture so we hugged him at the same time.

"Toni, I didn't know you would be with us today, and you know I can't forget about you." He reached into his pocket and pulled out his bankroll, counted out a grand and gave it to her with a kiss.

"Thanks Jamel, but you didn't have to do that," Toni said.

"Hell you've been a part of this family for as long as I can remember. Besides, that lil' shit ain't nothing."

"Jamel, watch your mouth please," Promise said.

"Toni, how is Big Ten? Have you talked to him lately?"

"He's good. Actually he's supposed to call me tonight at 7:00 p.m. Do you think we'll be back by then?

"I'll make sure of it, don't trip."

Lunch went well and what surprised me the most was how well mom seemed to enjoy having dad around. We have not seen them this close in years. I guess the money he's been flashing today really got her attention. Shit I don't blame her. Hell every woman loves her money. Within the last day and a half, I've gotten almost four thousand dollars from men, but hopefully if this shit Sandy has planned works out, I won't have to hustle these niggaz' anymore.

Hell, what does five million in cash even look like? Sandy had said there was stacks of it just sitting there. I don't know, TV will make you see all kind of shit that's not really there. But the government does like to hold onto shit like trophies. Then instead of them giving all that money to the poor where they can feed their kids, they rather burn it. I know one thing, we got a lot of work to do. Toni said she would get started right after graduation, but I don't think that's gonna' happen tonight.

She has to deal with Daishawn, take the call from Big Ten and no telling what else. But tomorrow I'm gonna' be on them both. Sandy started this shit and I plan to make sure we see it through. I know Toni is always layin' in the cut to shoot up some shit if things go bad, but I'm thinking seriously of suggesting to them we take Black and Yellow Bird along for back up. This is going to be big for us, and once we have all the cash we can get our hands on, we can let them go in and have their fill. Shit, them niggaz' would love all the drugs and guns that's sure to be in there. Shit, think safe and we'll be safe. By 5:30 p.m. pops had everyone fed and back home. Daishawn didn't eat much at the Panda Express, he wanted a Happy Meal so much that Jamel made the driver stop at the first McDonald's we came across. The boy is just so cute, not many people can say no to him.

Toni thanked Jamel for everything and promised to call later on that night. A few minutes later we were dropped us off at the house, we kissed our dad, told him thanks for being there for us today and headed upstairs. "Candy, why don't you put some music on that makes you wanna' make some money?"

"Like who?"

"Put some Ice Cube on. That Gangsta will take you there every time."

"Sandy you can't be getting ahead of yourself, we got a lot of work to do before we even find this money."

"I know, but we need this shit and I'm gonna' ball my ass off when we do find it."

"Whatever girl. Look I wanna' run something by you. I wish Toni was here so I could tell you both at once," I said.

"What is it?" Sandy asked.

"You know how I call Toni my bodyguard?" I said.

"Yeah," Sandy replied.

"Well, I was thinking that we could take Black and Yellow Bird along with us just in case there's any real trouble," I said.

"That sounds good, but I don't want anyone to know about this but the three of us. They're gonna' want to get paid, and everything I walk outta' that bitch with, I plan on keepin' for myself," Sandy said.

"I feel you, but it doesn't have to be that way. We can make them stand guard and watch over us. Toni is supposed to be our eyes and ears, but I don't see how she can do that if she's inside with us. She gonna' have to stay with the computers. Just look at it this way, if it's as much money in there as you say, there has to be just as much drugs and guns."

"Once we're in and out, we send them in. Girl all that dope, them niggaz' can slang that shit until they drop dead. The guns, their homies will love them for that. Then just for putting them up on game, we can charge them the price of fifteen kilos. That will be for me, you and Toni," I said.

"Damn sis, I thought this was my lick? It looks like you've been giving this a lot of thought," Sandy said.

"I have, I just want us to be safe."

"We still have a lot of information and equipment we need to find, so if you think this is a good idea, we can run it by Toni when we meet up for our Sunday run tomorrow at Compton College," Sandy said.

Sunday morning also came on way too fast, so my first mission was to call Toni and push our run time back until 10:00 a.m. After washing up I went downstairs. The limousine was long gone, but I could tell Jamel was still here. "Sandy come down here."

"I'm not dressed yet, what's up?"

"Will you just come here, damn," I insisted.

"What is it, Candy?"

"Tell me something, look around and tell me if you notice anything."

"No, why?" Sandy asked.

"Just look around and tell me if you notice anything."

"No they didn't?" Sandy said, with a slight grin on her face.

"Yes they did. Pop's still upstairs, and I know they're gonna' stay up there until we leave the house," I said.

"Mom knows we go running every Sunday morning, but that's not until nine. Man it's still too early, so what's up Candy?"

"Shit, I already called Toni and told her we wouldn't be there until ten. I know, just so they can finish doing their thang, let's go to Tam's on Long Beach Blvd, and have breakfast. It's right on the way to the college anyway," I said.

"You know it's right in Elm Street hood? And if niggaz' start shooting I'mma' kick yo' ass," Sandy said.

"Girl it's 7:45 in the damn morning, ain't nobody thinkin' about us. Now go finish getting dressed."

"Wait, wait, let's bust in on them."

"Girl we're not five anymore. Now go get ready."

For once Sandy insisted on driving, which was cool with me. Breakfast was greasy as hell, but for some reason I loved it. Since Sandy took so long getting ready, we only had about an hour before we were to meet up with Toni. But we did take the time to start a list of the equipment we might need. Sandy put most of it together.

"Candy, since I really want to go along with your idea of having Black and Yellow Bird watch our back, we're gonna' need to rent two SUVs, and an extra car for Toni since she's not going in. We know her computer is what's gonna' keep the police off us, so last night I went through some magazines and found some radar detectors called "Passports 9500-I". We don't need any company on our way there or coming home."

"We're gonna' need five two-way radios. There are some 'Casio GZ Ones' for three hundred dollars. They have a range of fifteen miles."

"You know I have no idea of what you're talking about, right?" I told her.

"Don't trip, we'll worry about that later. Also we're gonna' need some very large duffel bags to carry our money in. At least three apiece. Hopefully we will be able to drive the SUVs right into the place. The bags are just in case we can't. Toni will have to find the computers she'll need and then we can figure out how to power all her equipment from the car."

"What do you think so far?"

"Hey, it sounds good to me, what do I know? So when do we go on our first shopping trip?" I ask.

"We might as well go this afternoon once we've cleaned up from our run. Once we find our target, we can figure out what type of tools we need to get into the building, and our dry run will tell us that."

"Damn nigga, what you know about a dry run?" I said.

"Candy you would be surprised. You know how people call TV an idiot box?"

"Yeah."

"Well that's not true, but only if you know what to look for. Girl the Discovery Channel will teach you all kinds of good shit," Sandy said.

"I guess!"

By 9:50 a.m. we reached Compton College. Toni was already out on the track warming up. "Ah hell nah, she think she's slick. She's out there with them tight ass shorts on, and she has guys running right behind her," I said.

"Shit, what's wrong with that? Besides, as soon as you take yo sweat suit off, them same niggaz' are gonna' be running behind us," Sandy countered.

TONI

I saw them coming so I slowed down. The four guys finally passed me. I knew what they were doing, I was barely running and not once did they try to pass me. Some of these niggaz' see a chick with a lil' ass and they lose their fuckin' mind. "What's up y'all? I've been waiting on you."

"Well you shouldn't have gotten here so early."

"Sandy shut the hell up."

"What's up with you?" Candy asked.

"Just trippin' on them niggaz' over there, they was running behind me like they never seen a lil' ass before."

"First of all, it ain't nothing lil' about yo' ass. And second, you're probably prettier than every chick in this school, so what do you expect?" Candy said.

"Thanks, I think!"

"And", Sandy said, "them tight ass shorts ain't helpin' either." We all laughed.

"So what's good with y'all?"

"We've been over a lot of details of our venture and we plan to go shopping this afternoon. We think you're going to like what we came up with so far," Sandy said.

As we ran the twins broke everything down for me. I'm telling you now I wasn't comfortable about sharing my cut of the money, but they assured me I wouldn't have to. In fact Black and Yellow Bird would actually be paying us for coming along. "Everything sounds good, the only problem I have is, I might not have enough money to get new computer equipment," I said.

"I thought you made a come up at the Club Friday night?" Candy asked.

"Girl out of all them wallets, that shit was only twenty-two hundred bucks. That ain't shit, and the money Jamel gave me I sent to my Pop's, Big Ten, this morning. He wants to buy his own cell phone so he doesn't have to depend on his homies in there with him."

"It's a lot of people in there with cell phones, huh?" Candy asked.

"Yeah, he's been trying to get one for a minute."

"How much will it cost?" Sandy asked.

"Anywhere from five hundred to a thousand dollars. If he does get one I can pay for his minutes. Shit, them collect calls cost ten dollars each. With a prepaid it should be a lot cheaper. And I know he's got two or three females he's writing, plus his homies."

"Well whatever you need we'll cover it. Besides, we got a week or two before we'll be ready," Sandy replied.

"Even though I'd like to go shopping with y'all, I'mma' pass. I'll get started on my search and besides, I haven't spent much time with Daishawn in the last few days."

"Just remember", Sandy said, "during your search, keep an eye out for what we might need. If you think it's something we can find while we're out, just hit me on my cell phone and we'll try to find it."

"Have either of you ever heard of a long range Wi-Fi wireless unit?" I asked.

"Hell nah, Sandy lost me earlier talking about radar detectors," Candy said.

"Well it's a Motorola CPE-I 300, it has eight megabits, which means it's a Wi-Fi broadband on steroids. If I could put that in the car, I should be able to monitor everything going on inside that building and keep tabs on the police with a good police scanner," I said.

"Where are we supposed to find this stuff?" Candy asked.

"You've heard of Toys 'R' Us, well there's a store for nerds called Computers 'R' Us. There is one on Crenshaw right before you get to Stocker."

"Alright, I'll tell you what," Sandy said, "since what we're after is electronics anyway, we'll start there."

"This seems to be adding up the more we talk," Candy said, "and between Sandy and I, we got about seven or eight grand."

"Okay I feel you, so I'll tell you what, just open an account with them. You guys get what we need and after we make this money we can pay them off. Because if you think about it, we're still gonna' need money to rent cars and buy other things that's not electrical."

"So we're really gonna' do this?" I asked.

"Hell yeah!" Sandy replied.

After we ran our ten laps it was time to get cleaned up. But before leaving the track the four guys came within ten feet of us and followed as we ran. There was no need to give them any action, we had way too much to do today, and besides, I didn't see any cars in the parking lot that would indicate if they were ballaz or not. We had a good exercise,

It's Hard Being The Same

Candy and I agreed with Sandy on a lot of her ideas and they were ready for shopping.

Chapter 5

CANDY

Back home we got showered and changed clothes. Our mom was gone, I found a note saying Jamel wanted to take her shopping. "Be back soon, love mom."

"Damn, she must have put it on him last night."

"You think?" Sandy asked.

"I hope they do start spending more time together," I said.

"I guess, but I wouldn't get your hopes up lil' sis. Come on we need to make moves. Shit, if we get this money, you can buy them a new house for a wedding present," Sandy said.

"Do you really think it's that serious between them?" I asked.

"I don't know, but Jamel is gonna' have to get rid of them other females before she lets him get too close, but like I said, don't get your hopes up."

"Sandy I think it would be wise to dress like professionals. We are going to need to look like we're starting a business or something."

"You just better hope they don't go to asking a bunch of questions when we try to open this account," She replied.

"Shit the way you lie, you should be able to talk us right through the shit, so I'm not worried. You ready?" I asked.

"Yeah, let's go. Candy, you mind driving? My car is almost outta' gas."

"See what I mean?"

"What?" Sandy said, tryin' to look innocent.

"Bitch I was just in your car and that shit was damn near full of gas." All she could do was laugh. I grabbed my handbag, took some fruit from the kitchen, then we locked up the house and jumped in my Jetta. Since we live in Front hood I headed west down El Segundo Blvd towards Crenshaw. There's really no freeway close by so I took the surface streets. And just like clockwork, Sandy put on some music and fired up a joint. The shit blew up my car within seconds.

"Why don't you finish that half you left in the ashtray Friday night?" I asked her.

"I forgot about it, why didn't you say something before I lit this one?"

"All I know is you better stop leaving that shit in my car." She just rolled her eyes at me. It took us a lil' over an hour to get into L.A. and find the computer store. Ironically it was right next to a head shop called the Tender Leaf. "Ooh girl," Sandy said, spying the head shop,
"you know I have to go in there when we're done."

"Sandy, the last thing you need is to go in there."

The computer store was damn near the size of a toy store. As we wondered through the store I was surprised by all the gadgets. We found some two-way radios like the ones Sandy saw in the magazine. We also found some Samsung 830s with wireless headsets. These turned out to be a better buy. Each pair had a range of ten miles, and cost $150, so we took six, one extra just in case one failed to work. We got batteries and enough chargers to match.

We also managed to find some Passport radar detectors, so we got two of those as well. We found some Bosch infrared 500x binoculars, which would allow them to see us at night. "Sandy, what do you think? Black and Yellow Bird should be able to keep an eye on us real good with these."

"Yeah, get them." The good thing was, we found the thing-a-majig that Toni wanted. The Motorola CPE-I 300 cost $3,000 which was like half of what we had.

Since that shit didn't look like a computer, but more like a big ass orb with knobs and lights, we needed a sales clerk. The clerk was able to explain that, although Motorola was in fact a computer, it was actually a power plant for smaller computers. "Like laptops?" I asked

"Yes. You see this Toshiba here? Well if you add the power supply, the range of the laptop will almost triple," the clerk said.

"That sounds like what Toni needs. We'll take two of the laptops, along with the Wi-Fi Max," I said.

"One last thing," Sandy said, "we're gonna' need some extra cables and adapters for this, can you handle that?"

"Not a problem, give me a minute," I told Sandy I'd be right back. With my nephew on my mind, I came back a short time later with a remote control truck for Daishawn.

"You know you're gonna' spoil that boy to death," Sandy said.

"I know I just can't help it."

At the purchase counter our bill came to just over $14,000. We opened a line of credit and put down $6,500. And since I didn't wanna' get stuck owing these people by myself, I made Sandy sign her name as well. To my surprise, there was no questions. I guess the way we were dressed and our cash payment, screamed jobs. On our way back to the car, Sandy asked once more if we could go into the head shop. I took the bag she was holding. "Sis, if you wanna' turn yourself into a junkie, go ahead, I'll be in the car."

"Girl I ain't no junkie, I'll be out in ten minutes."

"Whatever Sandy."

TONI

Back in Compton, I was gathering some good information. Really, the shit was so easy. First I logged onto the DEA website. I wanted to see how many offices they had here in California, there were four. Two in Northern Calif., one on the Central Coast, and one in San Diego. I guess Sandy was right. Next I was able to find some information on recent drug bust. Five miles from the border, a black panel van was stopped, and due to prior surveillance, fifty kilos of black tar heroin was seized along with $15,000 in cash and two hand guns. And from what I could tell it was still waiting to be stored somewhere in the warehouse.

See that's what I'm talkin' about. That was good information, but not what I was looking for. Next I typed in storage facilities, not really expecting anything to come up from this, but there they were. I got the one in San Diego, which turned out to be located only three miles east of their main office. From what information I could get, the warehouse was 7500 square feet, so it was large enough to drive the SUVs into it. We still have to check it out to see the best way to enter. Next I hacked into their database where I found their inventory. After a good ten minutes of searching, all I could do was say, damn! The twins are going to cum in their pants when they see this shit. There was forty million in cash, hundreds upon hundreds of kilos of drugs, weed, cocaine and heroin. The weapons were in the thousands, and they even had a few high end vehicles in there.

The only problem with the money was, it was all over the place. I guess that was due to the different seizers. The largest amount I was able to find in one location was fourteen million. That was only one million less than what Sandy said we could expect, and I'm more than cool with that. Everything looked good, I knew where our money was, there's a van right there for Black and Yellow Bird, and to sweeten the pot, there's another thirty-five kilos of cocaine still on the floor of the warehouse. If they want, they can have that and throw it in the van as well. This was a gold mine of information. The twins are gonna' love me for this one. I printed out the inventory list, then went into an employee search. There were seven people there during the day that ran the place. They were not that important since we would be making our move sometimes after midnight. At that time there would only be one person guarding the place. Somehow we were gonna' have to find a way to catch him slippin'. My last task was their alarm system. I haven't even seen the building, but to be holding that type of inventory, they had to have a state of the art security system.

To my surprise, there was nothing state of the art about it. It was just a routine alarm system, with an alarm box on the outside of the building. I guess they thought, "Hey, we're the fuckin' DEA, who's gonna' rob us?" Just to test out my skills, I turned the system on and off a few times as if it had a short in the wiring. Since I couldn't tell how the police would respond, I figured that I'd do it before we were ready to go to work. If it's done too many times, they might realize something is up with their system and upgrade it before we make our move. By four thirty the twins showed up bearing gifts. Daishawn grabbed onto Candy's leg like he could smell there was something for him in one of the bags.

"What's up my lil' lover man?" Candy said, as he smiled up at her. She handed him his gift. But due to its size, when she let go, his lil' ass fell over. Even though I thought it was funny, I still told them.

"Y'all need to stop spoiling his butt."

"I know, I just couldn't help it, I saw this and I saw him. But don't trip, we got you something too. You gonna' say we're spoiling you too?"

"I can tell mine is about business, now show and tell."

"What about his truck?" Sandy asked.

"Leave it in the box, he can play with it like that until his dad comes to get him, then he can put it together for him. Say thank you Candy."

"T'nk u Candy."

"Where's your mom?" Sandy asked.

"Her job called and asked if she wanted to come in for some overtime, so she went. She should be in by 9:00 p.m."

"That's cool, 'cause I don't know how she would react to all this stuff and where it came from, not to mention what the hell we plan on doing with it," Sandy said.

"Look, before we go through that stuff, I'm dying to show y'all what I've found," I said.

"What is it?" Candy asked.

"When was the last time you had a major orgasm without anyone touching you?" I asked.

"Is it that serious?" Sandy asked.

"Girl I'm telling you, your panties might get wet when I show you this shit." I handed them the inventory sheet. "Look at what I highlighted."

"I knew it, I fuckin' knew it. Didn't I tell y'all it would be a boat load of money just sitting there?" Sandy said.

"Let me see that Sandy. Damn girl, Toni you sure you just didn't make this shit up?" Candy asked, skeptical of what she was seeing.

"Nah, that's what I found. Girl I'm telling you, there's forty five million dollars in cash in that place, and it's waiting on us."

"That means our fifteen million ain't shit. I had no idea it would really be that much. We might have to get a lil' more ya'll," Sandy said.

"No!" Candy said, "we stick to the plan. Hell, we don't even know if we can get fifteen million outta' there, now you want more. No, besides, we need to get in and outta' there as quick as possible."

"Sandy, I know you said we would each get like five million. Well if you look right here, there is fourteen million in one box or crate, we don't have to go running all over the place looking for shit, it's all right there and it's more than enough for the three of us," I said.

"Alright y'all," Sandy said, "I saw all them numbers and got greedy."

"Toni, you sure all we have to do is go to this one spot and our money will be there?" Candy asked.

"I'm sure," Toni answered and pointed at the computer screen, "but from the lay-out of things here, it looks like it's up off the ground, and in the air."

"Can one of you niggaz' drive a forklift?" Candy asked.

"No, but we can always work something out with Black and Yellow Bird," I said.

"No, no, and hell no!" Sandy said, "Whatever is in that box belongs to us."

"Sandy, you and I can handle it, even if one of us have to climb up there and cut the box open, then that's what we'll do."

"Okay Spiderwoman," I said, "what if it's a crate?"

"Don't trip, the Home Depot got all kinds of tools in there we can use. We'll just get tools for both," Candy explained.

"You think you're so smart," Sandy told her.

"Look fat head, being smart is the only way we're gonna' stay outta' jail," Candy declared.

"Look," I told them, "we still got a lot of work to do, but before we go any further I want to show you something else. This is really bothering me too. I got into their alarm system. I was able to turn it on and off a few times, so we're good on that end. But we need a police scanner."

"Okay, so what's the problem?" Sandy asked.

"The problem is, this shit was too damn easy! You would think a government agency like the DEA would have better security. There's millions in there and their system is bullshit. Something is not right, it's just too easy."

"Okay," Sandy said, "let's run it again, do everything you did before we got here."

"I know nothing is going to change. The building has no motion detectors on the inside, just your basic alarm system."

"Maybe it's as it should be," Candy asserted.

"What do you mean?" I asked.

"Look who this is? How often do you hear about people robbing, excuse me, ripping off government warehouses?"

"Never," I said.

"Exactly. But I'll tell you what, if you're worried, why not look at the other buildings around. Check to see if any of them are decoys. If they have ties to the DEA," Candy said.

"Damn sis, that's a good idea. Toni you think you can do something like that?" Sandy asked.

"I'll get right on it."

"I told you, if you think safe, you'll be safe," Candy said.

"Look y'all, before tonight is over I will work on that. It's getting late, I need to bathe and feed Daishawn before my mom gets home. I don't need her trippin'. I know if she didn't go to work she wouldn't care about doing it herself. But before you leave I wanna' see the stuff you bought."

"We found the Wi-Fi Max you wanted," Sandy said.

"Yeah, I figured they would have one. But what's up with the laptops? I have one here."

"The store clerk said, that together the two would triple the power of the laptop. Besides, I was thinking, once we're done, all this shit has to go. This stuff is gonna be like one big ass finger print," Sandy said.

"You know how long I've had my computer?" Toni asked.

"My point exactly. It has to go Girl. Here's two new laptops, top of the line. We use one for our mission and the other one, you can start to rebuild your system. Sounds good enough to you Toni?" Sandy asked.

"Sounds good," I reply.

"Okay you two, I'm tired, we can make our second shopping trip tomorrow for tools and what-not, or we can wait until we see the building. Because we still don't know how we're going to get in," Sandy said.

"Well whatever we do," Candy said, "it can't be too much 'cause we blew through most of our cash at the computer store."

"Shit I can fix that, here go $500 for each of you," I said.

"Thanks," Sandy said, "but I'm afraid this is not gonna' cover all the other things we're gonna' need."

"I feel you, we still need the police scanner," I said.

"You should have called us about that," Candy said.

"Don't trip, that was the last thing I worked on, and I know it would be too late to call, and we still need money to rent the cars."

"Leave that to me," Sandy said, "Black and Yellow Bird are going to kick in as soon as I see them."

"Sandy you know they're gonna' want more than what we're offering," Candy told her.

"Fuck that," I said, "how the hell are they gonna' get it? I'm the only one that knows where everything is. Believe it or not, I hold the key to this whole thang. Let them niggaz' trip, they ass will be running all over that place lookin' for shit, and we'll be on our way home."

We all laughed and high fived each other. "Besides, there's a van full of heroin sitting there for them. If that ain't good enough for them too bad."

"Go ahead wit' yo' bad ass," Sandy said.

"Alright, y'all gots' to get up outta' here."

"Cool, thanks for the money, I think I'll go buy me a stripper for the night," Candy said, as she thrust her pelvic and gave an erotic twist to her hips.

"Damn," I told her, "first it was some Mexican pussy, now you want a stripper, yo' ass is just nasty."

"You can call me what you want, I know what's up. Come here Daishawn and give auntie a kiss."

"Shit," Sandy said, "don't be tryin' to turn him out wit' yo' freaky ass."

"No you didn't. I'm not the one who was making all kinds of noises and had niggaz' staring at a bathroom door 'cause I couldn't take a lil' dick," Candy said. We laughed so hard, even Daishawn got in on the action.

Chapter 6

BLACK

"You know homie, we need to come up with a way to cut this dope-dealing shit loose. All day yesterday we was running around collecting money so we could pay off these fools and make this next run up north," I said.

"Well, what do you wanna' do? We make most of our money on these trips," Yellow Bird said.

"I know, but I'm about cool on this shit."

"Don't trip man, we'll come up with something. Have you been saving yo' money?" Yellow Bird asked.

"Hell yeah, why?"

"I don't know, Black if we stop this we're gonna' need something to make up for it. And you know them boyz' ain't gonna' wanna' let us go that easy." I didn't answer the homie, his words had me focused on the road. Before I knew it, we were in Bakersfield. My boy Voodoo was there waiting with the usual rent-a-car. Within its back seat there were fifteen kilos of cocaine, which was due in Sacramento in seven hours. I could make the drive in four hours and some change the way I drove, but riding this dirty could get a nigga on lock forever and a day. Before we hit the road, we made sure the dope was secure and that there was nothing laying around inside the car that would cause us to be arrested if we happened to get stopped.

Yellow Bird made sure the tags were good and that there was no broken tail lights. "Black, from what I can tell, everything looks good, the radar detector will have to do the rest. As long as you pay attention to it we should be alright," Yellow Bird said.

"Cool, I'm ready to push. Hey Voo, we should be back here by ten tomorrow, and back in Compton a few hours later. I want you to meet us at Rosco's Chicken & Waffles in Carson for lunch at 1:00," Black said.

"Alright I'll be there," Voodoo said.

"Yeah nigga, and when you get there I'mma' have a cool surprise for you."

"Yeah whatever nigga, just don't bring no bullshit," Voodoo said.

"When have I ever put bullshit in the game? Oh yeah, if you ride yo' bike bring an extra helmet," I said.

"What for?"

"I told you, it's a surprise. I peeped game last Friday and I'm tellin' you, I got something for yo' ass. We out my nigga."

About an hour after leaving Bakersfield, Yellow Bird's phone rang.

"What's up Candy?" Yellow answered.

"Hey, where are you?"

"About half way to Sacramento."

"I just called to say thank you again for the roses you brought me yesterday."

"Don't trip, I'm glad you like them. Shit the way you was smiling, I might have to buy you flowers more often."

"You know the one thing I liked more than the roses?"

"What's that?"

"Seeing you."

"That's always a good thing."

"When will you be back?"

"We should be back around noon tomorrow. Why, you wanna' hook up?"

"I might."

"Okay look, if you do, I want you to do me a favor," Yellow said.

"What's that?" Candy asked.

"I want you wear some stone washed 501 jeans and a white t-shirt. Also I want you to make sure yo' jeans are one and a half sizes too small."

"Why is that?" Candy asked.

"No questions, just do that for me," Yellow said.

"Hey my nigga," I said to Yellow.

"Candy, hold on a minute. What's up dog?" Yellow Bird asked.

"I was going to call Sandy, but tell her to take Sandy and Toni and meet us at Rosco's tomorrow afternoon at 2:00," I said.

"Candy, did you hear Black?" Yellow Bird asked.

"Yeah, I heard him," Candy answered.

"So, you'll be there, right?" Yellow asked.

"Yeah we'll be there."

"Okay, just make sure you got them Levi's on for me."

"Yeah whatever."

"Look, I'm out. I call you tonight."

"Yeah you do that, I like talking to you."

"You know I'm on a business run so I'll get at you later, K's up."

"Hey, I told you about that," Candy said, raising her voice in frustration.

"Damn, I told you, force of habit. Bye!"

A few hours later we were in Sacramento with time to spare. G Parkway was our destination. A ten-minute drive from the five freeway. It was surrounded by a rod iron gate with a guard station out front. Although they tried to clean this place up, this was still one of Sac's hottest dope spots. Next to Del Paso Heights, niggaz' out here were still willing to pay $16,000 for every brick. If this shit work out today, we stood to make $240,000. But it looked like some bloods out of Oak Park wasn't feeling how two Compton Crips was makin' moves in their city. Little did they know we had six young niggaz' staying in there. And we paid them real well to do one thing, dust anybody off that tries to interfere with our business. They know they are not to sale any dope, no gang bangin', all in all, no unwanted attention. And the $15,000 we pay them each month makes sure they comply with orders.

I called them five minutes before I got off the freeway, which gave them time to get themselves into position. When three bloods saw me and the homie get out the rental with blue Kansas City Royal hats on, they thought they had some easy victims. "What's up blood?" One of them said. Yellow played it cool.

"Hey fellaz', how y'all doing?"

"Where you niggaz' from Blood?"

"Is there a problem fellaz'?"

"Yeah nigga, I know y'all some punk ass crip's." I moved over to the passenger side of the car with Yellow Bird.

"Check this out home boy," I said, "we don't want no problems and you don't need the problem we're gonna' give yo' ass."

"Blood, you niggaz' gots' to get up outta' here."

"I plan to do just that in about fifteen minutes, so don't trip."

"Nah my nigga, I mean now."

"You know what home boy, I told you we would push in a few minutes, after we handle our business. But see, yo' ass want some shit you really can't handle. I'm tellin' you, be cool and we will do our thang and leave."

"Fuck that blood, you heard the homie," another one of them said. Yellow Bird took off his hat and threw it on the car, then he cracked his knuckles like he was ready to show off his boxing skills. One looked like he was going for a gun, but before either of them could react, six heavily armed men came from three different directions. It was only four in the afternoon, but no one saw exactly where they came from.

Each of the killers had a 357 Desert Eagle in hand and a fully automatic Bush Master across their back. Lookin' dumbfounded, I told them, "Now check this out cuzz', you was saying we needed to get up outta' here, right? We tried not to go there with you niggaz', but nah, you wanted to see how gang bangin' is really done. Now get yo' punk ass on the ground. # Six, pat these fools down for any weapons." Only two of them had guns. "# Four, we need something to move these dudes in."

"I'm on it boss," Soldier # Four said.

You four cuff they asses with zip ties and get them ready to move. Yo' hurry up, people are starting to take notice of what's going on." Just then, # Four came up with an old school K5 Blazer, they loaded the trio in the back, and I told # Six to go with # Four. "Y'all go down to Carl's Jr. on Florin Road and wait for us. Make sure you park where no one will pay you too much attention, we should be there in like twenty minutes."

"I got you, should we air these niggaz' out on the way there?" # Four asked.

"Nah nah, we got enough attention as it is. Hell I'm in a good mood, I just might let them go. Y'all push and we'll see you in a few minutes. Yellow Bird turned the car around while I opened the garage. As he did that, I told # One to stand guard. As we unloaded the car, the rest of the crew faded back into their surroundings. Ten minutes later we were done and I handed # One their pay for the month.

Things went well despite the run-in with them blood niggaz'. I was still going over in my mind what I wanted to do with them.

"Yellow," I said, contemplating our next moves.

"What's up?" Yellow Bird said.

"You know we really need to make an example outta' these niggaz'. You know how I feel about killin' though. Damn we've been doin' good on our runs up here," I said to him.

"Yeah I feel you, but I don't appreciate them getting at us like that."

"Okay, you make the call," I told him. "

"I got this. # One you got an extra car around here?" Yellow asked.

"Yeah, give me three minutes," Soldier # One said.

"What's up?" I asked.

"We're gonna' drive these fools to Modesto, then have they ass walk home ass-hole naked," Yellow Bird said.

"That ain't bad," I said.

"Yeah, well it will be after we put a bullet in one of their knee caps."

"Damn nigga, that's some cold shit."

"Cuzz', them fools will think twice about running up on some Compton niggaz' next time."

After making sure everything was locked up, we all met down the road as I instructed. "Y'all did a good job. We were gonna' push back to Compton tonight but tomorrow will be better. Besides we need the rest. # One, I want you to search them again, make sure they don't have anything they can use to cut their way loose. Then go park the blazer in a place no one can see them. Leave them in there for the night."

"You punk ass niggaz' get some sleep," Yellow Bird told them, "cause this might be the last time either of you wake up in the morning."

"Look, it's almost 6:00 p.m., y'all get comfortable, it's gonna' be a long night for y'all," I said.

"Damn boss, y'all some cold niggaz'."

"What, you want them to come sleep with you?"

"Nah, I'm cool," # One replied.

"They can stay in the trunk and you guys don't have to watch them for the night. You good with that?"

"Hell yeah."

"Cool. # Six, here's what I want you to do, make sure both these cars are gassed up, go ahead and put these niggaz' up for the night, then y'all go out and have some fun. We hit the road at 5:30 in the morning, so dress for the occasion. # One I also want you to bring two small caliber hand guns, but leave the rest of your hardware behind. We'll meet here in the morning. One more thing," I said, loud enough for them to hear me, "bring a can of gas, I got something special in mind for these fools." They all laughed, and the three in the truck began to squirm and moan. We left and took off down Mack Road. Just past the freeway we got a room at the Comfort Inn.

YELLOW BIRD

After we got our things into the room, Black went out for food. With nothing to do I started flipping through the T.V. channels. When porn popped up I started thinking about Candy, so I grabbed my cell phone. My shit actually got hard and it had nothing to do with what was on T.V. Thinking about her in them Levi's did it. Damn, I should have gotten some bud from one of them young niggaz'. Maybe the homie Black will come back with some.

With my shit still hard and frustration kicking in, I called her.

"Hello," she answered.

"What's up sexy?"

"Who is this?"

"Oh you got jokes now?"

"Oh what's up Keith? What are you doing?"

"Sitting here holding my shit thinking about you."

"Damn nigga, what am I supposed to say to that?"

"You ask me that same question tomorrow when we hook up and I'll give you a real good answer."

"Whatever nigga. How did things go today?"

"We ran into some dudes from Oak Park, but they walked into a bad situation."

"You're alright though?"

"I'm talking to you ain't I? Look, what are you wearing?"

"Shit, you think your dick is hard now, if I told you, yo' ass might blow a gasket."

"Don't trip on all that, now what are you wearing?"

"A lil' of this and a lil' of that."

"Why you playin' with the game?"

She laughed. "I'll tell you on one condition."

"What's that?"

"You gots' to pay to find out."

"What I look like, a trick?"

"Hey, you the one that wanna' know."

"Okay, how much?"

"I thought you would see it my way. It will cost you a C note for everything I tell you I have on then take off."

"Shit, with all the money I made today, I can handle that."

"Yo' shit still hard?"

"Oh hell yeah."

"Too bad, I gotta' go, here I come mom."

"That's fucked up Candy, you gonna' play me like that? Wait until I see yo' ass tomorrow."

"I can't wait, I love you too, Bye!" Damn, that was a first, I wonder if she really tried to say that shit?

CANDY

Damn, I hope he didn't catch what I just said. I don't know myself if I love him or not, but I know I can't wait to see him tomorrow. I could have easily played with myself just now while he was holding his dick, but that will have to wait. Although I haven't let him fuck me too many times, we have hooked up before and each time was off the hook. The way he seems to love eating my pussy was really making me miss him. I am so tempted to call him back, but instead I got up and went to my closet. If his ass wants to see me in some Levi's, one and a half sizes too small, the Apple Bottoms I'm gonna' wear is gonna' have that fool wanting to fuck me right through my jeans.

YELLOW BIRD

Black Bird came in the room with some Mexican food from Taco Rico's. "Cuzz', why you watching that shit?" Black said.

"Man you don't wanna' know. Check this out Black, I've been thinking and we need to go ahead and dust them three niggaz' off."

"Where did that come from? You said you agreed we shouldn't kill them."

"First give me my food, I'm hungry. "

"Here."

"Good lookin' out. Look, the more I think about it, the more I realize that leaving them alive will cost us in the long run, them fools saw too much," Black's eyes narrowed, but I went on.

"They've seen the drop spot, they've seen the hit squad we got stashed up in there, and they're gonna' know we're protecting something of value. All in all, they just seen way too much."

"Cuzz, them niggaz' don't have what it takes to fuck up what we got going," Black said.

"Maybe, maybe not, but even if that's the case, they will eventually talk about what went down today, even at the risk of embarrassment. If they don't come looking to check us out, someone else will."

"Man you seen how them young niggaz' took care of business today? That's what we pay them for."

"Yeah, that's just what I'm talkin' about. If they have to put in major work in that lil' ass area, eventually the police is gonna' show up, and if there is an investigation, you can best believe today will come up. If we allow that to happen, we're gonna' upset a lot of people, so we need to do this."

"Okay crip, you know how they say guns don't kill people, people kill people?" Black asked tapping the bull dog .347 under his shirt.

"Yeah."

"Well I'mma' prove them wrong, cause I'mma' dump a whole lotta' bullets into they ass." About thirty minutes later after taking a shower, I told Black to call or text # One, and tell them to get here as soon as they could with the soon to be murder victims. "Tell them they only need the blazer and some hand guns."

"Man what are you talking about? I thought we were gonna' take care of this shit tomorrow?" Black said.

"Shits changed. We were going to just hurt them a bit and send them on their way, but now they won't live through the night, and I plan to be in Compton when the sun comes up or very close to it. I'll be back in a few, I'm going to AM/PM to gas up the car. Make the call. You want anything? "

"Yeah, to get some much needed sleep," Black said.

"Man yo' ass can sleep in the car."

Chapter 7

BLACK BIRD

As Yellow Bird walked out the door, I couldn't help but think there was something else that made him want to take care of this shit now. The two of us grew up together and as far back as I can remember, his judgement was always good. Whenever I didn't listen to cuzz, things went bad. I wish that nigga had a way around this texting and cell phone shit. I knew from watching Judge Joe Brown, anything you say or text on these things is recorded and stored somewhere. But hey, what are you gonna' do? Niggaz' think they too good for a good old fashion pager and a phone booth. I made the call, fuck that texting shit, them lil' ass buttons always make me mess up what I'm trying to say. I got # One on the phone. "What's up boss?" he answered. I ran everything down to him in seconds.

"Check this out, why don't we take care of this shit and the two of you get to where y'all need to be."

"Damn yo' ass is country," I said.

"Shit I was born and raised in the Heights," # One said.

"Did you have a cow bell around yo' neck when you came out?"

"I see you got jokes. Look, we can be there in fifteen minutes if you want."

"Fuck it, go ahead and do the damn thang. Just make sure it's done far away from here and done right."

"I feel you, and I'll see you when I see you, stay up."

My boy was back and I put him up on game. Right off I could tell from the look in his eyes he wanted to have a hand in the execution. I asked him about it, but he said he was cool with my decision. Cuzz started gathering up his gear, so I did the same. I could tell this was gonna' be one long ass drive. A few minutes later we were in the car and heading south on I-5. Within an hour I was doing my best not to say anything, but this nigga was driving me crazy. His ass kept playin' "In Those Jeans" by Ginuwine. "Cuzz, what's up with you? Why the hell you keep playin' that shit over and over?" All he would say was:

"You'll see tomorrow."

"Where in the hell you find some CDs this time of night anyway? We didn't have any on the way out here."

"I caught somebody slippin' at the gas station. Lucky for me what I was after was in there," Yellow Bird said.

"That's my nigga, never pass up a good opportunity. There was a whole case?"

"You know it. Look back there."

"Cool, let's see what's in here."

During the five hours it took us to reach Bakersfield, we pretty much blew through all the CDs Yellow Bird came up on and I managed to get some sleep. I knew he has been awake almost two days straight, but so far his driving has been on point. As soon as we get back to the Escalade and our cash, which should be there waiting on us, I plan to drive the three and a half hours to the city. That should put us there in the morning.

SANDY & BLACK

"Candy, you sleep over there?"

"What do you think? What time is it?" she asked sounding annoyed.

"It's lil' after midnight."

"Man, I don't know why I never moved into the other room years ago. What do you want?" Candy asked.

"I can't stop thinking about what Black is gonna' say when I tell him about our plans."

"I don't see what you're trippin' on, them niggaz' are natural born hustlers, and I'm sure they're gonna' want in on this," Candy replied.

"I feel you," I said, "but I think what worries me most is, they might try to take over the show."

"Don't you remember, it's all about information, and they don't have it, and I don't see how they can get it. Unless they have a Toni of their own-that we don't know about, we're good."

"Shit, since you're so sure about this, why don't you tell them about everything?" I said.

"Not a problem, and since I forgot to tell you, the five of us are supposed to meet for lunch tomorrow. I'll tell them then," Candy said.

"When did all this come about?"

"Keith called me earlier, they want us to meet them at Rosco's Chicken & Waffles in Carson at 2:00. I'm not gonna' tell you what else that nigga wants me to do."

"What?" I asked.

"For some reason he wants me to wear some stone washed jeans one and a half sizes too small."

"I guess that explains it all, that nigga got ass on his mind," I said, laughing. Candy threw the covers over her head and turned over. I tried to do the same but it was not to be. Thinking of how Black had me all fucked up in the club last Friday night got to me. I grabbed my phone and speed dialed his number. After the second ring he picked up. "What's up kid? It's pretty late for you to be calling ain't it?"

"What do I look like, ten?"

"I'm just sayin'."

"Hey I heard you invited me to lunch tomorrow."

"Something like that."

"Well what if I didn't want to have lunch with you?"

"Oh I get it, you're still mad about the other night at the club."

"Nah I'm not mad, in fact I might want you to finish what you started."

"I didn't start nothing, you did when you let that nigga snatch yo' panties off."

"Oh you saw that, huh?"

"Yeah, and speaking of panties, do you have some on now?"

"Maybe, why don't you come find out?"

"If I wasn't three hours away, I just might take you up on that offer. Anyway, are you coming to lunch or what?"

"Yeah I'll be there, and I guess you want me to wear some tight ass jeans too?"

"Why you say that?"

"Cause Keith told Candy to wear some jeans and they had to be size and a half too small."

"I heard him earlier today, but I forgot about that shit. I knew something was going on."

"What?"

"When we first hit the freeway to come home, that nigga played "In Those Jeans" like ten times. You know I had to snatch that shit out the CD player."

"Well, it looks like somebody is going to get their freak on some time tomorrow. What do you think?" I asked him.

"Sounds like it, but the question is, are we gonna' be there?" Black asked.

"What, you want the four of us to sex each other?" I said.

"Nigga I heard that shit," Candy half yelled, "and the answer is hell no."

"Yo' ass is supposed to be sleep, and I didn't agree to no shit like that anyway," I said.

"No, but it sure sound like you was about to volunteer the both of us for some freaky foursome shit," Candy said.

"Shit, Baby girl, you know every man's dream is-to fuck two twins," Black said, as he laughed in a low tone.

"Well my nigga, it look' like your dream just got dashed fuckin' wit' me and my twin, cause it ain't goin' down," I said, adamantly.

"Look Sandy, it's late, I'm driving, and I don't want to get caught on this phone because they are gonna' impound the homies truck. Just make sure you come to lunch tomorrow, I got a surprise for Toni."

"Ooh, what is it?" I asked, excitedly.

"It's not a what, but a who."

"Well who is it?"

"Didn't you not hear me say the word 'surprise'"?

"Ah fuck you nigga."

"Yeah, that's just what I want you to do. Bye with yo' sexy ass." By 7:45 a.m. I came off the freeway on Atlantic Blvd and even though the Kellys' and the Atlantics' was beefing with each other like crazy, I still went down the Drive. Once I turned down Caldwell and passed White Street I felt safe. There was like twenty times more niggaz' from Kelly Park then there was from Atlantic Drive, but you had to give it to them, them niggaz' wouldn't back down from us or any other hood in Compton. Any gun play and they was wit' it.

I hit the block and pushed the garage door opener. The two Blue Nose Pit's, Black Jack & Friendly, who was anything but friendly, came from within the house. They have three doggy doors, so they're able to cover the whole house and yard. They can get in and out with ease if any of these neighborhood fools around here take leave of their senses.

"Hey my nigga, wake up, we're home." But before he could answer I was out and getting to work. There was two access panels at the rear end of the Cadillac. Within the two small doors, there was $244,000 I needed to divide into three. Sleep was still like an hour away for me. This is one time I wish I fucked with them 'X' pills. I know I won't have much time to sleep and I plan on fuckin' the hell outta' Sandy sometime today.

I'll be damn if I walk away from that pussy this time. But every now and then, niggaz' gotta' let these chicks know their pussy ain't all that.

Yellow Bird went right to his room with Friendly right behind him, and since there was no noise coming from the room, I knew he fell right into bed with the pit at his feet. The greatest invention ever made for drug dealers was the money counter, and I was happy as hell we had one. It only took thirty to forty minutes to get the cash divided into three. By now it was 8:30 a.m. in the morning and I've had it. I grabbed a half blunt from the ashtray, grabbed my Zippo, took one big ass hit, held it for as long as I could, then blew the smoke into Black Jack's face. Moments later I fell asleep on the couch.

TONI

A June morning in L.A. is but one thing, hot! It was 8:30 a.m. and I was trying to get Daishawn ready to be picked up by his dad. Even though it was his two days to have the baby, I knew Daishawn would spend most of that time being watched by his grandmother. "Come here lil' man and let me put your shoes on. Come on now, your dad will be here soon." I was finally able to get him dressed and fed. To my surprise, at 9:00 on the dot the door bell rung. Shawn was there looking good as ever. "What's up Shawn?"

"Chillin', tell me something good," Shawn said.

"I got enough of his things in here to last three days. Please make sure it's all in here when I come get him."

"You know that's not tellin' me something good, that's you barkin' orders."

"You always leaving half his stuff at your house."

"Okay we're not about to get into it. Look, I'll tell you what, why don't you come spend the day with us?"

"Sorry pretty boy, but I have work to do. Daishawn, come see who's here." He came towards the door dragging the box that was too big for him to carry.

"This is nice, you're pretty lucky lil' man. Hey, you said you have work to do, what are you working on Ma?" Shawn asked.

"Me and the twins are working on a project together. We're going to steal about twenty million dollars from the U.S. Government."

"Man, sometimes you so full of shit. Since you don't want me to know, and you don't want to spend the day with us, I'm outta' here, we'll see you next week."

"Next week, it's Wednesday and you only have him for two days."

"Check this out, who's his dad?"

"You are."

"Then don't be tellin' me when I can spend time with my son."

"But the court said..."

"Man fuck the courts. If I didn't want to have him around me yo' ass would complain about that. Now I want him longer than usual, and you want to complain about that. I don't need you or some white ass judge to tell me when to bring my son home. You feel me? Just know I won't let no harm come his way. So for the last time, you wanna' kick it with us today or what?"

"Sorry, but I can't."

"Alright we out. Give your mom a kiss lil' man."

"Bye baby, I love you."

Watching them leave, all I could only say 'Damn'. I guess I should feel lucky, most niggaz' wouldn't have spent time with their babies if you tied the kid to their backs. Shit, as long as he kept Daishawn safe, I'll have to live with this new turn of events. My mom left for work an hour ago, so I cleaned up the house and got to work on the computer. As it turned out, the surrounding buildings all seemed legit. I could find no signs that any of them had any ties to the DEA, and that made me start to worry again. Why would a place with so much valuable shit in it have such a bullshit security system? I guess I'll just have to run it by the twins again. Damn, I've been at this shit for almost four hours and I found all the information I could. I guess if the twins are serious about doing this, a day before we go in, I'll pull up the inventory list again to make sure nothing has changed. Black and Yellow Bird will have a van sitting there full of heroin, and we'll have a box full of cash. Let one of them niggaz' get greedy, I'mma' start bustin' with the 380. Noon came around and I got a call from Candy.

"What's up sexy?" she said, when I answered.

"Girl I told you about that shit."

"Bitch I'm just playin' with yo' ass. How did things go today? Was you able to find anything out?"

"Yeah, from what I can tell, we're all good. They are just ordinary places of business, but that worries me even more."

"Okay, look, we are meeting Black and Yellow Bird for lunch at 2:00 this afternoon. We'll be there to pick you up, we can discuss everything with them then, cool?"

"Yeah, I'll see you when you get here, bye!"

While I was getting dressed Big Ten called from prison, "What's up pops?"

"Hey baby girl, you know I had to call and say thanks for shooting that money."

"So I take it you got your cell phone?"

"Yeah, it came through yesterday," Pops said.

"Do you need me to buy you some minutes?" I asked

"Nah, you did yo' thang, I can handle the rest. The phone cost me five hundred and the other five I got something to hustle with, so I'm cool. Outta' that I can pay the $50.00 a month."

"I feel you, just be careful and you know I got you anytime you need me. Look Ten, I'm tryin' to get dressed, the twins are on the way to pick me up. We're working on something, and if it works out I'm going to buy your way outta' there."

"I don't know what that is, but it sounds serious, so check this out, don't get caught up in no bullshit on my behalf," Pop's said.

"I'm not dad, and don't worry, we're good. I love you. Even from in there you're still worrying about me."

"Hey, I love you too, and before you go, when are you going to bring my grandson to see me?"

"If our venture goes good, I'll be there in a few weeks, can you wait until then?"

"Yeah, that's cool. I'll talk to you later. Oh and tell your mom to get at me."

"Since I have your new number, I'll give it to her and she can call you."

"Yeah, do that. Alright baby girl, I'll talk to you later, and please be safe out there," he said, sounding concerned.

"I love you dad," I said.

"I love you more baby girl," he said, then added, "Be safe Toni."

Chapter 8

TONI

By 1:30 p.m. the twins were here, and I noticed something new. This was the first time they've dressed alike in years. "What's with the T-shirt and jeans? You two haven't done this in years," I said.

"Candy was told to specifically wear some jeans one and a half sizes too small."

"Okay, then why do they look painted on?" I asked.

"I guess she was tryin' to make a statement."

"Okay I can see that, now tell me this, what's your excuse?"

"Whatever it is", Candy said, "you can best believe Black had a hand in it."

"Shit, if he gets a hand in them tight ass pants, I'mma' know something," I said. We all laughed. "Look I'm ready but hold on for a minute."

Five minutes later I came back dressed like the twins. So for anyone walking behind us, all they would see was ass. I knotted my T-shirt at the hip so it wouldn't cover my butt.

"How do I look?" I asked.

"If your hair was more like ours, I'd say welcome to the family," Candy said.

"Toni, do you have the inventory list?" Sandy asked.

"I have all the information I was able to get. Before we go, y'all sure you wanna' bring them in on this?" I asked.

"We might as well," Sandy said, "what if we get there and find that we really need them? Now I just think things will work out better using them."

"I agree," Candy said.

"You better agree, it was your idea in the first place," Sandy said.

"Okay Sandy, don't start. You put this shit together so we know you're calling the shots, if them niggaz' go to trippin' and tryin' to flip the script, I'mma' trip myself. Let's go!" I said, grabbing my bag, keys, and cell.

BLACK

"Good lookin' out Black," Voodoo said, "it ain't nothing like being handed a wad of cash this early in the day. Did you two run into any trouble up north?"

"Somewhat, but it wasn't nothing major. Although yo' boy over here decided to have three niggaz' executed," I said.

"Damn my nigga, what's up with that?" Voodoo asked.

"Fool don't go trippin' 'cause you would have done the same thing if them niggaz' pushed up on you like they did us," Yellow Bird said.

"Yeah, you're probably right. I guess I'm glad I wasn't on this run."

"Well you can best believe you'll be on the next one," I told him. "But hey, just follow protocol and everything will go smoothly."

"Check this out Black, and this goes for you too Voodoo. We need to cut down on wearing so much blue when we make these runs. Oak Park is big as fuck and them blood niggaz' are all over the place," Yellow Bird said.

"But my next run is to Del Paso Heights," I said.

"It doesn't matter, them dudes out there are so mixed up, it's hard to tell the Crip's from the Blood's."

"Look when the three of us put this shit together, it was supposed to be highly profitable and easy, so no more crippin' on our runs. Y'all cool with that?" Yellow said.

"Hey," I said, "I always trust this niggaz' judgement. Why you think I never go to jail?"

"We good my nigga," Voodoo said, "Hey my nigga, we been here almost an hour and I'm still waitin' on my surprise, what's up with that?"

"Just hold on, it'll be here. And that reminds me," I said, looking at my watch, "we need to move, this booth isn't big enough. Excuse me," I called to the waitress.

"Yes sir?" answered the waitress.

"I have three more people joining us for lunch in a few minutes, do you think I can have this area back here and have these tables moved together?"

"Sure," she replied.

"I appreciate that," I said, handing her a $50 bill.

"Hey y'all come with me, we need more room."

I noticed Candy's Jetta pulling into the parking lot, so I told Voodoo to check this out. "You wanna' see some magic?"

"Man what the hell is you talkin' about?" he asked.

"Watch me make three fine ass chicks get outta' that car right there. Ta dahhhh, how you like me now?" I said, demonstrating a magician's sleight of hand.

"Ah yeah," Yellow Bird said, "that nigga good."

"Cuzz, that's oh girl from club Vault," Voodoo said.

"I told you I peeped game that night. Nigga the shit I just did for you right there is easily worth a thousand dollars," I said.

"Man you got that comin'," Voodoo said.

"Come on y'all let's move," I said.

"Black, you know I got major love for you."

"Don't trip my nigga."

YELLOW BIRD

The six of us met at the rear of the restaurant. "Ladies, thanks for coming. Candy, Sandy, this is Donnie Walls, we call him Voodoo. Toni, you guys already know each other."

"How you guys doing? Well well, if it isn't miss many names. Your other name is Layla, right?" Voodoo asked.

"Yep," Toni answered.

"Everyone have a seat. Candy come here." I leaned into her ear as she sat down. "You did yo' thang wit' them jeans."

"I'm glad you like them."

"Yeah Toni," Black said, "I saw y'all talkin' and since I mess with this dude real tough, I figured he would like to see you again."

"Yeah, and you figured right," Voodoo said.

"I hope you don't mind me playing match-maker?" Black asked with a grin.

"I'm good with that," Toni replied.

"Well," Sandy said, "you picked a fine time to wanna' play Mr. Hook Em' Up."

"Why you say that?" Black asked.

"Because we came here to talk business with you two," Sandy said, motioning to Black and Yellow Bird.

"So what's stoppin' you?" Black asked.

"We just wasn't expecting him," Toni said, "this is some serious shit, Black."

"Check this out. I trust cuzz like I trust Yellow Bird. Whatever it is, it couldn't possibly be worse than the shit we do three or four times a month. Shit, if only you knew, each of us could get struck out just walkin' across the street. I said that to say this, whatever you got planned you can say it in front of cuzz."

"Alright nigga," Toni said, "you asked for it. I sure hope you niggaz' ain't scared of the Federal Government? Sandy, you're up."

"Shit, since you put it like that, I'll let Candy tell you," Sandy said.

"Oh scary ass Sandy," Candy said.

"Look, here's the deal. Sandy got it in her head to break into a government warehouse and steal some money."

"What part of the government?" Black asked.

"The Drug Enforcement Agency."

"So what's the problem?" Voodoo said.

"See, I like the way you think already," Sandy said.

"You telling us you want to rob a DEA warehouse?" I asked leaning over the table so only the six of us could hear. Then, I added, "where in the hell she get an idea like that?"

"Keith if I told you, it might make it sound even worse, but we've been going over this and it's turning out to be a good looking plan," Candy said.

"And believe me," Sandy said, "yo' ass is gonna' think it's a good idea too when you see the building's inventory sheet we got our hands on."

"And how did you manage to do that?" Black wanted to know.

"Ancient Compton secret!" Toni said.

"Black I like this one. Ancient Compton secret, that was a good one," Voodoo said.

"Toni let Black see that list. There is something specifically we want, we know right where it is. Then there's a van in there full of heroin, and it has your name written all over it," Candy said.

"Man, you three have lost y'all minds," I said, "Sandy, come on now, you can't be serious about this."

"Oh we're serious, and we want you for security," Sandy said.

"Let me see that," Voodoo said.

"Look y'all, I hacked into their computer system and got this information. I got into their alarm system, which was easy as hell. I even went as far as to check out the surrounding buildings, and from what I can tell, none of them have any ties to the government," Toni said, proudly.

"Toni, do you know for sure what's in there?" Black asked.

"We have not done a visual yet, but according to their computer, that's what's in there and a whole lotta' other shit. Now give that back, thank you!" She said, taking the list back. The waitress came to take our order.

"Look, since I wanna' say thanks to Black, I'm buying lunch. Also, because I really like where this conversation is going, I'm going to order the house special for everybody. Six specials and a pitcher of orange juice. Thank you," I said, nodding to the waitress.

"Black let's hear some more of what they have to say,"
Voodoo said.

"You sure you wanna' hear the rest?" Candy asked.

"Yeah," Black said.

"Okay, this is what we want from you guys. You're basically going to watch over me and Sandy while we go in and get our cash.
For you doing this, we're giving you the opportunity to take the van that's holding fifty kilos of Black Tar Heroin that's sitting in there. Plus, the price of fifteen of those for the three of us."

"Man, at $17,500, that's like six million dollars. Toni will you marry me? Homie, if they talkin' like this I wanna' be a part of that, ain't no tellin' where we could go," Voodoo said.

"Toni, you said you were able to get into their security system, right? Tell me about it," I asked.

"I'mma' be honest, it was so basic it worried me. So Candy told me to look at other buildings but they came up clean. I couldn't find any motion detectors, there's just nothing to suggest we can't get in and outta' there without the police showing up."

"I noticed, Candy said, that her and Sandy are going inside, where will you be?" Black asked, pointing at Toni.

"She'll be in a rent-a-car with her computer and police scanner. She's our eyes and ears," Candy said.

"Yeah," Sandy said, "we already bought some of the equipment we'll need. We were also hoping you would help us out with some supplies."

Our orders came and as the waitress retreated, I wanted to know what type of supplies they needed, so I asked.

"We were thinking two suburban's', one for us and one for y'all. Then we'll need something for Toni, it needs a lot of room for batteries," Sandy said.

"Look," Voodoo said, "vehicles are not a problem. I can take care of that. Are you two squares with this shit or not?" Voodoo said, looking directly at Black and I.

"Keith, we looking at six tickets here, what's up?" Black said.

"Man you know I'm always about my money, but we need to check this shit out," I said.

"That's why we plan to drive to San Diego to see what the place looks like before we buy anymore supplies," Candy said.

"What did you buy so far?" Black asked.

"Toni's computer, six two-ways with wireless headsets, we got some infrared binoculars and three passport radar detectors," Candy said.

"Okay, so what else is needed?" I asked.

"You know about the vehicles, we still need a police scanner, and we didn't wanna' buy any tools until we see what the building looks like," Candy said.

"Well, when did y'all plan to go check out this building?" Black asked.

"Hell," Candy said, "it's only Wednesday, we could go anytime between tomorrow and Sunday."

"Hold on," Sandy said, "before we go anywhere, we need to get a few things straight. This was my idea and I'm in charge, feel me?"

"Baby girl," Black said, "in those jeans you can call all the shots you want." We all laughed.

SANDY

I needed to let them know this was my show. As we ate there was still some discussion about the lick. And from what I could tell everyone was willing to play their part. I was thinking of mentioning the guns that would be in there, then I thought, why give these crazy niggaz' out here even more reason to kill each other? "So tell me Black, what do you think?"

"Sandy I don't mind doing this, shit money is money and I don't care where it comes from. But Toni, it looks like everything is really riding on you, and before I let anyone step one foot in that place, I wanna' know what's gonna' happen when you turn that system off. I wanna' know how long we can leave it off, and what's gonna' happen if one of us walks around in there. Just because you didn't find any motion detectors doesn't mean they're not there," Black said.

"Black, I've made two searches already and they're not there, I'm tellin' you," Toni said.

"I feel you, but we won't know for sure until we get there and check it out," Black said.

"Man that's easy," Voodoo said.

"How so?" Black asked.

"All we have to do is make a hole in the building, then throw some dog food in as far as we can. Then send a hungry puppy in there that hasn't eaten in two days. His ass will move around in all different directions. After thirty minutes if no police show up, we know we're good to go," Voodoo said.

"I like the way you think pretty boy," Toni said, "but I don't think that will be necessary, I'm tellin' you, their system is bullshit."

"We'll see," Black told her.

"Okay," I said, "if everyone is on board with this we can take our first trip down there Friday morning. After we check out the building we'll go to the Home Depot and get whatever tools we might need. I'm telling you now, I'mma' make you niggaz' rich as fuck."

"I'm already rich," Voodoo said, "but you can never have too much money. Now I have a question. I know you two are twins, but what's up with the jeans?"

"You can blame that on those two. He wanted Candy in jeans today, then I guess Black talked Sandy into wearing some, and me, I didn't wanna' be left out," Toni said.

"Well I'm sure glad you felt that way," Voodoo said.

The waitress came to check on us. Voodoo said everyone was good and asked if he could get the check. "I'll be right back," she said. When he pulled out his cash, Toni's eyes lit up like diamonds. He counted out $1500 and handed it to Toni.

"This is for any more supplies the three of you might need." Then he counted out another thousand and handed it to Black.

"Thanks my nigga, she's smart and beautiful."

"Hold up, I know you didn't just buy me?" Toni said.

"Nothing like that, that was strictly appreciation money." After the bill was paid and a lil' more small talk, the six of us headed outside.

VOODOO &TONI

I knew I was expected to have Toni come with me. 'Bring an extra helmet' Black told me, and now I see why.

I peeped out what was about to happen and I made it sound like it was my idea. "Voodoo, I've never ridden a bike before, you mind taking me home?"

"I can handle that, go put that helmet on. Black, Yellow, y'all wanna' hook up later?"

"Not me," Yellow Bird said, "I'm about to find somewhere real secluded and enjoy bangin' all that ass over there, and I suggest you do the same."

"I heard that shit Keith," Candy said.

"Homie," Black said, "you're on your own, get at me tomorrow, we can go find some SUVs for this lick they got planned."

"You think this shit is a good idea?" Yellow Bird asked.

"Fuck it, if we can get our hands on that much heroin, and it's free, how can we not win? Hit me up tomorrow, I'm out," Black said.

KEITH & CANDY

"Candy, give me your car keys."

"Nigga you know I don't let nobody drive my baby." He pulled out a butterfly knife.

"Nobody will be driving this shit for days if I stick this in your tires."

"You wouldn't dare."

"Of course not, I actually got this to cut your clothes off."

"Ah ah, very funny. Yo' ass bet not come near me with that thing."

"Baby girl, do you plan on being this difficult the rest of the day?"

"No but..."

"But nothing, give me the keys and get in the car, we're the only ones still standing here."

Before Black could pull off, Keith went to grab his overnight bag from the back seat of his Escalade. "Don't let nothing happen to my sister fool," Sandy said.

"Don't worry she's in good hands. Don't let nothing happen to the homie."

"Fuck you nigga."

"That's what you got cuzz for, later." When he got in the car he threw his bag on the back seat. "What's that for?"

"Don't feel left out, we're about to go to your house and get you one, you're spending the night with me."

"First of all, it's after 4:00 p.m. and my mom is home, so we're not going there to get nothing. Second, you didn't ask me if I would spend the night with you." When he gave me that devilish grin I knew I was in trouble.

Chapter 9

KEITH & CANDY

Keith drove us out of Carson and into Torrance. He first took me to a small boutique, handed me $300 and told me to get whatever I might need to get me through the night. Since I knew what was in store, I got some lingerie in his favorite color, Royal Blue. I also got a short set to wear home tomorrow, along with a few other necessities. When I came out, Yellow Bird had the whole car smelling like Chronic.

"Damn nigga, that shit is strong."

"You want some?"

"Maybe later. Where are we going?"

"This morning I reserved a suite at the Holiday Inn."

"So you just knew you was gonna' get you some pussy today?"

"Don't say it like that, I've been thinkin' about enjoyin' your beautiful body since I saw you last Friday night. And I got big plans for you when you come outta' them sexy ass jeans."

"Oh really, and what might that be?" He gave me that grin again and said, "Does K-Y Jelly mean anything to you?"

All I could do was stare at him. Something told me that's what he wanted when he told me to wear these tight ass pants. I heard that shit hurts like hell. Shit, his dick barely fits in my pussy, now he wants to stick it in my ass. Damn, what am I supposed to do now?

"From the look on your face I know what you're thinkin'. Don't worry beautiful, I will never hurt you. Believe me Candy, this is one night you're going to love, trust me."

I still couldn't say anything, so I just nodded my head and turned to stare out the window. When he put his hand on my thigh, real close to my pussy, I instantly got hot.

"Don't be nervous."

"I don't do nervous, I'mma' gangsta." He laughed at me.

"Gangsta, man you get mad when I tell you K's Up."

"That's because I'm not from Kelly Park, we live in Front Hood."

"You know what? Yo' ass is crazy. But fuck all that gang shit. Why don't you come over here and give me a kiss?"

"I can do that." But I should have known better, when my lips touched his, his hand went right to my pussy. "You better pay attention to the road before you run into something."

"Baby girl I can multi-task with the best of them. Just watch all the shit I'm going to do to you once we're locked inside our room."

"Okay I hear you, but I might have a few surprises of my own."

"I know I like the sound of that."

Smiling I thought to myself. There's not much a woman can really do to a man but suck his dick, unless the couple is into some off the wall type shit. I've sucked on him before, but only a lil' bit. Tonight however, will be totally different. I'm talking about sucking on his balls and letting him cum in my mouth different. I know he will love that. Just to act like I was going to play hard ball when we got there, I slapped his hand away from my pussy. "I thought you said you had a few surprises for me? Then you slap my hand away. Man, I can tell this is gonna' be a long ass night."

As he pulled into the Holiday Inn, he reached for me again, but this time I hit him pretty hard. "Damn, like that? That's alright, 'cause the more you fight me, the harder my dick is gonna' get."

After finding somewhere to park, we gathered up our things and headed for the front desk. Right before we reached the counter she hit me in the rib cage again, it didn't hurt but I knew what the gesture meant, and my dick knew what it meant too! "Hi, do you have a reservation for Keith Sloan?"

"Just a moment sir."

I told Candy to walk over to the newsstand and grab me a paper. I didn't need nor want it, I just wanted to watch her ass move.

"Mr. Sloan, I have you right here. Do you have a major credit card?"

"Yeah, here you go." After verifying that the card was valid, she handed me a key card to room 470.

"Please call room service if you should need anything, and enjoy your stay."

"Thank you, we will." Upstairs in our suite, I got right to work on my first task. "Do you like it?"

"Very much, it's nice."

"Good, now don't move, I'll be right back." I made my way up to the second level, dropped our bags and went into the bathroom where I ran Candy a hot bath.

Back downstairs, I told her to go up and get ready for her bath. Seeing her go up the stairs almost made me say fuck it, run up after her and rip her clothes off. But I moved on to my next task. I found some nice R&B on the stereo system, then I called room service to order two bottles of Champagne and a platter of fresh cut fruit. "Candy," I called.

"Yes," she answered.

"Keep an eye on that tub, make sure it doesn't overflow, okay."

"Alright, but the shit is like a small swimming pool, it's gonna' take a while to fill."

"Just make yourself comfortable and I'll be up there as soon as room service gets here."

I don't know what's gotten into him but he has never treated me like this before, and so far I'm lovin' it. I walked back into the bathroom that looked twice the size as the one we have at home. There were bath oils on the counter, which I added to the hot water. After I really looked around, I found that there were candles and the lights could be dimmed. I turned down the lights, lit three candles and hurried to fold my clothes once I was undressed. I eased into the water, and was like damn, even the water felt sexy. The Peach aroma from the candles and the Mary J. coming from the sound system was making me want to smoke a joint. Not more than five minutes later, Keith came in carrying a serving board. The board held everything that could make a night like this exquisite. Champagne, fresh fruit, two glasses and a blunt.

"Keith, you must have been reading my mind."

"I could say the same thing about you. You're so beautiful, I was hoping to find you like this when I came in here."

"I hope you're not just saying that 'cause I'm naked Keith."

"Not at all."

"I see you have a blunt for me. I didn't expect those other things."

"What you sayin', I don't have no class Candy?"

"Not at all, you've outdone yourself with this one. There's just one problem."

"You can't get in."

"Okay hold that thought."

He sat the serving board down next to the tub and began to undress. I've seen him do this before, but this time he looks almost other worldly. All of a sudden my nipples started to harden. He did as I did and took the time to fold his clothes, then climbed into the tub. I haven't even touched him yet and his dick was rock hard, which made me smile. "Oh you like that huh? Don't trip, you're going to get real up close and personal with it tonight." He had me thinking hard with that one.

"Keith, I wanna' tell you something."

"What's up?"

"Two things actually. Thank you for calling me beautiful, and also for bringing us here." When he kissed me I felt the first signs of an orgasm coming on. I reached for his dick and he throbbed in my hand. But he acted like he didn't want me to stop kissing him, so I pushed away from him. "Hold down slick, why don't you pour us a glass of that, while I light this and we can meet in the middle."

After I drank two glasses of champagne, he sat down what was left of the blunt, grabbed a Mango wedge and told me to sit on the edge of the tub. He pushed my legs open and stuck the fruit inside me, and before he went after it, he washed off the bubbles with champagne. Then he ate my pussy in a way I never felt before. The shit felt so good, I damn near fell off the tub. He wrapped an arm around my back and sucked on my pussy until the fruit was all gone. When he came up for some air, he took a wedge of Pineapple this time, told me to get on my knees and turn around.

Without hesitation I did as I was told. Again he stuck the fruit inside me and this time it wasn't my pussy, and just like the first time he chased it with his tongue. He stayed at it until I could no longer feel the fruit in my ass. The shit was so intense I had to turn the tide on him. I pushed away from him breathing hard and made him change places with me. I washed away the suds as he had done me. I took a quick drink, then took three Mango slices, surrounded his dick with them and slammed it all in my mouth. At once I tasted his salty pre cum mixed with the sweetness of the fruit.

I sucked on him until they were all gone. Then I took him out and just looked at it. I smiled up at him then started sucking on his balls. I could tell he loved it, 'cause he leaned back and closed his eyes. After a few more minutes I went back to sucking his dick. He tasted so good I got faster and faster with it. I guess it became even too much for him, because he came in my mouth so much and so unexpectedly I couldn't swallow it all. What surprise me next tho' was how eager he was to kiss me after swallowing his cum. I loved the way his dick felt so much I grabbed for it again. I knew after that first nutt, if you let a dick get soft it will stay that way for at least fifteen minutes and I had no intentions of letting that happen. I licked and played with him until all was right with the world again. I started to suck his dick under the water, but I don't swim that good and I couldn't hold my breath that long.

So I did the next thing that came to mind. I stood up, did a couple of slow sexy turns, then eased down on his dick backwards. "You like that?" I asked.

I guess it was her turn to do some cummin'. She started riding me so fast the water was splashing from the tub. Her pussy felt so good I wanted to cum again. Then she started talking to me. Saying how it felt like I was in her stomach. She rode me faster and faster, and when she came, I swear I could feel the temperature of the water get hotter. Continuing to pound into her, I realized that her pussy was not where I wanted to be… so I put her on her knees again then bent her over the side of the tub. She looked back at me and smiled as I eased right into her ass. At first she was so surprised she tried to resist it, but the bubble bath was like a lubricant, and I pushed into her as far as I could go and held it there. Slowly I started easing in and out of her until she started to relax.

I grabbed her ass cheeks and pulled them apart, then pulled out of her until just the head of my dick was still inside her. Enjoying how I had her opened up, I started hitting her as hard as I could.

I couldn't believe this shit, I didn't know whether to scream or bite my fuckin' tongue off. I've never known anything that could hurt so much and feel so good at the same time. After the initial shock I started to relax and enjoy him inside of me. His dick felt so good, but he was fuckin' me like there was no tomorrow. I caught his rhythm and begun to fuck him as hard as he was fuckin' me. I wanted him to cum in my ass so bad, and only because it would be a first for me. I told him over and over, "Cum for me baby. That's right, fuck me. Fuck me Keith. Put that big ass dick on me." I looked over my shoulder, and saw him in pure beast mode. As he came for the second time I screamed out in pure ecstasy, and all I could think was-damn, we should've had this shit on tape.

As I exploded in her for the second time, she screamed her ass off but was still tryin' to fuck me some more. I begged her to stop, for her not to move. She felt so good the slightest movement from her made me shiver. I was finally able to pull out of her and kick back for a minute. I poured us each a drink, sat back and pulled her close to me. "Do you have any idea how amazing you felt?"

"So you like that, huh? Are we done?"

"Not by a long shot. I'm just getting started." At the sound of that she took a sip of her drink and started playin' with her nipples. Needless to say that got my attention, and for the first time tonight I put one of her titties in my mouth.

Every woman has their one spot that will push them over the edge and right into an orgasm and my chest was mine. My titties are just big enough for him to put both my nipples in his mouth at once. He pushed them together and tried to swallow them. He sucked them so well I began to shiver, and then I came once again. The water was cooling off so I grabbed him by the hand, pulled him from the tub and told him to follow me.

Man, this was a totally different Candy, even though I've made love to her before, there was something way different about her tonight. This was some grown woman pussy here. She was completely open to me. I knew she just came again, and all I did was suck on her titties. But as she led me into the bedroom, all I could see was her ass and I wanted some more of it. Before we reached the bed I turned around. Back in the bathroom under the towel on the serving board was the K-Y jelly. When I returned I told her to get on her hands and knees. My dick was reaching out to her from where I stood. I wanted to lick on her some more, but maybe later. Instead I put some of the jelly on my dick, then with two fingers I put some inside of her.

I could tell, just from that lil' bit she enjoyed it 'cause she started pushing back onto my fingers. So I substituted my hand with my throbbing dick. I think she liked it more than I did. I stood at the edge of the bed and pushed in and out of her. I hit it so hard she bit down into a pillow and let me have all the ass I wanted. I thought of when she punched me in the ribs and I tried to make my dick come out the top of her head. She reached back with one hand and pulled herself open and that made me explode deep inside of her once more. After that one, all I could do was fall on top of her and we laid there until my dick got soft and came out on its own.

I finally made him get off me. "Keith will you do me a favor?"

"Anything sexy."

"Will you call room service and order me some cake and ice cream?"

"You got that comin'."

"Anything but chocolate." While he did that I took my bag and headed for the shower. My ass was so sore I was hoping a cool shower would help. The shower helped somewhat. When I was done, I dried myself off and put on some baby oil. Wanting to look sexy for him once again, I put on the Royal Blue bra and panty set.

When I came into the room I knew he liked the way I looked. He started smiling and asked me to turn around for him. Although he had a sheet covering him, I could still see his dick jump up and down. "Is that ice cream any good?"

"Yeah, but it's missing something." I knew what was coming, but I asked anyway.

"What might that be?"

"Your pretty ass nipples."

"I just put this on, you don't want to enjoy it some?"

"You don't have to take anything off, but I do want to put some of this on you and lick it off."

"On one condition."

"What's that?"

"That I get to put some on yo' dick and lick it off."

"Shit, for the whole night my dick belongs to you and you can suck this shit until the sun comes up in the morning if you want." Looking at his Rolex. "It's only 9:20 p.m., so you better pace yourself."

I smiled at him and came over to the bed, pulled out one of my breasts and allowed him to put the cold dessert on me. But I surprised him by lickin' it off myself. "Ooh this taste good. You want some?" Even though he said no, I knew he was lying. So I put my tittie in the bowl, then put it in his mouth. Within a few minutes I found myself naked and on the floor with cake and ice cream on my pussy. He licked and sucked on my pussy and ass until I had to back pedal away from him.

After that round of pushing out cum and cake it was hard to breathe again, and suddenly I wanted to sleep. "Look baby, we've been at this for some time and I need a time out. You won, I give! It's not funny either Keith."

"I'm not laughing, but what am I supposed to do with all this?" I said holding my throbbing dick. She was so fuckin' sexy tonight, it felt like I took a whole bottle of Viagra. Maybe I should give her some time to rest. It's 10:10p.m. and we're not checking out until noon tomorrow.

"Okay sexy, I'm sorry, I got carried away. Come over here and lay down for a while. Close your eyes and listen to me tell you how beautiful you are." I pulled a sheet over her and I started to lightly kiss her face. Within minutes she was asleep. "I love you beautiful." I hit my blunt a couple of times, finished off my glass of champagne and joined her in sleep.

Chapter 10

VOODOO & TONI

I headed West towards Venice. I planned to spend as much time with Toni as I could. So when she told me where she lived I took off in the opposite direction. I could tell she didn't mind by the way she would put her hands on my thighs when I stopped for a red light. That was always a good sign of things to come, and they most certainly did. After we walked along the Board Walk, ate ice cream, and talked for a couple of hours, we headed back towards Compton. As we pulled up to Toni's house her mom was just getting in her car to leave. Since I wanted to meet her I blocked the drive way. When she got out the car I couldn't believe what I saw. Moms was fine as hell.

She looked like an older Toni.

"Hi baby, and who might this be?"

"Hi mom, this is Donnie, Donnie Walls. We met last week and we had lunch today."

"Lunch, it's 7:00 p.m., where have you been?"

"After lunch we rode out to the beach."

"He's kinda' cute."

"Mom weren't you just leaving?"

"Yeah, me and Promise are going out for a while. Where are the twins?"

"I don't know, I haven't seen them since we finished lunch."

"Oh, they were with you?"

"Yes, also Keith and Taylor."

"Alright baby, Promise is waiting on me, I'll see you later. There is dinner in the kitchen, and you know the rules."

"Alright mom, later. Oh yeah, Big Ten said for you to get at him. I have a number for him."

"How am I supposed to do that?"

"I bought him a phone. I'll explain later, 'cause I see you about to go on one."

"Alright. Bye Donnie, can you move your bike?"

After Stacy left I kept Voodoo outside for like ten more minutes just to make sure she didn't double back. Once I was sure she was gone I took him by the hand and told him to follow me. I peeped game all the way, but I asked anyway. "She told you to remember the rules. What are they?"

"That when she's gone there are no rules." Believe it or not, when she said that my dick got hard instantly. Once inside, she pointed towards the den and told me to go make myself comfortable while she headed off down a hallway. Five minutes later she was back wearing some cut off sweats and a half sweat top. Looking around they were living pretty good. "Hey, you have any brothers or sisters?"

"Nope, it's just me and I have those two," I said, pointing at the twins picture on the wall, "They're just like my sisters."

"Say um, would you like something to eat or drink?" When she said that, I told myself, fuck it. Her ass came in here lookin' like an Island Goddess, and I wanted a bar of her sexy ass.

"I'm cool on the drink, and what I want to eat you won't find in the kitchen." When he said that I swear my nipples got hard.

"I take it you're talkin' about me?" But before I could answer, she walked over and started pullin' off my shirt.

We started kissing, which was like sucking on some tropical fruit. When I grabbed her ass I could tell she had nothing on beneath her shorts. With every passing moment of kissing her, my dick got harder and harder. This was turning out to be a hell of a day. Black gave me like $80,000, and now I was about to knock down one of the baddest chicks in Compton.

Spending time with Voodoo today showed me a lot. He's smart, he knows how to talk to people and like he said, he was rich as hell. Most gangstaz was all about fuckin' every bitch they came across and finding other dudes to shoot at. I could tell he was about his money above all else. Each time his cell phone rung, I expected it to be some female, but it was always about business. While riding behind him today I had to hold on to him and he was totally solid, so I was happy when I took his shirt off. He was so ripped up, it was just sexy. And a real sexy man will always make my pussy wet, even if I'm not about to fuck him.

Toni was radiating heat from her body like crazy, and I guess she could feel my dick thumping against her thigh 'cause she made my pants and boxers fall down around my ankles. What surprised me was, without a second thought she went down and started sucking my dick like it was her favorite candy.

I knew every man wants a woman to suck his dick and hopefully until he cums in her mouth. But just like he's done most of the day, he surprised me by pulling me back up. "You need to be first," he said, kissing me passionately. While he got out of his Timberlands and his Levi's, I just took off my shorts.

Damn. I can't believe this shit is about to go down. She is so fuckin' sexy I didn't know where to start. "Look, go over to the couch and get on your hands and knees." She did as I said and I followed her. "Now put your left leg up on the couch." When she moved her pussy opened up and I went down and started eating her in such a way she would never forget. She had some oh melt in yo mouth type pussy. I could taste the subtle changes in her too. She was so wet I could tell she was ready to cum, so I took my middle finger and pressed down on her clitoris. When she let out her next moan I pressed a lil' harder and sucked in really hard and there was an explosion of cum in my mouth.

Man, this nigga'z tongue was like a Magic Wand. Within the first few minutes he had my pussy so hot and wet it was crazy. By minute five he did some shit I never felt before. It felt so good I was ready to cum all over his face. Then he hit me with some shit that felt like a vacuum cleaner was sucking on my pussy. I came so hard he couldn't take it all in, and some actually dripped onto the couch. Thank goodness for leather, I thought. After he had his fill of me, he turned me over onto my back. I could see how his dick was standing up and it was enormous. I could tell this was going to hurt so I wadded up the front of my sweat shirt and stuffed it in my mouth. When I did that my titties came out and his dick started bobbing up and down like it had a life of its own. He pushed my legs up and apart, and when he entered me I would have screamed if it wasn't for my shirt. This was just too much, so I grabbed his ass and when he pushed in again, I held him there until I could get use to him being inside of me. "Are you okay?" With my eyes closed tightly, I just nodded my head. As I held him there, I could feel the thumping of his dick. As the pain started to subside, I started thinking about cumming again, so I began to move him into a slow rhythm. I loosened up, relaxed and let him go for what he knew.

Cuzz, this was one of those times when a nigga wish he was a Contortionist. I was knee deep inside her and I still wanted to lick her pussy some more. But since I couldn't reach it without pulling out of her, I just licked and sucked on every other part of her I could reach. Her tight ass pussy really had me going. I was working her so good we were both sweating. I know I have a big dick and I knew I was almost too big for her, but her fine ass was taking it like a champ. I kept hitting her harder and harder, and she took it all. I pulled her shirt from her mouth just so I could hear her moaning louder. Then she moaned one too many times, 'cause I released about a whole ounce of hot cum deep into her pussy.

Although I'm only eighteen, I've gotten my sexy-on before and I even had a baby, but this shit was something else altogether. I don't even think he knows it, but since we started this, he's made me cum three times already. This has never happened to me before. After fifteen minutes of him pounding away at my pussy, he finally came. "Baby that felt so good, but you know what? I'm not done, I still want some more." Since I could still feel his dick throbbing away inside me, I pulled his dick out, I leaned back on the couch and told him to come fuck me in the mouth. When he got close I took his dick, and him knowing what was about to happen, he got hard again. I licked the length of it all the way down to his balls and back up, and it damn near jumped out of my hand. Before I put him in my mouth, I stuck my tongue in his hole and tried to lick out the last bit of cum that was there.

After I did that it was his turn to do some moaning. I put his balls in my mouth and started rubbing his dick all over my face. For the next ten minutes I played and sucked his dick like it was my best friend. I was trying to make him cum, but it was not to be, I gave his huge dick one more good lick, then told him I'd be right back.

The girl was turning out to be a cold freak, she actually told me to keep my shit hard until she came back. Fine as hell, but a cold freak. I already seen how smart she was, so with those facts, maybe I'll stick with her for a while. Like I said, she told me to keep my shit hard, so I started slowly stroking myself thinking about how she was just suckin' on me. She actually had the best head game I've seen. She was back a short time later with a hot towel and some K-Y Intense jelly. This shit was supposed to make a woman's pussy feel like heaven on earth. She saw what I was doing and said. "I like a man that can follow orders." She got down on her knees and cleaned me with the hot towel.

When she was done, she took me into her mouth once again to make sure I was nice and hard. Then she pulled me to the edge of the couch, rubbed some of the jelly onto my dick and I swelled up even more. Next she turned around, squatted down and guided my dick back into her pussy, which felt like hot silk. She asked for it so I gave it to her. Moments later, she leaned forward, reached back and pulled her ass and pussy open as much as she could. From underneath she watched as my dick pushed in and out of her. Her pussy felt tight as it did when we first started. And seeing her sexy ass move up and down, and the way she had herself open like this really made me wanna' bust a nutt. Man, I see why they call this shit Intense. I wanted to stick my tongue in her pretty ass, but I couldn't reach it.

So I did the next best thang, I licked my finger and stuck it in her ass. That damn near made her jump off me, but again, she hung in there like a champ and kept bouncing up and down on my dick.

I never had any dick this good before. I could fuck this nigga all night. When he stuck his finger in my ass I screamed but kept right on fuckin' him. I was lookin' under us, watching his dick. He actually had me wanting to be as freaky as I could. For another five minutes he fucked me so hard I had to put my shirt back in my mouth. When he took his finger outta' my ass, I said, "Do you wanna' fuck me in my ass baby?"

"I don't think you're ready for that yet. But I do wanna' do this." He pushed me on the floor. I wanted to see what he was about to do, but I felt it instead. He stuck his tongue in my ass. Shit I had a baby by Shawn and he's never done this to me.

This was a first for me, and I loved it. I began to push back and forth like his tongue was his dick. I got so caught up in the moment I actually had a fourth orgasm, or was it my fifth? Whatever it was, it was another first for me. I guess he felt it too, 'cause he took out that vacuum cleaner again and sucked the gooey cream from my pussy. After that nutt, I fell to the floor and rolled up in the fetal position, closed my eyes and said. "No Mas! No Mas!"

There are so many different types of females out there. Beautiful, fine, sexy, gangsta, freaky and the exotic. I wanna' say Layla was a mixture of them all. The way she was balled-up in a fetal position let me know I put in major work. But it was nothing compared to what I would really like to do to her sexy ass. It was getting late tho' and I knew her moms would trip if she found us like this. If I stayed I might really go into beast mode. Besides, I still had to dodge these Compton niggaz' to get back to the hood. I snatched up my clothes and the towel, found the bathroom and washed up real quick. After I took a leak and got dressed, I went back into the den and Toni was still rolled up on the floor.

When I knelt down beside her, she reached up, put her arms around me and said, "Thanks for spending the day with me."

"You said that like I'm never going to see you again." When she smiled, I kissed her. She moaned and I moved to her chest. After hearing her moan from that, I moved down to her pussy. After a few moments of this I moved on down to her legs and back up. "You taste so perfect, you know that? From this day on, I'm going to make it a point to eat yo pretty ass pussy every time I see you. On that note I'm out. Now get cleaned up before your moms get home. Hey I forgot, let me see your cell phone."

"It's over there next to my purse." I used hers to call mine. When it rung I hung up.

"Call me some time tomorrow and we can talk some more about this lick y'all putting together." Then he was gone.

I think I'm in love, I thought to myself. The whole day now seemed so complete and perfect. I think more than anything, what was perfect was his body and how he used it to control mine. It was time to clean up this crime scene. But when I stood up I almost fell back to the floor. My legs and pussy hurt so much I could barely move. I must have been crazy asking that nigga to fuck me in the ass. I'm glad one of us had some common sense. I finally made it to the door to lock it, I found the towel we used in the bathroom. I washed it out with hot water and went to wipe down the couch. After that was done, I grabbed my clothes and the K-Y jelly and went to take a hot shower. Soaping up my body, I started thinking about Voodoo and how he was fuckin' me. My nipples hardened and one of my hands made its way to them.

Somehow I got turned on again and my other hand made its way to my pussy, but the shit was way too sore for that. Man, what he said really got to me though. He wants to eat my pussy each time he sees me. Shit, if that's the case I thought smiling to myself, that nigga will be obese by the end of the year. Since I couldn't work myself into another orgasm like I wanted to, I washed off and stepped out of the shower. I dabbed myself dry with a clean towel and went to eat. I warmed and ate a half plate of spaghetti. Once I was done, I made my way back to the den, still wrapped in my towel and passed out on the sofa.

Chapter 11

BLACK & SANDY

Just like clockwork, when the clock turned twelve, deep inside me Black came for the third time. I've been riding his dick for the last twenty minutes. After lunch today he drove us to the Lake Wood Mall and told me to get a few things that would get me through the night. Then we went to see Tyler Perry's new movie. Sitting all the way in the back, we stayed true to form, that black folks don't know how to act. About five minutes after the movie started, Black fired up a fat ass joint, hit it really hard then made me do the same. We blew the whole theater up, then I heard someone say, "Damn that shit smells good." I was just happy no one got up to go get security. We both took another hit and put it out.

The movie turned out to be the bomb, as to be expected, but I didn't get to see it all. When he put his arm around me, he started playin' with my tittie. I could tell he was more into the movie than he was me, but the shit really turned me on. He tried to push my hand away when I went to open his pants. "Stop," I told him and went back to my task. I moved his hand out the way, which he put right back, so he got a shot in the gut. A moment later I was able to get his dick out. "For you not to want me touching you, why yo shit so hard?" I whispered in his ear. He ignored me. He was ready for action 'cause he pushed up and his dick started pulsating like a heart beat in my hand.

I only got glimpses of it from the changing lights of the movie, but his dick was so perfect I was drawn to it like a magnet. You would have thought I never seen his shit before. I could tell he wanted me to put it in my mouth because he kept pushing it towards my face. So I gave him what he desired. First I licked around the top of his dick which looked like a mini football helmet.

When I came up to ask if he liked that, there was a long line of pre-cum still on my lips. Then I licked just below his pee hole, which really got his attention. I went for broke from there and started sucking on him like my life depended on it. I sucked on his balls for a few minutes and the nigga actually stuck the head of his dick in my ear. It seemed like the longer I stayed down there the bigger he got. I was taking nice long and slow strokes on him, all the way up and all the way down. After about five minutes of this I grabbed him just above his balls and pulled down, stretching it as far as it would go, he was huge, I jammed it back in my mouth, which barley fit. His shit seemed to grow another two inches. He throbbed once more with the down stroke of my head and exploded deep in the back of my mouth.

After a few more well placed strokes to make sure he was done cumming, I took some napkins and cleaned him off. As he fixed his clothes, I grabbed the popcorn and curled up next to him to watch the rest of the movie.

Now you would think after all that cum he wouldn't be able to nutt again for days, right? No, because once we got to the Hotel it was' on and crackin'. He cummed two more times, and with just as much intensity too. The Days Inn was not some big' ass fancy hotel but it was nice and clean.

After that major workout, we were both sweating and I collapsed on top of him. He put his arms around me and held me close.

Within minutes, his ass managed to flip us over without taking his dick out of me. I just couldn't understand how this niggaz' dick was still rock hard. "Black did you take some Viagra?"

"Nah baby, this is all yo sexy ass." I could still feel him throbbing inside of me and knew he wanted to fuck some more. So my way around that, I asked him to please go run me a bath. He took a few more good strokes inside me, but he finally said okay. He kissed both my nipples, smiled at me, then we both watched as he pulled his long ass dick out of me.

When I pulled out of her it felt like it took a full minute just to do that. After I left her high and dry last Friday, well maybe not so dry, it seemed like she didn't want me to stop fuckin' her, so I gave her the business. She went from one position to another, it was crazy. When I put two pillows on the corner of the bed and told her to lay on her stomach, I fucked her in her ass so hard, it seemed as though with every stroke she got louder. For a minute there I thought for sure someone would come knocking on the door. I eased up on her, and started taking long deep strokes. My dick felt like a cord of wood it was so hard. When she started talking to me I knew it was over. By the seventh time she said my name I slammed into her and unloaded. She screamed so loud I had to pull her by the hair and kiss her just to get her to stop.

From her kiss I could tell she still had some fight in her. So after playing with each other for about an hour, my dick came back to life and I put her on top of me. While she rode me I was making her titties do all kinds of tricks. I took the right one and made her lick it, which I think she liked. After we finished sucking on them pretty titties, her nipples were hard enough to cut glass. I think it was something about her nipples, 'cause when I brought them together and started sucking and blowing on them she went nuts. She started riding me so fast I actually came again. But I had to give it to her, she didn't stop until she got one last nutt as well. Her insides were on fire.

When she collapsed on top of me all I could do was hold her. While I was holding her I could feel her heart beat, then I started making my dick jump to the beat of her heart. I flipped her over and slowly begun to push in and out of her again. But I guess she'd had enough, 'cause she asked me to go run her a hot bath. Although we put in some serious fuckin', and Sandy looked like she'd been in a prize fight, she was still sexy as fuck. I didn't want to, but I pulled out of her. My dick looked and felt like it was a mile long. She watched as it came out and I had to smile because she had a look of pure relief on her face. "Now that's how you lay pipe!"

"Ah shut up nigga and move."

Black went into the bathroom and turned on the hot water in the tub. I could see most of what he was doing. Next he went to the sink and brushed his teeth. When he was done he stuck his head out and told me to keep an eye on the tub, he was about to take a quick shower. By the time he was done, my overly sore body was in the hot water soaking. I don't often get to see him like this, fully naked and in the light. He looked so nice. What surprised me was the fact that his dick was back to its normal size, then I wondered how did that grow into the monster it was earlier? "Girl, I know you not over there playin' with yo'self?"

"Ain't you over there doin' something? Why you watchin' me?"

"I'm just sayin', if you need some help with that I'm here for you," he said, laughing.

"Ain't you had enough?"

"Shit you the one over there making waves in the tub."

"Baby will you pour me a drink?"

Wrapping a towel around himself, he said, "You got that coming." He was back moments later and handed me my drink and jumped up on the counter. Watching me, he asked, "Did you get one?"

"What?"

"A nutt of course!"

"Ah shut up fool."

"Sandy I need to know something. Where in the hell did you get this idea of yours?"

"You really wanna' know?"

"Yeah, 'cause this shit sounds like something me and Yellow Bird should have come up with."

"I know, you're gonna' think this is crazy, but I got it from watching this show called, 'Black Market, The Elicit Trade' on the Discovery Channel."

"I guess they call it Discovery for a reason."

"The question is, do you think you can pull this shit off?"

"Why you sayin' me, I thought we were in this shit together?"

"Check this out, and this is some real shit. When you appointed yourself the boss, that means you're out front. You got five niggaz' following yo' move, and if something goes wrong it's on yo' head. I'm not too worried about me and the fella'z, but you got your sister and Toni depending on you, not only to make them rich, but to keep them safe."

"No, it's your job to keep us safe, and if you gotta' kill somebody to do it, that's what I expect you to do. As far as worrying about them, this is more money than any of us ever dreamed of. I came up with a plan, I had no real idea if the money would be there or not, and now that we know for sure that it is, we're going to get it."

"Okay I feel you, but there's one thing we didn't go over at lunch earlier. How many people work there and how do you plan on getting around them?"

"I think there's seven or eight during the day and one at night."

"Hold down, this is not a guessing game. You need to know everything there is to know about this place, and if there's something you already know, you need to remember it."

"Yeah I feel you."

"I hope so, 'cause if something goes wrong, we're looking at major football numbers in the feds. If that happens, instead of me licking on that pretty pussy of yours, you're gonna' have somebody name Bertha doing it."

"Ah shut up nigga."

I went to kick back on the bed. I ate a slice of cold pizza, then fired up my blunt. Then I started wondering why she didn't answer the second part of my question. There would only be one-night guard, and something told me she had no clue as how to get around him. I should ask her about it again just to see what she would say, but I knew it would still fall in my hands since we were the ones that are to keep them safe. I'm sure I could get close and try to knock him out, but I'm no knock-out artist, and I don't want a big struggle with the dude. I thought about it some more, then it hit me. My nigga Voodoo has an uncanny knack for getting his hands on just about anything. It's 1:30 a.m. in the morning, damn. I grabbed my cell phone to call 'em. On the second ring he answered.

"What's up Crip? What can I do you out of?"

"What's up homie? Check this out. I'm going over this shit we talked about at lunch, and we got one person standing in our way and I wanna' be able to get rid of him from a distance. You think you can handle that?"

"I take it you just need him to go to sleep for a few hours?" Voodoo asked.

"Exactly."

"Don't trip, I'mma' find some Pixie Dust for him, and when the time is right, I'll send his ass to La-La Land."

"Alright cool. Hey one more thing, when was the last time you got us new phones?"

"Damn nigga, it's been less than thirty days, you ready for a new one already?" Voodoo said.

"Cuzz you know how I don't like or trust cell phones, period! But nah, I'm cool, get at me tomorrow."

"Alright later my nigga."

I know he will take care of things. I want this shit to go down as much as Sandy does. No one seemed to notice what else was on that inventory sheet. There was a shit load of weapons in there too. The fifty kilos would make us about two million each, but six million each sounds much better. I need to get some one-on-one time with Toni. Besides, we're like a week away from hitting this place. The van and its contents might get moved at any time. If I can find another fifty kilos, or enough shit, our share could double, and we need that. Sandy came from the bathroom looking beautiful and sexy. I looked at the lil' patch of hair on her pussy and my mouth started to water. She got into bed next to me and instantly my dick got hard. It was amazing how she could do that.

But getting some more pussy was not to be. She leaned over, whispered in my ear. "Tell that thing to go back to sleep." Then she took the ashtray and fired up the weed I was smoking. She wasn't trying to hear nothing I was saying, my dick was jumping all over the place and it wanted some attention. "Damn Black, I know I shouldn't have come in here naked, and I told myself to wrap a towel around myself."

"I can't help it."

Yep, I fucked up, as soon as I walked in the room that nigga started lickin' his lips. But me and my pussy needed a rest. So to keep him from taking me then and there, I lit up the weed that was in the ashtray next to him. I took a good hit and blew smoke at him. Damn, why did I do that? I could see his dick jumping up and down under his towel, and it was like a sign to attack. "Man I thought I told yo' ass to put that thing back to sleep?"

"Yo' ass shouldn't be so sexy."

"See you sayin' shit like that is not fair Black." I reached under his towel and grabbed his man hood. "I'm telling you Black, after this I'm going to sleep." After pumping on him a few times with my hand, I went down on him and gave him the best head job I could. I jacked him off as I sucked on him. He took his hand and wrapped it around mine and we pumped it faster. We pulled down and held it there. I took his dick out and it was swelled up with blood.

Stretching it as far as it would go, he was huge, and I jammed it back in my mouth, which barely fit. Together we worked his dick so fast, that when he came in my mouth, cum ran down over his hand, and not wanting to be wasteful, I licked that up too. "There, I hope you're satisfied?" I kissed it once more, then turned over to go to sleep.

"Not so fast." He said. And the next thing I knew, his tongue was trying to find its way into my pussy from behind.

"Come on Black." But he didn't stop. So I said fuck it and raised my leg up. "If you want it, you better eat my pussy until I cum all over yo' face. Ooh shit Black, that feels good. I know you're back there lookin' at all that ass, you might as well lick some of that too."

He did as I said, and after going back and forth for the next ten minutes, I clamped down on his head and pushed out I think my biggest orgasm of the night. "Did you like that?"

"Yeah, more than you know."

"Okay, now can you go to sleep, please?"

Chapter 12

CANDY

Thursday morning turned out really nice. Keith ordered us a big breakfast. We fed each other, talked about the upcoming robbery and whether or not it was a good idea. After we ate I went to take a shower, but before I could even get in the water he was there. He really surprised me when he said, "Baby girl, I don't know when we'll be able to do this again, so will you make love to me one more time?" I was so touched by the way he said it. I helped him out of his bath robe and pulled him into the shower with me. Last night he fucked me every way possible. I think he would have fucked me on the ceiling if he could have gotten me up there. But this morning he was a totally different person. He took the time to wash my body. He kissed me like I was the love of his life. He had me so hot, I had to fight to keep my hands off him.

I wanted him to be in control, and whatever he said do, to the best of my ability I would do. But he kept it simple, He kissed me some more, then he moved down to suck on my breast. A few moments later he moved down further. He parted my legs and licked on my pussy in such a way, that when I came I almost pulled out some of his hair. I was sliding down the back of the shower but he put an arm under one of my knees, then the other and lifted me up. I wrapped my arms around his neck and he slid his dick so far in me I had to bite down on my arm just to keep from screaming. But again, he took his time, and in a slow and gentle way he moved me up and down on his dick he made me wanna' cry. It was so amazing. I was trying to move faster, but he was in charge and he slowed into a steady rhythm. I knew he was reaching his peak because he started telling me how good the pussy was, which made me kiss him with all the love and passion I could find within me.

Although he insisted that I slow down, he was now pushing into me with more and more urgency. The more he talked to me the harder he seemed to drive into me. But lil' did he know, I was just waiting, waiting, then when he closed his eyes I knew it was time. I quickly jumped down and put his beautiful dick in my mouth. I pumped and pumped on him until he could take it no more, then he exploded like the Big Bang Theory. His cum was so hot in my mouth but I wanted it all. All down the back of my throat I could feel his dick pumping out the last bit of cum. When I knew he was done, I finally came up for air.

YELLOW BIRD

I've known Candy since she started high school. We've kicked it a few times, even fucked, but last night she let me have my way with her like never before. Today, though', what we just did was not the same, I felt like we were making love for the very first time. Even though she just let me bust a major nutt in her mouth, it still felt different. Like it was more love than lust behind every move we made. Everything she's done since we got up this morning said I love you Keith. And what's wrong with that? She's almost beyond beautiful. She has a body that won't quit, and last night she proved she's willing to share it with me in any way I want. I don't see her fuckin' with a lot of niggaz', so why not make her mine?

"Look Candy, I wanna' tell you something. From this moment on, and as long as I'm alive, you will never let another man touch yo' body. I love you and I'm going to make you love me." When I kissed her she started crying and that let me know I made the right choice.

VOODOO

Even though Toni made me put in some serious work last night, when I got home I still set my clock for 7:00 am. Man, I wish I could have brought her home with me. It's rare to come across someone like her. Other chicks make me just want to fuck 'em then fuck over them. But I know one thing, if she was able to find this kind of information once, she should be able to do it again. Shit, I need to get at Black and Yellow Bird about this. We're out here movin' dope all over California, and for what? Sandy saw all that dope sitting there and was smart enough to know if she took it, she would then have to move it in these streets.

Double hustling is just an extra rock throw at the penitentiary. But these fifty kilos are gonna' put us up though. Black's call last night is another reason why I'm up so early. I need to find a Veterinarian Office, or some kind of Animal Control Facility. I should be able to find a tranquilizer gun in one of them. I bet if I called Toni she would be able to get into their computer system in no time. I grabbed my phone to google a location. There was so many to choose from, but I found one in a rural area. The country has more wild animals then the city. I found two good choices. I grabbed some cash, the keys to the Ford F150, a couple of other things and headed to Riverside.

TONI

When I woke up this morning I wrapped my arms around my pillow like it was Donnie. You know I love me some Crip's, but this one was more than that. Last night came back to me and I had to squeeze my legs together. Somehow I have to make it to where, when I wake up in the morning I can hold him and not this damn pillow. What am I saying? He might be just like most niggaz', he got to fuck a mix female with some ass and now he's cool. I don't know, even though we went at it like crazy, he seemed to really enjoy being with me. We had such a good time during lunch and our walk along the beach too. I guess only time will tell.

Tomorrow we're all going to San Diego, and spending that much time with him will tell me if I was suckin' that niggaz' dick for nothing. Fuck it, I gotta' stop thinking about his ass, I have too much to do today. But damn I want another bar of that nigga sexually. When I got up I wanted to scream, my inner thighs felt like I'd been through a Torture Chamber. How in the hell am I supposed to get around like this today? I made my way to the bathroom and found some pain pills. I am so glad this is not Sunday, there's no way I could run some laps in this condition. After I did what I could for my legs, rubbing them and what not, I washed up and went to my room to get dressed. This felt like a Nike day. So I put on a Nylon warm up suit, blue and white of course. Some blue Nike Cortez, then put my hair into a ponytail.

I checked my computer for any emails, there were two, but nothing I had to respond to. Next I went into my mom's room, it's after seven and she was still sleep, knowing her ass is supposed to be at work. "Mom, mom, wake up, aren't you supposed to be at work?"

"No baby, I changed shifts with someone, I go this evening."

"You and Promise have fun last night?"

"Yeah, it was nice. The question is, did you have fun last night?"

"Why you say that?"

"What time did Donnie leave here?"

"Not long after you did." To hurry up and change the subject, I asked if she wanted me to make her something to eat.

"No I'm good, I just need a couple of more hours of sleep and I'll be good to go.

"Alright, I'll see you later." And I eased out the door. I knew she was getting ready to start fishing for information, but I was not having it.

I went to clean up my mess I made before I went to sleep last night. When I was done I took some fruit and a power bar and headed for L.A. with the money I got from Voodoo yesterday. I could have easily gone shopping for some new clothes, but I was on my way to try and find a good police scanner. If I can keep us outta' jail, and we get this money, I can buy all the clothes I could possibly want. I can even get matching outfits for me and Voodoo. Smiling to myself, then I was like, what the hell, I sound like I'm fifteen again. What makes me think he would wanna' dress like me? I don't even think niggaz' do that type of shit any more. I wonder what he's doing right now. Thinking about him my free hand actually went to my inner thighs. Last night came up again, this shit was like a DVD stuck on repeat. Somehow my hand went from my thighs to my pussy. I opened my legs a lil' more and rubbed myself.

Damn I thought, if nothing else, I gotta' at least let him fuck me one more time. I got so caught up in thinking about him, I damn near ran a red light. Shit, they say texting while driving will kill you, try driving while having sex with yourself. Now how was I going to explain that one? I thought laughing.

VOODOO

Man I can't get this chick off my mind. I was on the 15 Freeway heading South and she was there like a damn sexual ghost. I should have called and asked if she wanted to ride with me. When my shit got hard from thinking about how we got down last night, instead of grabbing my dick, I grabbed my phone, put the phone in the hands free device, and called her. "Hello." just the sound of her voice made me wanna' grab my dick and squeeze it.

"What's up sexy? Are you busy?"

"Not really, I was just pulling into the Fox Hills Mall."

"What, that money I hit you wit burning a hole in yo' pocket?"

"Nah, it's nothing like that. I don't need a man to buy me the things I want. Actually, I came to find a police scanner."

"Oh I see, you got money on yo' mind then?"

"I have to, how else am I going to buy us a house when we get married?"

"Hold down a see, did you just ask me to marry you?"

"Nah I was just playin' with you. But what if I was serious, would you?"

"Shit, after that performance you put down last night, I might have to give that some real serious contemplation."

"Whatever nigga. Anyway, why are you up so early?"

"I'm doing the same thing you're doing. Right now I'm half way to Riverside. And I should have brung' you with me."

"Why didn't you then?"

"Shit after last night, I thought you might not be able to move for a couple of days."

"Oh you think you got it like that? Well for your information I was probably up and on the road before you. Why are you going to Riverside?"

"You know when we hit this joint there's gonna' be one person standing in our way so I'm going to find some Pixie Dust."

"Do I dare to even ask?"

"We need to put this dude to sleep, and to do that I'm gonna' need a tranquilizer gun."

"Okay, but why Riverside?"

"That's simple. The country has wild animals, whereas places like L.A. and Compton has cats and dogs. An Animal Control will use a snare to catch them, but where I'm going they're more likely to use a dart gun if there's a problem with an animal."

"So you're going there to buy a dart gun?" Toni asked.

"Baby girl, why you think I have so much money? I very seldom buy anything."

"I thought you work with Black and Yellow Bird?"

"I do, and we're clockin' a major end, but I found out a long time ago, most people are too preoccupied to pay attention to what's going on around them."

"So you're going to steal the gun?"

"Actually, I'm going for the tranquilizer, without it the gun is useless. And I know if I find one I'll find the other. Any more questions?" You don't have to worry sexy. I'll be there."

"You really think I'm sexy?"

"Did Jesus walk on water?"

"Yo' ass is crazy, I gotta' go, call me later, Bye!"

Chapter 13

SANDY

After a night of sex, sex and more sex, I was worried about what my mom would say about stayin' out all night. Just because we're outta' high school now, don't mean she would be all smiles when she saw me. It's after 9:00 a.m. and she should be at work, but I called Candy anyway just to see how upset Promise was. After the third ring big head answered the phone. "What's up sis?"

"Hey, where's mom? Does she know I didn't come home last night?"

"Ooh, you nasty heifer, you with Black aren't you?" Candy asked.

"Man fuck all that, where's mom?"

"I don't know, most likely at work."

"Wait a minute, what do you mean you don't know, where are you?" I asked.

"Actually I'm in Torrance at the Holiday Inn having a strawberry breakfast. Where are you?"

"In Lake Wood. Look Candy we need to figure something out."

"What do you mean we? You're the oldest, and you know when mama start kickin' ass, she's gonna' start with you."

"Ha ha, very funny. Look call Layla and let her know we spent the night with her."

"Hold on, I'mma' call her on three way."

"What's up Candy? Speak on it," Toni said, answering the phone.

"I got Sandy on the line."

"Alright. What's up ugly?" Toni said.

"Fuck you nigga. Anyway we got a problem."

"So why you callin' me?"

"Toni don't make me kick yo' ass." I said.

"Fool it ain't that much kickin' in soccer."

Candy started laughing. "Toni, if our mom asks, we stayed with you last night."

"I don't think that's gonna' work y'all, Toni said.

"Why? It always works," I said.

"Yeah well, Stacy and Promise went out together last night, and my mom saw when Voodoo brought me home, and she also saw me before I left the house this morning."

"Where are you now?" Candy asked.

"The Fox Hills Mall, I came to find a scanner. Oh yeah, and before y'all get any more bright ideas, Stacy changed shifts with somebody, so it's a good chance Promise is still at home too."

"I don't believe this shit, can this get any worse?" I said.

"Sandy, I say fuck it. Tell Black to take you to his house and Keith and I will meet you there," Candy said.

"Alright, we should be there in about an hour," I said.

"Just remember, you gotta' go in first," Candy said.

"Candy, I gotta' go, with yo' scarry ass. Bye," Toni said, and hung up on us.

"Candy, y'all hurry up, this nigga is lookin' at me with lust in his eyes," I said.

"Are you dressed?" she asked.

"Yeah, but I don't think that will stop him," I said.

"Oh well, you better run out the room or something. Bye," Candy said, and hung up.

BLACK BIRD

Last night was one for the history books. But this morning didn't get off to a good start. Sandy was frantic about being out all night, and now there was no one to cover for her. Then if that wasn't bad enough, when I woke up, my dick woke up as well. I guess she knew right away, 'cause as soon as I put a hand on her ass she jumped outta' bed. "Nah nah nigga, you jumped around in my ass all night and I didn't say shit." I ignored her. When I got outta' bed and she saw how hard my shit was, she moved to the other side of the room. Looking at her I just took my dick in hand, shook it at her and said, "You know yo' ass is gonna' wish you had some of this before the day is over." But before she could say anything, I walked in and closed the bathroom door on her ass.

I took a gangsta, then jumped in the shower. When I came out she was dressed and on the phone with her sister. While she was doing that I got dressed too. I guess Candy didn't get home either, and Toni can't cover for her, so Sandy was on one. But fuck that, all I saw was that ass in them shorts. I walked up behind her, I moved her hair from the left to the right side of her neck. I started kissing the baby hairs that were there. I knew I should have wrapped my arms around her. I guess she felt my hard ass dick thumping up against her ass, 'cause she took off across the room again. How can one woman be so damn sexy even when she's not tryin' to be? When she hung up the phone she began to gather her things and said, "Candy wants me to meet her at your house."

"Which one?" I said.

"How many do you have?" she asked with an astonishing look on her face.

But I answered by smiling. "When you say I do, you'll find out." I grabbed up my stuff, took a quick look around and headed for the door.

KEITH

Before we could finish breakfast Sandy called, and from what I could get, she was worried about going home to face their mom. My girl Candy was acting like it was no big deal, but I heard her say, "You gotta' go in first." That tells me moms wasn't no joke. I looked at her and said, "Hey sexy, you know you might be on lock for a while, so you might wanna' let me hit that one more time before we go."

"I guess you wanna' stick strawberries inside me and eat them?"

"You know, I didn't think about that, but I'm sure glad you did, now come here."

"Keith we don't have time, you know we have to meet Sandy in an hour, and something tells me, if yo' dick gets any harder it will stay that way for hours."

"If you love me none of that would matter." As she walked into my arms, she said, "I thought you said you were going to make me fall in love with you? That means you have a lot of work to do."

"That's just what I'm tryin' to do."

"Well I hope you got something else planned besides using yo' dick?"

"I thought you like my dick?" She gave me a kiss, rubbed the front of my pants and asked, "Didn't I act like I liked yo' dick last night?"

"That you did lil' mama, that you did."

"Then let me go so we can get outta' here."

CANDY

Forty-five minutes later Keith had us back in Compton, and before we could make it out the car, Black and Sandy pulled up in the Escalade. He was playin' Jaheim's, Ghetto Love. The shit was so loud and clear I had to roll up my window. But then it got too hot so we got out the car. When Black Jack and Friendly came out, I ran around to the other side of the car and jumped in. They're so big, they both look like they would eat through the car to get to me. Keith came back to me and said, "Come on Candy you're safe."

"Nah nah, you been with me all night, and Black has been with Sandy, and them dogs ain't ate all night and they look mighty hungry." Then Sandy came over to get her clown on.

"Girl, will you get yo' scary ass out the car."

"Look who's talkin', I thought you was so in a rush to get home?"

"Keith will you please make them go inside or something?"

"Baby they're not going to bother you."

"Fuck that, if you love me like you said, you'll do it."

"Damn," Sandy said, "what did you do to this nigga last night?"

"None of yo' business, now get yo' ass in the car, I'm ready to go home. Keith will you call me later?"

"Girl you got it so good, I might just call you before you reach the end of the block," Yellow Bird said.

"Damn you really are in love with her big headed ass."

"Something like that. Candy I'll get at you later, tell your moms I said hi."

"Nigga you really tryin' to get us killed," Sandy said.

Sandy went over and rubbed the two pit bulls, then kissed Black Bird good bye. He came over to the car. "Look y'all, we got a whole day of nothing to do, is there anything y'all can think of that you might need?" Black Bird asked.

"When I called Toni, she said she went to buy a police scanner. We wanted to take some duffel bags just in case we can't drive into the place," Sandy said.

"How many you talkin' about?" Black asked.

"I think two apiece, so six total. They have to be pretty big. Hell I don't know, what will fourteen million dollars fit in?" Sandy asked.

"Don't trip, I'll take care of it. Now y'all get on home so you can collect yo' ass whoppin's."

"Fuck you Black!" I said.

SANDY

Even though I was worried about seeing my mom, I noticed something on the fifteen-minute drive to the house. Candy was a totally different person. She looked different and sounded different, so I said, "Candy, I don't know what happened to you last night, but you better hope mama doesn't see what I see."

"I don't know what you're talkin' about," Candy said.

"Yeah whatever nigga." When she pulled up in front of the house, Promise was out on the porch watering the grass.

"Maybe we should not be trippin', if she was worried about us she would have called one of us," Candy said.

"Yeah you would think," I said, "but that's mom you're talkin' about, and all I know is, you better hurry up and think of something."

"Shit, what's wrong with yo' thinkers?" she shot back.

"Candy, this shit is not funny."

"Man you trippin', let me show yo' ass how to lie."

We got out the car, went through the gate, and said, "Hi mom," in unison.

"Hi baby, did y'all come up with a good one?" Promise said.

"One what?" I asked.

"A good lie. That's what y'all was just in the car talking about, wasn't it?" Promise asked.

"It was Candy's idea."

"Damn," She said, and pushed me.

"So where have the two of you been? You know what? Never mind, I wanted to put foot to ass when I came home this morning and you two wasn't here."

"This morning, what time did you get home?" I asked.

"About 2:30 a.m., but you know what? The two of you are young women now, and you sure as hell look like you became a woman last night."

"Ooh I told you she would notice."

"Will you shut up, please!" Candy said.

"I can't really put the brakes on when the two of you come and go anymore, so all I ask is, that you never disrespect this house, and know this, until you move out on your own, this will always be your home, even after you're gone. So make sure you always come home if you need to, I love you girls," Promise said.

"Mom I know you not workin' with no feelings?" I said.

You know Candy couldn't help but laugh.

"Oh you got jokes, huh? Let's see how funny you think this is. You're grounded for two weeks," Promise said, in a stern voice,

"But you just said..."

"Sorry baby, I forgot. But I'm serious, y'all promise me you'll always come home."

"We will mom," I said.

"Look, we're together more than we're apart, we look after each other well," Candy said, "Plus we have our own personal body guard, Layla."

"Yeah mom-we're good," I assured her.

"Alright, with all that being said, let's hear it."

"What?"

"The lie y'all came up with."

"Candy, she talkin' to you."

"What lie? We spent the night with daddy."

"Girl, you ain't spent the night with yo' father since you was what, ten?"

"Let me show you how to lie." This time I pushed her ass.

"Candy", Promise said, "you need to step yo' game up!"

Chapter 14

VOODOO

I turned onto the gravel road at 1:30 pm. The Animal Control Office was more like a small house. The gravel made a complete U around the place. I made the short trip around the building. There was a pickup truck and three county vehicles. Already I could tell what I was after was in one of the trucks. By the time I reached the other side of the building there was a county officer standing there. I stopped and rolled down my window. "Good afternoon, can I help you with something?" he asked.

"I hope so. Actually I'm looking for work."

"Well there's three of us that work out here, and today is my shift. There's not much work out this way though."

"I understand, do you think I could come in and submit an application? I mean since I came all this way, I'd like to think I at least tried."

"Sure, come on in."

When I cut the engine and opened the door he turned around. I followed him a few steps and just as he entered the office I shot him in the back of the head. His skull muffled the sound of the 38 revolver. I put the gun behind my back and pulled on some gloves. I told Toni I steal most of the shit I want, I just didn't tell her a lot of the times I kill to do it. I took him by his shirt and pulled him away from the door and closed it. I took a quick look around, there was a key rack, so I took two sets. There was a metal cabinet, and I was surprised to see it unlocked. Inside there was three hand guns, two shotguns and two dart guns. Bingo! On a rack on the cabinet door were five bottles of tranquilizer.

I took one of the rifles and shook it. I got worried 'cause I didn't see any darts at first, but I later found them in the butt of the rifle. The hand guns were some nice semi-automatic 9mm's, with sixteen round clips in them. But since taking things from a murder scene is never good, I left them and put the keys back where I found them. Closing the door as I left, I went back to my truck, put the gun in the tool bin in the bed of my truck and locked it. I started up and made one more slow loop around the building. I took my time focusing on the upper corners of the place. All four corners were clear of any video cameras, so I made my way back down the road, turned left onto the highway and headed north for home. "Toni, here I come lil' mama."

TONI

I found the scanner we would need, and I probably have less than a week to learn how to identify certain calls signs. I can only assume that if the local San Diego police are alerted, the DEA will show up too. This shit is crazy, everyone is depending on me to keep the police at bay. What if there's something I've missed? Actually, I've done everything I could think of, I guess tomorrow will tell us if we need anything else. What's good is, I get to spend another day with Voodoo. Maybe we can even stay the night. I wondered around the mall awhile longer. Had something to eat just to kill some time, and just like clockwork, they started coming.

Any woman sitting alone in a mall will draw men like fuckin' flies. Within ten minutes four guys were there giving me their best lines. Three were black and one Hispanic. I gots' to say, his ass was fine as hell. I gave them all the same answer; I have a girlfriend. One even said, "You make me wish I was a woman right now." All I could do was shake my head and laugh. When I was done I grabbed my things and headed for the parking lot. Outside I took the two-minute walk to my car, but I went down the wrong row. I moved over to the next row and made my way back, but this didn't look familiar. About half way down I cut through some cars and then

I saw it. "Ah' hell nah," was my first reaction. There was a white SUV there and broken glass on the ground. Bitch! Somebody stole my fuckin' car. This can't be happening. I took out my phone and called the police. I was assured someone would be here soon.

Next I called Candy, I told her where I was and what happened. "I'm on my way," she said. Standing there alone I wanted to cry. I sure hope this wasn't a sign of things to come. A few minutes later a patrol car came towards me. I stopped it and a female officer got out. I showed her where my car was parked, gave her all my information and answered all her questions. I wanted to tell her about my 380, but I didn't have a license for it. I just knew the mention of a gun would have made them really look for the car today. Before she left she gave me a copy of the report and her card. Then I wondered back into the mall to wait on Candy.

I was so fucked up in the head I really felt alone. I took my cell out and called Voodoo. When he answered he knew right off something was not right. I told him my car was stolen, but for some reason he acted like it was no big deal, which upset me even more. "Hey, where are you now?"

"I'm still at the mall waiting on Candy."

"Okay, check this out baby girl, I know where you live, but what's your address?"

"Why? You were there last night."

"I know, I just wanna' make sure I find it again," he said.

"It's 1231 W. 134th and you know it's in Compton. So you're coming by sometime today?"

"Yeah, I'll be there in a few hours. Don't worry Toni, the police will find your car. Look I gotta' go, I'm still like two hours away and I wanna' try to turn that into one."

"Alright, I'll see you later. Bye!"

VOODOO

I could tell she was hurting, some punk stole her car and I wanted to make things right for her. So I thought I would have a lil' surprise waiting for her when she got home. I turned on phone and called lil' Voo. When he answered I got my usual greeting, "What's up nigga?"

"What's up kid? You at home?"

"Yeah."

"Look, I need you to do me a favor. Get something to write this address down."

"Alright I'm ready." I gave him Toni's address and told him, "I want you to go to my place, get my white Lexus, take it there and park it out front. Have Bad Luck follow you out there."

"Hey, ain't that Front Hood?" he asked.

"Yeah, why?"

"You know them niggaz' in Compton be trippin' if they don't know you," Lil Voo said.

"I feel you," I started to say, "y'all should be alright, but go heated just in case. Look, Lil Voo, leave the driver's door unlocked. Leave a short note saying, 'Toni, look under the seat. This is you until they find your car. Just think of something special for me." Then drop the car off and leave the key under the seat for Toni. Don't give anyone time to ask questions,' I finished.

"Alright I feel you. I'll have it done before the hour is up."

"Good lookin' out cuzz, later!" Wait until she gets home and see what awaits her ass. Fuck brownie points, these are straight up pussy points. Which one would you rather have, a brownie or some more of Layla?

CANDY

"Sandy you wanna' ride out to the Fox Hills Mall with me? It's Toni, someone stole her car."

"Is she alright?" Promise asked.

"Yeah but she needs me to go get her."

"Okay, I'm on my way, just let me go to the bathroom real quick," Sandy said.

"Yeah make sure you wash yo' hands too."

"Yo' butt lucky mom is right here."

"Yeah yeah," I said.

"Why didn't she call that boy Donnie?" Promise asked.

"Hey, how you know about him?" I asked.

"Stacy told me about him last night. She said he was cute too," Promise said.

"I'mma' have to agree, he's real cute," I added.

"Alright, let's go. Mom we'll be back later," Sandy said.

"Did you wash yo' hands?"

"Momma look at that," When mom turned her head in the opposite direction, Sandy hit me in the arm.

"Hit me again, hear," I said ready to take her down.

"What you gonna' do?"

"Will y'all cut it out, that girl is out there waiting on you."

"Bye mom."

"Bye baby!"

PROMISE

The twins will be gone for lord knows how long, so I grabbed my cell phone to call Jamel. He surprised me when he answered on the first ring by saying, "Well if it isn't the love of my life. I was wondering when you were going to call. I started to think I disappointed you last weekend."

We haven't slept together in ten years. But last Saturday night was really nice. We're both in our early forties, but he was making moves and freaking me like we were twenty again. I don't know why I'm even doing this, his ass haven't called me once since he left here Sunday. But last night made me horny as hell. Stacy and I danced with some nice looking guys, I even got up close and personal with one, but there was no way I was gonna' bring a stranger home with me. So here I am making what I know is a mistake.

"Why did you say that?" I said.

"Cause I've been waiting for you to call me."

"Shit, what's wrong with you calling me?

Laughing, he said, "Baby I have loved you from the first time you shared your beautiful body with me. And I was trying to show you that last weekend. I know I messed up with you, but Promise I love you still. I love you today, I'mma' love you tomorrow, and even sometime next year-I'm gonna' love you woman. All I can do is wait on you, and you know what?"

"What?" I said.

"It looks like my wait is almost over."

"Don't go ruining shit being conceded. Anyway, where are you?"

"I'm on Wilmington and Alandra getting some BBQ. You want me to bring you some?"

"Yeah, bring me a Shredded Chicken sandwich, a big bag of Lays and a Coke."

"Alright."

"Thank you."

"Yeah, that's just what I'm hoping you'll do."

"Whatever Jamel."

"Alright, I'll be there in like twenty minutes."

"Alright, I'mma' take a quick shower so I'll leave the side door open, so just come on in."

"Cool."

Since I had some time, I did some prepping. I went into the den and put on some 'Loose Ends', I turned up the volume to where I could hear it throughout the house. Next I went into my room and took my weed box from my closet. On my bed I packed my lil' bud pipe, and took a few good hits. The Chocolate Thai was sweater then any candy bar. I hit it a couple more times, then headed for the shower. "You Got Me Hangin' From Strings" played in the background. I turned the hot water on, and before it got too steamy I pined up my hair. I was actually taking my time. I wanted him to find me in the shower. I knew I still had about fifteen minutes, so again I took my time getting undressed. Once I was done I went and stepped in. While washing my body, I started thinking about what I was doing.

Jamel was Gang Bangin' right through high school, and right into adult hood. He sold drugs and I can't tell you how many times he cheated on me.

But he gave me my beautiful twins and I love him for that. Last weekend showed me how much fun we use to have together. And thinking about him being here now made me hotter than the water ever could. Thinking about a man like I was, I did what any woman would have done. I had my first orgasm like three minutes before he walked in the bathroom and called my name.

JAMEL

After our short conversation, I damn near said screw the BBQ. She pretty much let me know what was up without actually saying she wanted to make love to me. I told them to put a rush on my order. I didn't wanna' seem too eager, which I was, but when I crossed over Rosecrans, I had to make myself slow down. I knew it would only take five minutes to get to the hood. When I pulled up to the house I saw Sandy's car was there. But when I walked into the house I could tell that both of the twins were gone. I locked the door and called out to Promise. No answer. I dropped our lunch on the kitchen table and went towards the bathroom. The music was on and sounding good, so I called her name loud enough to be heard over that and the shower. Her silhouette turned at the sound of my voice. She shimmied down and back up, and my dick came alive like a light switch went on.

She was doing a slow dance, and through the frosty glass she was telling me to come join her. As I got undressed, I couldn't take my eyes off of her. At forty-one, she could give any twenty-five-year-old a run for their money. As soon as I stepped into the shower, she wrapped her arms and one of her legs around me like the last ten years we've been apart has been sheer hell. "Hold me," she said. I did and her body was like fire. The next thing I knew, she pushed me to the back of the shower and went crazy. She kissed me from top to bottom. On her way back up, she took my dick in her mouth. You know it always feels good when a woman is tryin' to blow yo' socks off, but when it's someone you love, it's almost indescribable. The sounds of her working my dick with her mouth and hands could be heard, and it was driving me crazy.

Her hand and mouth were working in tandem. I grabbed the back of her head and started pumping my hips, working my dick in and out of her mouth. I wasn't ready to cum, so I tried to pull her up but she wasn't havin' it. She was sucking on me faster and faster, and jacking me off at the same time. If this is what she wants, no problem. She had me feeling so right I was trying to push my dick all the way down her throat, even over the running water I could hear her working it.

"Promise I sure hope you like the way this taste." And I emptied a bucket full of hot cum in her mouth.

Chapter 15

PROMISE

When I heard him call me I did the first thing that came to mind, I started a slow dance, enticing him to come join me. Then I got so emotional for some reason, I just felt like I needed him to hold me. But I felt his dick thumping against my thigh, and all that sexual heat came back like a flash. I pushed him against the back of the shower and started kissing him all over. Then I found myself sucking his dick that I really needed. I forgot how good this nigga taste. I knew he didn't want to cum so soon. He tried to pull me up, but I held on and worked him in and out of my mouth so good he couldn't help but to explode down my throat.

Before I took his dick out, I looked up at him and saw pure joy on his face. I worked him over a lil' more, and when I came up I said, "You miss that shit, don't you?" He answered by sticking his tongue in my mouth. While he kissed me, my hand found his dick that just grew for me the more I squeezed it. Once he was nice and hard again, I threw my leg up and rubbed my pussy lips with his dick. I think the more I moaned the harder he got. Then he managed to turn me around, now I was up against the wall. I let his dick go and made him suck on my titties as I pushed them up to his face. Just like a mind reader he put one in his mouth, and as he pulled it out his teeth caught my nipple and bit down, I damn near came again.

I could barely stand it. "Bite them baby." And when he did, I said, "You're gonna' make me cum." But then he let them go. He played with them some more then he turned me around and bent me over. I tried to relax myself for what was to come. Looking back at him, he lathered up his dick with soap, I reached back with both hands and pulled myself open for him, then he put his whole dick in my ass. I cried out and not because it felt good, but he held me in place. "You know I'd never hurt you."

"Yeah well, this shit hurts," I said.

"Just relax." As he started talking to me, he also started hitting me more and more. Then the shit got good to me, I bent over even more and started fucking him back. Together we fucked each other like there was no tomorrow.

It felt like he was growing more and more, and my ass hole had had enough. I pushed off of him and took a moment to catch my breath then made him lay down in the tub. I took him in both hands and squatted down on him. First I moved one hand and was only taking him in halfway. But I could tell he wanted more, he was trying to push up further but my hand was blocking his full thrust. Finally I moved my hand and let him in. I thought he came-because of the way his eyes rolled up in the back of his head, and the pleasing that he made. But a moment later he took my right breast in his mouth and started suckin' and fuckin' on me at the same time. I got his rhythm and bounced on his dick for a good ten minutes, all the while telling him how good his dick was. I'm telling you, it felt so good I was squeezing my own titties.

JAMEL

I couldn't believe it, this was like the days of old when she loved me and couldn't get enough of me fucking her. Not wanting to be in the shower any more, after she came all over me, I said, "Come with me." She got up and turned off the water. I pulled her from the shower and grabbed a towel. Slowly I dried her off, kissing her in several places as I went. To me Promise had the prettiest breast known to man. I've always enjoyed sucking on them, but at that moment there was another part of her body I wanted to suck on, so I picked her up and sat her on the cold sink. My dick was still hard as hell and she was trying to reach for it, but I wouldn't let her have it. Yeah I wanted back inside of her, but before I plunged back in, I parted her legs and put one of her feet on the sink.

Then I dipped down and stuck my tongue in her pussy as far as it would reach. I guess she liked it because she took the back of my head and held me there. I moved my tongue around in a circular motion and she moaned and pushed on my head even more. I damn near couldn't breathe. I pulled away and looked at what I had in front of me. Her pussy was succulent and delicious. I took my thumbs and opened her to where I could almost see inside of her. Her clit jumped out and I devoured it. After five minutes of sucking on her she tried to push me away, but I knew she was enjoying it, and when I bit down on her clit she slammed her legs close on my head. When she came I let go and she let me go. I pulled back to admire her pussy again and some more cum came outta' her, so I went back to finish the job.

Then she reached down and pulled on her ass so I went there next. When I stuck my tongue in her ass she threw both her legs up and grabbed even more of her ass cheeks. I went back and forth between the two trying to drive her crazy. She finally pulled me up, and with both her legs on my shoulders, my dick took over. She had me so hard I came within minutes. Then she pulled me in, held me as tightly as she could and released her own stream of hot cum.

PROMISE

I must say, the boy still got it. Two good orgasms in an hour, shit, what more can I ask for? Now it was time for him to go. But how do I do this where he's not upset? I took a hot towel and cleaned myself, when I was done I did the same for him. Cleaning him I couldn't help but wanna' suck on his dick again, but instead I told him to get dressed. "Jamel, I need to get ready for work." I could see a bit of disappointment in his eyes, but hey, there's nothing I can do about that. I put a towel around myself and headed for the kitchen. Our lunch was there so I put it on some plates and put it in the microwave.

When I turned around he was right there, so close he made me jump. "Promise, I know this doesn't change all my years of fuckin' up, but I do wanna' thank you for spending some time with me, and any time you want me to come suck on yo' good ass pussy, just call." I thought he was going to get all deep and shit, like, "Oh baby I want us to be together again," Or something like that. But I didn't get none of that. It actually made me smile from being so turned on.

"So you saying anytime I want you to come eat my pussy, you'll come, no questions asked?"

"No questions asked."

I pulled my towel open and said, "Shit, you can do that right now."

He smiled at me and dropped to his knees. When the bell on the microwave went off he got up. I fucked around and did what he was supposed to do, got emotional. I put my arms around him and said, "You know I'll always love you, right?" Again he surprised me by not saying a word. While we ate, we talked about the twins some. I told him how someone stole Toni's car today, and a few other things. When he was done eating, he gave me a kiss then made his way to the door.

"Don't be no stranger," he said. Then he was gone. I closed the door and locked it behind him. Standing there for a moment, I wondered if I had done the right thing, by pushing Jamel away. Oh well, I reasoned, at least I had myself some well-deserved orgasms.

TONI

I had been sitting in the food court playing with my phone and trying to ignore everyone around me. Then to my relief Sandy and Candy walked in. I gathered up my belongings and went to meet them. "What's up y'all?" I said, pushing my bag at Sandy. "Here, this was your idea, you can carry this."

"Damn nigga, I didn't steal yo' car, why you trippin' on me?"

"Somebody took my baby, I gotta' trip on somebody."

"What did the police say?" Sandy asked.

"What could they say? My shit has already been in a drive-by shooting or is in somebody's chop shop by now."

"Don't think like that Toni, the police will find it soon," Candy said.

"Yeah", said Sandy, "don't trip, you can have my car until you find yours."

"That's sweet of you, but I'm cool, I just wanna' go home."

"First of all, I'mma' gangsta, I don't do sweet, and the first time yo' ass call talkin' about you need a ride, I'mma' tell yo' ass to take the bus," Sandy said.

"First of all, yo' ass ain't no gangsta, and second, if she calls you, yo' ass better go get her, or I'mma have somebody steal yo' shit," Candy said. That got a smile outta' me, but I told them not to trip.

"I'll just use my mom's car."

"Nigga please, you know Stacy worked too damn hard for that BMW. Toni, I hate to tell you this, but there's no way she's going to let you use her car."

"She's got a point there, girl." Candy said.

"Y'all forget I got the gift of gab. I can talk an elephant into taking flight," I said.

"Well that shit is gonna' sound like gibberish when she tell yo' ass no," said Sandy.

"Sandy will you please stop being so negative, damn," Candy said.

"I'm just sayin'. No matter what happens, I just want you to know you can always count on Candy," Sandy said, as we all laughed, "Toni, did this thing come with a book of codes?" she continued.

"No, just instructions. And don't ask that dumb ass question Sandy, 'cause I don't know," I said.

"I'm sure if we listen long enough, we can figure out the different calls," said Candy.

"Yeah", Sandy said, "but are they going to be the same in San Diego as they are here?"

"Didn't I just tell you not to ask that? I don't know. Shit Sandy, you the boss, aren't you the one that's supposed to have all the answers?" I asked.

"Good point sis," Candy said.

"Let me hear one more good point outta' you and I'mma' put yo' ass out," said Sandy.

"Nigga how you gonna' put me out my own shit?" Candy snapped.

"Man I swear, you two argue like an old married couple," I said, shaking my head in disgust.

"I'm sorry girl, this is not about us," said Sandy, "and I got just the thing to make you feel better." She reached into her bag and came out with a fat ass joint.

"Damn nigga, where do you keep getting all this weed from? We've pretty much been together since last week and you ain't bought shit, but you steadily pullin' shit out yo' purse," Candy said.

Sandy grabbed the lighter, lit up, took a big hit and said, "Weed is nature's medicine, so I grow it in my purse." She took another hit and passed it to me. After taking a good hit myself, I held it for as long as I could, and when I blew the smoke out I coughed for the next minute. "Damn girl, where did you get this shit?"

"What was it you said, Ancient Compton Secret," Sandy said, smiling from ear-to-ear, "Shits good, huh?"

"Hell yeah, they should just call this shit Choker." I took another hit and passed it to Candy.

CANDY

Lucky for me it was a red light. Almost immediately I got high, and just like Toni, when I exhaled I got to choking which made me even higher. Then my dumb ass went into race mode. When the light turned green I hit the gas and threw them back into their seats. I had the Jetta in third gear before I knew it. I pushed around a few cars and when I hit Imperial I was in fifth gear.

"Will you slow yo' crazy ass down," Sandy hollered. But my response was to turn up the music and then I blew through a yellow light.

"Girl, just let her do her thang. Just make sure your seat belt is on tight," Toni said.

Before anyone realized it, we made it all the way back to Compton, and just before I turned onto 134th street, I got pulled over by a Compton Sheriff.

"See that's what yo' crazy ass get." Sandy said.

"Man will you shut up and close the ashtray." I wasn't really trippin', everybody had their seatbelt on and I had all my paper work, so the most I could get was a ticket for speeding. But as it turned out, the officer saw a car full of women and he thought he could get lucky.

"Good afternoon ladies," he said, as he approached the car, "may I see your license and insurance please?"

"Here you go officer, is there a problem?"

"Yes there is." He said, fanning, "First do you know how fast you were going? And second, have you ladies been smoking marijuana?"

"First, yes I know how fast I was going, and second no we were not smoking marijuana. That's my newest perfume you smell. Do you like it? It's called Choker." Sandy and Toni fell out laughing. "Officer, can I see your identification please?"

"Let me see, Miss Jordan, maybe I should pull you out and have you walk a couple of straight lines."

"Are you going to walk with me or are you going to kick back and watch all my curviness?"

"Miss Jordan, are you being flirtatious with me?"

"Do you want me to be?" Before he could answer, Sandy leaned over and whispered Yellow Bird's name. I shooed her away.

"Oh I see it's two of you, maybe I should pull you both out. I think I'd like to see you both do some walking."

"Since you didn't show me your ID officer York, I guess I'll just have to ask. What's your first name?"

"Devan, Devan York."

"Look Devan, I know why you pulled us over, and not because I was speeding, but because of who you saw in here, and that's cool 'cause you're cute as hell. So how are we gonna' do this? You're gonna' write me a ticket or are you going to write me your phone number?"

"Can I do both?"

"Nah nah baby boy, I may be young, and I can handle either one, but not both."

"Here you go," he said, handing me back my paper work. Then he gave me his cell phone and told me to put my number in it. I took it with the prettiest smile I could give him.

"Devan," I said, handing him back his phone, "I want you to do two things as soon as you get off work tonight. Clock out and call me. You think you can handle that?"

"Candy, you got that comin'. Shit I should arrest yo' pretty ass just so I can spend some more time with you."

"I was wondering when you were going to say my name. And since I know what you're thinking, yes I taste like candy." He shook his head smiling.

"Look, you ladies slow down, I'd hate for anything to happen to that amazing body before I get to it."

"Don't worry, when you're good and ready, this will be waiting for you," I said, opening my legs very seductively. "Now are we free to go officer?"

"Yes, you ladies have a nice day."

Chapter 16

TONI

Damn, I thought I had the gift of gab. "Girl, she just sweet-talked her way out of a ticket. Yo' big head ass would be on yo' way to jail by now," I told Sandy.

"Yeah I got game, and his ass gonna' trip when he makes that call," Candy said.

"What I wanna' know," Sandy said, "is why is yo' ass still sitting here?"

A few minutes later Candy was at my house, she pulled up in back of a Pearl White Lexus. The shit was sitting on low profiles rims and tires, looking clean as hell. When we got out I told the twins, "Stacy must have met someone while they were at the club last night."

"Well if she did, he might have a son our age," Sandy said.

"If he's pushing this he might have some deep pockets." I just looked at her. Out of curiosity I looked inside and I could see there was a note on the front seat. I moved to the other side and peeped in the window. I was surprised when I saw my name.

"Hey y'all come here. Look."

"What?" Candy said.

"There's a note with my name on it."

"Are you serious?" Candy asked.

"I'm telling you, look," I said, pointing at the window.

"Shit," Sandy said, "try the door."

When I did, it opened. I took the note and read it.

"Toni, don't trip, this is you until you get your car back, I got you, Voodoo. P.S. Look under the seat!"

"Ooh shit, read this," I said, handing them the note. I sat in the soft cream color leather and reached under the front seat. There was a digital key and an alarm pad. I hit the alarm button and the shit said, "Please stand back, now arming."

"Ooh shit, did you hear that?" I said.

"Fuck that," Sandy said, "I want one and I want it now."

"How did he even know?" Candy asked.

"I called him right after I called you. You know what? Now that I think about it, he asked for my address."

"I thought he brought you home last night?" Candy said.

"He did, and that's what I told him, but he said he wanted to make sure he found the house when he came by today."

"Oh he found it alright."

"But there's no way he could have done this. He was two hours away when I called, and I know he didn't drive all the way from Riverside, pick this up, drive all the way from Duarte to here and drop this off."

"Girl that nigga knows where you live, he just needed it so he could have someone else drop it off," Sandy said.

"That's so sweet of him," Candy added.

"Yeah well, just make sure you don't wreck his shit, 'cause you think you gave up some pussy last night, yo' ass gonna' be fuckin' a long time if you fuck this ride up."

"Sandy shut yo' ass up," Candy said.

"Fuck all that," I said, "how you know what I did last night?"

"Hello, it's a fuckin' Lexus sitting here. You do the math," Sandy said.

"Toni, she got a point there girl."

"There you go with them bullshit points again. I'm really trippin' right now, what am I supposed to do with this shit?"

"Shit," Sandy said, "push this bitch like yo' shit don't stink."

"She got a point there too girl," Candy said again, and we all laughed.

"All I wanna' know is," Sandy said, "where we going tonight?"

"We're not going anywhere until I talk to Voodoo. This shit is gonna' sit right there."

"This nigga is doing way too much. Call him," Candy insisted.

"Nah nah, he'll be here before the night is over, if for nothing else, just to gloat on how much money he has."

"Well I love you, but I'm going home, and since you didn't buy me lunch I'm hungry and I need something to eat. Let's go ugly," Sandy said.

"Bye baby girl. Call us if you wanna' get into something," Candy said.

"Hold up, I got something for y'all." I reached in my purse and handed Sandy $500. "Y'all split that," I said.

"Thanks girl. Big money, new Lexus, nigga you sure yo' ass didn't hit our lick yet?"

"Bye Sandy, and when I do hit, I'm going right to a car lot."

"Well make sure you take me with you, we out!"

TONI & VOODOO

The twins left and I locked up the car and went into the house. It was 2:36 p.m. and I was so happy Stacy wasn't home. I just couldn't go through the whole explanation thing. The day was still young, but I felt totally drained. I went to my room and fell across my bed. As soon as I thought I was sleep my cell phone started complaining. I took it from my back pocket, and without opening my eyes, I answered. "Hello." It was Voodoo.

"Hey sexy, where are you?"

"I'm laying on my bed. Why, where are you?"

"Never mind all that, do you want some company?"

"If I thought you were close I'd say yeah."

"Is your front yard close enough?"

I threw the phone on the bed and ran to the front door. He was out there in all gray looking sexy as fuck. He had a towel and was wiping down his motor cycle, which was sitting in the drive way. I thought to myself, this nigga sure knows how to make a good impression. I walked up on him and said, "You think you got game don't you?"

"You like the car?" I nodded. "Do you like me?" Again I nodded my head. "Then there you go, I got boss game."

"Whatever nigga. I love the car, but you need to take that back where it came from."

"Then how do you plan to get around?"

"I'll use my mom's car."

"Is she home now?"

"No, but..."

"No buts, if you needed to go somewhere right this moment you couldn't go. Look, I thought you was feelin' me the way you shared your beautiful body with me?"

"Yeah, I am."

"Then accept my gift. All I ask is one thing."

"What's that?"

"That you don't have no niggaz' in my shit."

I nodded my understanding for the third time, then walked into his arms and thanked him with a kiss. "That's what I'm talkin' bout."

"Can we go for a ride?"

"You haven't drove it yet?"

"No, I told the twins this car was not movin' until I talked to you, and now that I have, I'm ready to see what this baby can do."

"Well let's go."

"Hold on, let me go lock up the house."

Watching her walk towards the house made me want to follow her, her blue sweat pants wasn't that tight but her ass still looked nice on the move. I said fuck it and went after her, but before I got halfway to the door my cell phone rang. It was Black. "What's up homie?"

"Hey where you at my nigga?"

"Over here in Front Hood kickin' it."

"I know you ain't with Toni?"

"Well yo' ass wrong. What's up?"

"I was just callin' to see if you wanted to come out here and kick it, I'm doing some grillin'."

"I like the sound of that. Shit it's after 3:00 and I ain't ate yet. I was about to go eat some pussy but you stopped that."

"Don't blame it on me nigga, and besides, if you're there now that means you got all year to suck on her."

"I'm ready Voo."

"Alright, just a minute."

"Hey Voo," Black said, "I got one question for you."

"What's up?"

"Does she taste good?"

"Does she taste good? Shit, is water wet?"

"I know you're not talkin' about me?"

"You're exactly who I'm talkin' about." And I gave her a kiss.

"Hey you got the twins over there?"

"No, but I'm about to call them. So you coming or what?"

"You know I got Toni with me right?"

"I ain't trippin'."

"Cool. We'll be there in a few, later."

When he hung up the phone I punched him. "Don't be talkin' about me like that."

"I don't know what you're talkin' about."

"You just said you were talkin' about me."

"I did, you got that shit on tape?"

"No!"

"Then you can't prove it," he said, kissing me again.

"Ah shut up nigga, let's go. I wanna' test out my new wheels." While I went to the car he pushed his bike further into the drive way.

Sometimes I swear, this nigga is one big mystery, but I'm really feeling him more and more. When I hit the alarm to the Lexus, it said, "Disarming" and beeped three times. Once we were inside the car everything went silent, I couldn't hear shit. I started the engine and it ran so quietly I barely heard that. Already this bitch made my Camry look like a bucket. I adjusted everything and then just sat there. For some reason I got really nervous. He put a hand on my leg and said, "Don't trip, it's just a car." I smiled and nodded. When I took off the car showed me one more thing. The shit had major power. At the corner I just sat there, and again he had to get me past my nerves. This time I said fuck it, like he said, it's just a car.

"So where we going?"

"You know where Black and Yellow Bird stay at?"

"Yeah, and in this baby I'll have us there in ten minutes. Are the twins there?"

"No, but I think Black's gonna' call them. He said he's cooking BBQ."

"That's good. I'm hungry."

"Yeah me too. I was actually on my way into the house to eat on you when he called."

"I knew something was up."

"What?"

"When I went inside you were wiping off your bike and when I came out you had one foot on the porch."

"I couldn't help it, when you walked off yo' booty pulled me like a magnet."

"Yeah right. Anyway did you find what you were looking for this morning?"

"Yeah I got it, that shit was easier than I thought it would be."

"So that's one less thing we have to worry about."

"Yep. What about you, did you find a scanner?"

"Yeah and I want to give you yo' change."

"Man I don't need that shit."

"Good, 'cause I forgot I gave it to the twins."

"I ain't trippin', y'all gonna' make us a lot of money soon. Hell I could light a blunt with that lil' shit I gave you. But you know what I think about when I think of money?"

"What?"

"Sex," he said, reaching between my legs.

Her pussy felt so soft I wanted to stick my finger inside of her, but she was already nervous about the Lexus. "Donnie will you stop," she said, moving my hand away. When she turned right on Long Beach Blvd, I moved my hand back to her thigh. I'm telling you, the feel of her leg alone made me want to put my head between her legs and eat everything in sight. As we came up on Alandra I pointed to Jack Rabbit's and told her, "Pull in over there so I can get some brew. Do you want anything?"

"Yeah," she said, pulling into the parking lot.

"Get me a Sex on the Beach."

"How about sex on the hood of the car?"

"Will you stop it."

She didn't notice them but I did. There were four of them, they came from the wash house next to the liquor store, and since I didn't have a gun I used the next best thing. I took out my phone and pulled up Black's number, then opened the door. The four of them had blue Kansas City Royal hats on so I knew they were from Kelly Park. When I closed the car door I hit the send button. Black answered on the second ring. "What's up homie?" They were coming right at me, an outsider with a fresh Lexus. I screamed victim.

"Black Bird," I said, louder then I needed to, "I'm at Jack Rabbit's, you and Yellow Bird want anything?" Black didn't get where he was by not being able to pick up on things.

"How many is it?"

"Four." Two of them walked up on me.

"Where you from cuzz?" One of them said.

"Black Bird, hold on a sec. Homie I'm from Due Rock," I said. But this time at the mention of Black's name I could see a change come over him.

"You know the big homie Black?" he said.

"Yeah, we're going to a BBQ at his house. What's yo' name crip?" "Lil' Sandman."

"Black you hear that?"

"Yeah, I know him, you good. Now get yo' shit and get off that corner before yo' ass get dusted off," Black said, on the other end of the phone.

"Alright, I'll be there in a few minutes."

I hung up and went into the store, and as I might've guessed they followed me. I got two large bags of chips, four bottles of Old English, and at the counter I got Toni's Sex on the Beach. I pulled out a $50 and paid. When everything was bagged up, I peeped out what the four of them were doing. Since none of them bought anything I thought I might still have a problem. I know if any of my young homies went against my orders I'd hang his ass by his nutts, and I'm sure Black would do the same. Bangin' was about following orders, but sometimes the lil' homies tried to buck the system. They went out the store before I did, so as soon as I stepped outside I called Sandman.

"What's up cuzz?"

"Here you go homie," I said, handing him a 40oz.

"Good lookin' out cuzz."

Then he pulled up the front of his shirt showing me the butt of his 9mm. "You be safe now, you hear?" When I got in the car I gave Toni a deep kiss.

"What was that for?"

"Baby my life just flashed before my eyes, them niggaz' was about to kill me."

"Ah nigga please, you wit that drama, I know you called either Black or Yellow Bird."

"You peeped that huh?"

"Yeah, now if you wanna' kiss me like that, next time do it 'cause I'm sexy."

"Okay you asked for it." I kissed her for a whole minute, as my hand found its way back to her soft and silky inner thighs.

Chapter 17

TONI

This nigga just will not stop. In every situation he seemed to handle himself like it ain't nothing. That nigga just showed him a gun and he smiles and gives him a cold beer. At the same time, he puts his hand on my thigh's again and the temperature in the car went up like 20 degrees. Shit, the second kiss really had me ready for a motel. I had to pull away from him and start the car so we could get going. I shot down Long Beach and turned left on Caldwell. It being the middle of summer, kids were out in force. Music was coming from houses and cars alike. I hit Black's street, Harris- and it looked like a low rider car show. There seemed to be three houses where people were gathered. Yellow Bird was standing in the front yard with his huge pit bull.

When I pulled up the dog put its front paws up on the gate. "Why these niggaz' gotta' have such big ass dogs?" I said.

"Come on Toni let's go, Friendly is like a puppy," Voodoo said.

"Puppy my ass, he looks more like a bear."

"You'll be alright. You've been here before and you made it out alive." When I got out the car I told Yellow Bird, "You really need to put his ass up somewhere."

"You safe, he ate already." They laughed at me but I wasn't convinced.

When I moved to come in the gate Friendly got down and came over towards the entrance. "See what I mean. Why he do that?"

"I told you not to worry," Yellow Bird said. But just like a sign from above, the black Jetta hit the corner, followed by Sandy in her grey one.

"Yeah nigga, I bet you put his ass up now, won't you?" I said. Candy got out and locked up her car.

"What's up y'all?" Candy said.

"Girl I'm tryin' to get this fool to put his dog up."

"Girl that's easy, watch this. Keith I got a question for you. Y'all standing guard like you own the place or something."

"We do..."

"Okay then, would you rather rub on all this ass in these shorts or would you rather rub on Friendly?"

"Shit my nigga," Voodoo said, "I'd take door # One." And I punched him in the arm. Yellow Bird called for Black Jack, and when the second beast came he took them both out back to their kennel.

"Yep yep, the power of the booty will work every time," Candy said, laughing.

The twins were dressed alike but in different colors. When Black saw Sandy he closed the grill, walked over and picked her up off the ground kissing her. "Damn," Candy said, "I sure wish I got that type of love. But nah, I gots' to make you choose between me and the family pets."

"I'm sorry baby girl, come here and let me show you some love," Yellow Bird said.

"Nah nah, lover boy, you need to go wash yo' hands."

"Damn," he said, veering off to go in the house.

There was a cooler full of beer and ice. Voodoo put his beer in there and asked if he could make me a drink. "You sure can."

"Sandy, Candy, y'all want something to drink?"

"Yes please," Candy said. But Sandy's ghetto ass took a 40oz. from the cooler, popped the top and took a big gulp. Then her nasty butt let out a big belch.

"That's what I'm talkin' about," Voodoo said.

But Candy walked over took the bottle and poured Sandy some beer in a cup.

"You are not about to be walkin' around here filthy drunk," she told her. "It's still early so take it easy. Black will you keep an eye on her?" Black nodded to her.

Voodoo handed me my drink and I gave him a kiss in return. Then I spotted something on a smaller table, I walked over and there was a mixing bowl full of weed. It was mint green with purple hairs. You could probably get high just smelling it. There was all kind of shit to smoke with too, blunt papers, orange zig-zags and two bud pipes. I took one of the pipes, packed it and lit it with a wooden match. The shit was so strong, it was even stronger then the shit Sandy had earlier. I got mad tho', 'cause by the time I was done choking, the shit went out. I choked each time I hit it, and even though I was high as hell, I was determined to finish the whole bowl. When there was nothing but ashes left I stood up and had to sit right back down. Candy came over and said she wanted some. "No the hell you don't, leave that shit alone, I'm tellin' you." But being the hard head she is, she packed the bowl and lit up. I must have been trippin', 'cause she hit that shit again and again like she was a fuckin' Jamaican. Then somebody put on some Scarface and I came alive. I found Voodoo and started dancing around him. My drink turned out to be too much for me, so I made him drink the rest of it. I gave him a nice kiss and told him thanks again for letting me use his car. He just smiled and held onto my ass. I didn't see Black and Sandy anywhere, then I thought I was having a bad reaction to the weed, 'cause Candy was over at the kennel letting the dogs lick her hand. "Yellow Bird, will you get my girl before her ass gets eaten alive."

"Don't trip, she's good." I pushed away from Voodoo and went to her side, if she can do it, so can I. But when I walked up they started growling. Okay maybe I was wrong.

BLACK BIRD

I called everyone to the table to eat. "First, thank you greedy niggaz' for coming to kick it with me and the homie. I was actually calling all of you here for a reason. Earlier today I made some calls and put everything together. Tomorrow we were going to drive to San Diego and check out this building. Well we're still going to do that, but we're not coming back without our money and dope."

"Hold up," Sandy said, "I thought I said I was in charge of this thing?"

"You did and you are, but I see no reason to wait. Tomorrow night or Saturday night we're going in."

"But we still don't have everything we need," Sandy said, with a little agitation.

"Okay, what else is needed? Toni has all the computer equipment she needs, right? We have the two-way radios, and y'all got radar detectors. We have the location of the building and we know how many people will be there. Voodoo went to find something to take care of the lone guard, so as far as I can see, all we need now is the police scanner," I said.

"Actually, I found one of those this morning, and some bitch stole my car for my troubles, but that's another story," Toni said.

"Well there you go, we got everything," I said.

"What about the vehicles?" Sandy asked.

"I told you, I made a few calls. I got us three non-descriptive vans. The one for Toni has more batteries than my low rider out front.
Toni, sometime this evening you're gonna' need to get all your equipment and bring it back here. In the morning before we leave, it will all be hooked up and ready to go for you. Sandy I'm not trying to step on yo' toes, but Voodoo is due in Sacramento with a load of work Tuesday, and I want what's in that warehouse to be what he takes with him."

"Black, I feel you right," Voodoo said, "and I know what you're really trying to do. But what's in that van is just not enough, and you moving up our date is stepping on my toes."

"How so?"

"I was going to ask the mad professor here to locate us another fifty keys."

"Hold up," Sandy said, "we had a plan and we're sticking to it."

"I agree," Toni said, "it's a lot of shit in there I'd like to get my hands on too, but we have two targets pin pointed and that's what we're going to get."

SANDY

Somehow I knew I was going to lose control of this shit. These niggaz' couldn't have put this together in a million years. Watch, something is going to go wrong. I don't know, maybe I'm just trippin', today, tomorrow or next month, either we're going to find this money or we're not. Candy and Toni don't seem to be trippin', so who am I to stand in their way? We all been wanting something like this since who knows how long, and we need this money! After I was done eating I got up and made myself another drink, then I wondered over to the weed table. Maybe I should call this whole thing off. Then I thought, that wouldn't work, Voodoo would just fuck the information we have right outta' Toni, and they would still do the job without me, and I'll be damned if I'm the only one walkin' around here broke. I rolled myself a joint, fired it up and just sat there staring at them all.

I guess Black could feel what I was thinking 'cause he came over and knelt down in front of me. "Look baby, I'm not trying to take over yo' operation, you came up with this shit and I love you for what you've done, but I'm trying to get out from under some people and you've given me the opportunity I've been looking for."

"But what if something goes wrong?"

"We can't do much about that, but deal with it. If something goes wrong, it's gonna' happen whether we go in tomorrow or next year."

"Black I'm not trying to mess things up for everybody, but now that all the pieces are in place, I'm scared."

"Didn't you bring me into this to keep you safe?"

"Yeah."

"Well that's what I intend to do."

Then he gave me what I think I needed the most. He kissed and hugged me and I felt most of my tension fade away.

CANDY

When my sister got up and walked away from the table my twin radar kicked in. But lucky for me Black went to be with her. I know she didn't like losing control of this thing, but it happened anyway. Actually, they needed to take over whether she knew it or not. These niggaz' are in the streets every day dealing with situations that could get you killed or thrown in jail, and what do we do? Come around when it's all good and spend their money. I understand Sandy wants her own money, I do too, but hey, they need to be out front making this shit happen. Yellow Bird hasn't said anything about it, but I'm sure he had a hand in this. Hell, what's wrong with doing it this weekend?

Sandy hasn't even given us an actual date we could make our move on the building yet. Keith was done eating and was sitting there rubbing his stomach, so I got up and went to fix him a drink. I then went to sit on his lap.

"Here you go baby, I thought you could use this."

"Thanks, I'm full as hell. You know for that nigga Black to be so ugly, he sure can cook."

"You bet not let him hear you say that," I said, laughing. "Keith, do you think what we're doing is a good idea? I mean all we really have is some information on a piece of paper."

"What, you not getting cold feet on me, are you?"

"Cold feet, hell my shit feel like blocks of ice."

"Hey, y'all the ones that came up with this remember? I really don't see how anything can go wrong."

"We got one bullshit security guard patrolling the place. Toni will be monitoring everything else with her computers, we'll be alright."

"I guess I just needed to hear you say this is gonna' work out," I said.

"You know I love you right?" Yellow Bird said.

"Yeah."

"Okay, and I'm gonna' keep you safe, I promise." It's the middle of summer and his words still managed to make me feel warm inside. He gave me a kiss and said he needed to take care of something. When I got up he kissed me again, and this time his hand found my butt. When he left me I thought to myself, loving him is gonna' be easy, and somehow I needed to spend the night with him. Last night came back to me, how he made me feel like a woman. Yeah nigga, whether you know it or not, I love you too.

YELLOW BIRD

I just made a promise I wanted to keep more than anything. I know my killin' skills are up to par, but we're talkin' about the DEA here. "Hey Black, Voodoo, check this out," I said, motioning them to come with me. I took them over to the kennels. Black Jack and Friendly were panting with anticipation. "Here y'all go," I said, giving them some bones, "this oughta' keep you two busy for a while."

"What's up?" Voodoo asked.

"Look, these girls are really nervous about this. Toni I'm not too sure, but the twins are shakin' in their boots and they both got on tennis shoes."

"So what's yo' point?"

"My point is, we're getting ready to go up against the fuckin' government, and I'm not tryin' to let anything happen to the three of them."

"Look," Black said, "we've been over this, we got one guard to deal with and cuzz," he said, pointing at Voodoo, "already went out and found something to put him to sleep with, so what's the problem?"

"The problem is, we're still walkin' into an unknown situation."

"So what are you suggesting?" Voodoo asked.

"Why don't we bring in our boyz' we have stashed in Sacramento? They work good together and they're good at killin' when it's needed."

"There's two problems with that," Black said, "one, that six million dollar figure Voodoo came up with is gonna' turn into like one and some change for each of us. Second, they really didn't wanna' let us in on this, there's no way they will accept six more people," Black added.

"I agree," Voodoo said, "and we still promise to cash them out on fifteen keys. So that one and some change might turn out to be some change."

"Well that extra fifty bricks you was talking about, we're really gonna' need that, do y'all agree?" They both said yeah. "Well yo' ass better get over there and sweet talk Toni into telling us where it is."

VOODOO

I'm not a big weed head but I will blow. I was about to come at her with a cold ass deal, so I rolled a cool sized joint, knowing a blunt would've been too much. I set fire to the joint, took a cool hit and headed over to Toni. I held the smoke until I reached her, I bent down and mixed my kiss with the weed smoke. When I was done she was actually able to blow smoke out. I took another hit and pulled her away from the twins. "Here hit this." She pulled on the joint and returned the favor by blowing smoke into my mouth with a long hot kiss. When she was done I looked into her pretty eyes and said, "We need to talk, but first I wanna make you a deal."

"You wanna' make me a deal, huh?" she said.

"Yeah."

"Okay pretty boy, let's hear it."

"I wanna' sell you that Lexus out front. When was the last time you seen a car that can talk?"

"You wanna' sell me your car?"

"That's right, and all it's gonna' cost you is some information."

"I'm not following you, what kind of information?"

"I need you to go back into their inventory and find us another fifty keys or close to it, and for that you can be the proud owner of a 2013 Lexus."

"But I thought we all agreed on the two specific targets?" she said.

"We did, but there's other factors that are coming into play that you can't see, and keeping the three of you safe is at the top of our list.
If we do this, you still gotta' keep in mind who we're fuckin' with. If there's any gun play the three of us may not be able to hold them off while y'all get away."

"Shit I know how to shoot."

"I'm sure you do, but I'm just getting use to you, and like the homie told Candy, I plan to make sure you come home in one piece."

"So what are you proposing?"

I told her about our six-man crew up North and half of what they do for us.

"But why do you need the extra fifty keys?" she asked.

"Simple, if we bring them in, and stick to our original plan, I don't think the three of us will clear a million each."

"Baby I'm telling you the six of us can handle this ourselves. I'll tell you what tho', if it's like you say I'll do it. But somebody better talk to the twins about this shit," Toni said.

"Yeah we need to tell them, but I think it would sound better coming from you."

"How did I know that was comin'? I'll tell you what, it's 6:30 p.m. and as far as I can tell the only thing we'll need for them is some two ways to match ours. That means I need to make it all the way to Crenshaw and Stocker, and get some more radios."

"Then I have to get back home, hack into their system again, find the next biggest stack of drugs, and not only that, I have to pack up all my equipment and get it back here. And I still have to talk to the twins. What the fuck, do you see a cape on my back?" Toni said.

"No, but you can be my superwoman."

Chapter 18

TONI

I pulled the twins together and ran everything down to them, and trust me, they didn't like it. "Look," I said, "we can do this y'all, we still get our fourteen million, and we got enough fire power watching over us to start a small war. Sandy I know you started this, and it's not turning out how you planned, but hey, the shit is what it is. Now for the last time, are we going or not?"

"Yeah we're going," Sandy said, "just no more surprises."

"Hey y'all come here. Look, you three are not to change or add anymore bullshit scenarios. I'll find your extra fifty keys and that's it, if you so much as dream about another change, we're out, understand?" They all agreed and Black told Yellow Bird to make the call.

"Look y'all, I got a lot of shit to do before it gets too late. Voodoo you coming with me or what?"

"Black, you need me for anything?" Voodoo asked.

"Nah I'm cool, but she needs to take care of whatever it is and get back here tonight."

"Candy, do you have the computer store account number with you?" I asked.

"Yeah, it's in the trunk of my car, come on I'll get it."

"Look, I'll be back here as soon as I can," I said, as I followed Candy and Voodoo out front.

SANDY

You just don't know, these niggaz' had me so hot, I could have shot all they asses, but since I didn't have a gun I did the next best thing, this time I loaded up the bud pipe and got high as I could. Yellow bird was over there clearing the food from the table so I went over and tried to help. I was moving so slow, he ended up doing most of the work himself. He took some more bones and other scraps over to the dogs. After these niggaz' make me rich I might have to get me some pit bulls. Black came from the house carrying two guns. I knew one was a hand gun, but for the life of me I couldn't tell what the other one was.

"Sandy come here, it's time for school."

"Cuzz, I don't think it's cool to be doing that right now, she just got high," Yellow Bird said.

"Shut up nigga, ain't nobody high. Hey baby, you bring me some toys to play with?" I said.

"Yeah, you can play, but these ain't toys." Candy came up as Black was handing me the hand gun.

"What are you doing?" Candy hollered.

"Don't worry I got one for you too."

"Hell nah nigga, is you crazy? First of all, we don't know the first thing about shootin' no guns. And second of all, you niggaz' got a fuckin' police station in the park right around the corner."

"'First of all' smart ass, they're not loaded, yet! And second, fuck the police. Now do you wanna' learn how to use this shit or not?" Black said sternly.

"Let me see that," Yellow Bird said, taking the gun. "Come with me," he said, taking Candy by the hand. Black took me further away from them still. "Baby you really need to pay attention to what I tell you." I nodded my understanding. "This is a seventeen shot 9mm, it's pretty simple to use. This here is the safety switch, the red dot means it's on and you can't pull the trigger. No dot means it will fire. This is the slide, when you pull it back and let it go a shell will move into the chamber. This here is your hammer, it has three positions. Here it's open and ready to fire. You can also hold the hammer, pull the trigger and it will semi close. You got all that?" Again I nodded my head. "Here, take this," he said, handing me the gun. He told me to pull the trigger, when the hammer fell, the click made me jump. "Sandy, you can't be scared of this."

"I'm not scared of shit," I told him and pulled the trigger again, but nothing happened.

"When there's no clip you have to pull the slide back."

"Oh." I did as he said, then did it several more times until I was used to it.

"You got it now?"

"Yeah I got it."

"Hey Candy come here. Did you get what the homie showed you?" Black asked.

"Yeah, that was easy."

"Oh really, okay tough guy," he told her, "it's time for today's second lesson. Yellow Bird, run inside and turn up the music." Moments later the bass that came from the house was so deep I felt it in my bones. When he came back he was holding a black bag that he dropped at our feet. From within he took out two clips, he gave one to Black and kept the other one. Black took the hand gun from me and loaded it.

"Candy what kind of gun is that?"

"A Tech-Nine and it holds a thirty round clip," she said.

"Why she get that one?" I said.

"Don't worry you'll get your turn." She smiled and stuck her tongue out at me.

"You two are not to point these guns at anything but the ground," Yellow Bird told us. Black moved us away again, then from behind me he took both my hands in his. "Okay, is your safety on or off?"

"Off."

"Now pull back on the slide."

"Why does it feel heavier?"

"Cause it has bullets in it now. You ready?" I nodded my head. He guided my hands down and out just passed my knees. He kissed me on the ear and said pull the trigger. The gun went off and I damn near jumped outta' my shoes. Because of the music it was not loud at all, but it still scared the shit outta' me.

"Relax baby girl. Do it again." The gun fired and my hands came up. "Again," Black ordered. I fired three more times. He let me go and I held my arms in the same position. I pulled the trigger again and again, but I had to tell him to take the gun because my hands were hurting.

"Here, this shit hurts."

"That's because you're holding it too tight." He took the gun and pointed it at the ground with one hand and fired off three quick rounds. "Look, as long as you don't point the gun at yourself it can't hurt you, so just relax." I took it back, held it one handed like he did and fired off three shots. After pulling the trigger six more times, the slide locked back.

"How you like me now?" I said confidently.

"You did good, but you need to do it again. Change out yo' clip and start again," he said.

YELLOW BIRD

Candy was so nervous; she was shaking like Don Knotts in a gun fight. After the first shot it took me five minutes to talk her into taking the gun again. The Tech-Nine has a built in silencer and that mixed with the music, you couldn't hear anything from the weapon. "Baby you trust me right?" she nodded her head. "Okay then you need to relax for me. Spread your feet, hold your arms steady, now squeeze the trigger." The gun fired. "Again," I told her. She got off five shots and smiled at me. "See there's nothing to it, now we're gonna' try something a lil' different." I moved the selector switch to automatic.

"What's that?"

"Remember I told you the gun has three ways to fire? Now every time you pull the trigger it will fire three rounds."

"That's too much, I'm not ready."

"Yes you are, now relax and hold it with both hands and squeeze the trigger." She managed to get nine rounds out without killin' me or the dogs.

"Baby I don't wanna' do this anymore."

"Look, I know you don't like it, but we're tryin' to teach y'all this for a reason."

"Nigga I don't know what reason you're talkin' about, but I ain't about to be shooting at nobody, so you can hang that up!"

"Candy this is some serious shit we're about to do, we need to be ready for anything and that includes you, now start shootin'."

BLACK BIRD

After a few more times of going back and forth, the twins got use to firing both weapons. I could tell Candy was not feeling any of this shit, but she learned well and was able to load each weapon and empty the clip. My girl Sandy on the other hand enjoyed herself like crazy. When she put the Tech-Nine on fully automatic and emptied the clip this last time, I could have sworn she had an orgasm. "Alright you two, you're done, I'm proud of both of you, any questions?"

"Yeah, do I get a Tech?" Sandy asked.

"Damn sis, you sound like you ready to go do a drive-by shooting or something," Candy said.

"Don't trip," I told her, "when we're on our way into the building you'll get this, until then it stays here with me."

"Ah man, I can't take it home?"

"Man yo' crazy ass will commit some kind of felony before you get off Long Beach Boulevard," Yellow Bird said.

"No I won't."

"And that's why you can't take it with you," Yellow Bird told her.

"This shit is for committing major felonies and since you're not about to go put in work, there's no need for you to take it. Yellow, will you and Candy gather up these empty shells so the dogs don't eat them? Sandy, run inside and turn down the music, and when you come back we're gonna' clean these weapons." I took the bag and went over to the table. I poured myself a cup of Old English, and sat down.

From the bag I took out some rags, some oil and two push rods. By the time Sandy came back I had both guns broken down and laid out on the table. "Sorry I took so long, I went to the bathroom."

"That's cool. Look, I started without you. Here's the 9mm, and even though they're different guns most of the parts are the same." Over the next hour we went through the different parts cleaning them. I tried to explain what was what as we went. In the end, she was able to put the hand gun back together.

"How did I do?"

"Excellent."

"I sure hope you not trying to turn me into no killer?"

"Nope, but you can shoot me with some of that killer pussy."

"You just might have action at that, but right now I'm going over there and roll me another joint."

TONI & VOODOO

My new Lexus got us to the computer store in no time. We ran in, got the extra two-ways and to be on the safe side, I got a couple of more chargers. Voodoo insisted on paying the bill, but after some back and forth with me I was able to put it on the account Candy opened. "I thought you like to pay for everything by not paying for it?" I whispered in his ear.

"Baby girl it's not what I steal, but the how you might have a problem with." That was a crazy thing to say, but before I could question him, it was my time to pay up. The bill came to $360.00, I paid

$100 and put the rest went into the account. "You know I could have paid that, right?"

"Yo' ass sure is tryin' to be helpful, I hope you not tryin' to buy you no pussy tonight?"

I took the two bags and headed for the door. He didn't say anything, he just smiled and put his hand in my back pocket and squeezed my butt. When we reached the car he gave me a soft kiss, took the bags and told me to open the trunk. Then with a surprised look on his face he asked, "Is that what I think it is?"

"Yep, and they got some bomb ass shit in there to smoke weed with too."

"I don't believe it, all these years of cruising up and down the Shaw, I've never noticed this place. Can we go in?"

"Man will you get in the car, you know we need to go so I can get on the computer. Yo' ass want this information don't you?"

"Alright, you win." We jumped in the car and I headed back to Compton. I know I was racing against time, I had a whole lot of shit to do and I needed to get it done before Stacy got home, so I hit the gas.

When she looked at her watch then hit the gas, I knew she was trying to get home. We had a lot of work to do still, but I was still thinking about the two of us going into business together. "Toni I wanna' run something by you." She put her hand on mine and said, "Speak on it." This shit was crazy, all she did was smile at me and I almost told her that I loved her. Because I was just staring at her, she had to say, "What is it?"

"Um, I was thinking that after we make this move the two of us can go into business together."

"Doing what?"

"The same thing we're doing right now. Baby this city has money laying around all over the place, all you have to do is find it on your computer and I'll go get it."

"But this is supposed to be a one-time thing."

"I guess it was for the three of you guys but for me, I'm about money and I wanna' get all I can while the getting's good."

"I don't know Donnie, what's wrong with this one job? We're about to come outta' there with like twenty million dollars. As a matter of fact, it's more than that, you say you need another fifty keys of dope, that's what, another six or seven?"

"I know what you're sayin', and after we get rid of the drugs I'm cool on the dope game."

"So what's the problem?"

"The problem is I still wanna' make money. Toni, I know what you're thinking."

"Yeah, what's that?"

"You're thinking you're about to come up on like five million, plus your share on the sale of the fifteen keys."

"That's exactly what I'm thinking. Do you have any idea what I can do with that kind of money?"

"I feel you right, but I'm telling you it won't last. Within twenty-four months you're gonna' need more money."

"That's easy for you to say, you got money. Watch this, how much money do you have on you right now?" I reached into my pocket and pulled out my cash, took a quick count and it was $8600."

"See what I mean, I think I barely have $400 on me, and yo' ass got damn-near ten G's in pocket change."

"Here you want it?"

"Nah I don't want it, you gave me some money yesterday, remember?"

"Yeah I remember, but that was nothing, I enjoy being able to look out for you."

"Hold up, you haven't known me that long, I appreciate what you've done, but I can take care of myself, and when I get my hands on this money, me and Daishawn will be straight for a very long time."

"Daishawn, who is that?"

"Ahh shit, I thought you knew, that's my son. Now that I think about it we haven't talked about him, have we? You didn't notice his picture at the house?"

"No, but it's cool, where is he?"

"On Wednesdays and Thursdays he's with his dad, but for some reason this time he said he would bring him home when he was ready. You don't think he's getting ready to flee the country with my son do you?" He just laughed. "I wanted to argue with him, but you can't pay most of these niggaz' to spend time with their kids."

"How old is he?"

"He's one and a half."

"Well it looks like I have two of you to spoil now." I guess that was the right thing to say, 'cause she leaned over and gave me a quick kiss. She was now heading down Imperial Boulevard, when she crossed over Vermont I said, "Look, I really need you to do this for me, actually I need you to do this for us."

"Why do we have to keep throwing rocks at the penitentiary?"

"I'm talking about stealing some money, going into a few places and taking what's just sitting there. That's throwing rocks, but the shit me and the homies are doing right now, hell I'm not just throwing rocks, I'm throwing whole slabs of concrete."

"So stop, you got plenty of money now. Hell open up a strip club like all the other big D-Boyz'."

"You know I like the way you think, so I'll tell you what, you find us twenty million in cash and you and I will do just that."

"You wanna' open a club with me?"

"You'd be surprised at some of the things I'd like to do with you, and to you."

"Well the doing part is gonna' have to wait, I'm trying to get in and out the house before my mom gets home, if she's not already. Hell she doesn't even know about my car yet, and if I tell her then I'll have to explain this one."

"Well you better think of something 'cause this belongs to you now."

Chapter 19

VOODOO

"Toni you know yo' ass is gonna' have an accident if you don't slow down."

"You want me to pull over so you can get out and walk? Shit, you wait until I get all the way back to the Compton to complain, what's up with that?" She said laughing and turning onto her street.

"Let's just say I like my life more then I like you're driving." We pulled up to the house and her mom's BMW was not there. But knowing where we were I was just happy to see my motorcycle was still there.

"Come on," she said, "we're going to pack up my computer system."

"Hey, I thought you were going to find that additional information?"

"And I plan to do just that, but not here. Besides, I already know where it is."

"You do?"

"Yeah," she said, dragging me into the house and right into her room. I tried to ask her about it, but she said, "Later! Start unplugging everything in that corner and put it in the car." She went to her closet and gathered some clothes. Even though I knew the reason, I still had to ask her.

"What's that for?"

"We're staying in San Diego for at least two days and I wanna' have something to wear."

"Okay I feel you, just make sure you put something sexy in there."

"Ah shut up nigga."

But a moment later I saw her pull out a one piece and a two piece, then she looked over her shoulder to see if I was watching. "I like the black one, now let me see yo' car keys, I'm ready to take this out."

"Here, and when you come back you can take this out," she said, pulling out two bags. Although it took us about fifteen minutes to get everything out to the car, and before we left she wrote her mom a note saying she was going to a job interview in San Diego and would be back Monday. "I don't know how that's gonna' work."

"What?"

"Baby girl it's Thursday, where are you gonna' interview on the weekend?"

"It was all I could think of."

"Okay don't trip, just leave your cell phone so she can't call you."

"But..."

"But nothing, nothing is gonna' happen to her or your son and you know it."

She gave me a kiss and said, "You better be right. Come on let's get outta' here before she shows up."

"Look, I'll follow you back to Black Bird's house."

TONI

"Alright, just don't stop at any liquor stores, we don't need you getting shot," I said, laughing. I made it over to the East side of Compton just before dark, as I turned off Long Beach Blvd. onto Caldwell, I heard gun shots, I closed the sun roof and sped up. When I reached their house both Jetta's were still there. Voodoo came up right behind me. Candy came out to meet us. Just looking at her I already knew my mom called.

"What's up Candy?"

"Girl you know Stacy is looking for you."

"Yeah I kinda' figured she would be, and big head over here convinced me to leave my phone at the house."

"Why was she saying you went to a job interview in Diego?" Candy asked.

"Cause that was all I could think to say. I damn sure couldn't tell her what we're really going for."

"Damn, I didn't think of that, Promise is gonna' flip the hell out when we don't come home the whole weekend."

"I'm sure glad I don't have these types of problems."

"You're not helping Voodoo. We don't need to hear that shit right now," I said, getting frustrated.

"Sorry, but check this out. I know y'all think y'all grown, and believe me, when you get yo' hands on this money everything in your life will change, so that anxiety and shit you're feeling, let it go. You're about to do the most grown up shit in yo' life, and if you go to trippin' off yo' moms and what they think, believe me, you're gonna' fuck up and we don't need that. So from this point on, you need to turn them phones off and concentrate on this weekend."

"I guess he has a point," Candy said.

"Girl with you, everybody has a point," I said.

"Toni hit yo' trunk so we can get this stuff inside." She hit the alarm pad just so she could hear it talk again.

"Man don't you just love that shit?" She turned it off and opened the trunk. After the three of us got everything into the house, her first words were, "Black will you park my car in your garage?"

"Hell nah, you can put that bucket of bolts in the front yard with their cars."

"Fuck you nigga, my car is all that."

"Where in the hell yo' ass get a brand new Lexus from anyway?"

"I got friends in very high places."

"Okay smart ass, I'll leave that shit out on the street, and you know it ain't nothing but vultures around here," Black said.

"Voodoo!"

"Hey that's your car now, don't look at me," Voodoo said laughing.

"Black will you leave her alone," Sandy said.

"Cuzz you gave her that shit?" Black asked.

"Actually she brought it. Speaking of that, is there somewhere she can hook all this up? She has some work to do before it goes into the van."

"Nah, as a matter of fact I wish you would have left it in the car. We need to get it over to the wrecking yard on Alameda, that's where the vans are," Black paused, then said, "Voo, don't worry about the info. Toni can work on that while we're driving or once we get there, either way it goes, we'll make sure she has time to look. But like I said, I wanna' get this stuff into that van. Toni, you cool with that?"

"Yeah, however it works out, and like I told him, I pretty much know where the dope is now, but to be on the safe side I wanna' go over everything again."

"Okay ya'll. I need to get outta' here," Voodoo said.

"Where you going baby?"

"I need to get my gear and that Pixie Dust I found this morning."

"Alright," Black said, "it should take a couple of hours to get all this hooked up and tested. Somebody should be here when you get back."

"Alright, but before I forget, did anybody call out to Sacramento?"

"Yeah they should be here in the morning."

"Cool. Check this out, I've been on the road since early this morning, so make sure this couch is ready for me when I get back. Does anybody need anything while I'm out?"

"Nah my nigga, we're good," Black said.

"Alright, I'll be back in a couple of hours. Toni, come here," as I was embracing her, Yellow Bird walked into the living room and said,

"Cuzz if you don't get yo' hands off my woman." Hearing that, Candy elbowed Yellow Bird in the stomach and said, "Nigga' what?!"

"Oh sorry about that, I thought that was you Baby."

"Whatever nigga," Candy said, giving him the evil-eye, while everyone laughed. Voodoo gave me one more kiss and headed for the door. Over his shoulder he said, "Black thanks again my nigga."

"Toni, you know his ass is really feelin' you?" Candy said.

"Yeah, I got that impression."

"Man fuck all that mushy shit, we got work to do," Yellow Bird said.

"Keith, it ain't nothing mushy about us," Candy replied.

"Yeah yeah, whatever," Yellow Bird replied.

"Sandy let me see the keys to your car," Black said.

"You taking my car?"

"Yes I'm taking yo' car."

"Black, you better put some gas in her shit," Candy said, "'cause she thinks that shit runs on good looks."

"I do not," Sandy cried.

"Candy, you and Toni put your cars side-by-side on the grass," Black said.

"Also y'all can clean up around here while we're gone," Yellow Bird said.

"Oh hell nah," Sandy cried, "nigga this ain't the Jefferson's and my name ain't Florence. I'mma' find that bowl of weed, roll me something to smoke and kick the fuck back."

"Yeah, that's just the same lazy ass shit Florence would have done," Keith said.

"He has a point their girl," Candy said.

"Man fuck both of y'all," Sandy said.

"Black let's go, I'm sleepy as hell," said Keith.

They got everything into the Jetta and took off down the back streets of Compton.

BLACK BIRD

The back streets might not have been such a good idea, even in a new car. Greenleaf was bumpy as hell, and when I made a right on Alameda, it was just as bad. They've been remodeling this whole damn city since 1992 and ain't repaved one fuckin' street. When I hit Rosecrans I looked at the gas gauge and sure enough Candy was right, it was on E. The junk yard was only a few minutes away but I still pulled into AM/PM and filled up the tank. Ten minutes later I hit Alameda again, I wanted to see what kind of power the Jetta's had, so I jammed down on the gas.

"Man this shit got a lil' engine under the hood."

"Lil' is the key word my nigga," Yellow Bird replied.

I reached 115th in a couple of minutes, made a left then a right into the wrecking yard.

"Man," Yellow Bird said, "I don't know how Chico does it? I bet if we had asked, a fuckin' helicopter would be sitting there. We've been coming to Chico for the last few years, and any request we make, before the day is over he would have it here. Shit, from drugs to guns, to extra cars. Whatever, hell, we even got Black Jack and Friendly from his ass."

When I got out to greet him, I gave him $6000. "Black, you not even gonna' check out the vans?" Chico asked.

"Man we been fuckin' with you a long time and you always on yo' game. Did you get the battery rack set up?"

"Yeah, you can run stuff for days, and if they start to get low, start the engine and the auxiliary power will charge them back up." We walked over to the three vans. There were two black ones and one gray.

"Is your nephew here?"

"Yeah, he's around here somewhere. Echo," he called out. The boy came out of the darkness like a fuckin' ghost. He was so pale, he looks more white than Mexican.

"Chico, this the one that knows about computers?"

"Like the back of his hand."

Cuzz tried to ask where the computers were, but he stuttered so bad, I just pointed at the car. "That's why we call him Echo, case you was wondering."

"It's all good, as long as he can hook everything up and make sure it works."

"That he will do mi amigo, that he will do." After we got everything into the van Echo got right to work. I thought it would take much longer than it did, but within the hour everything was up and running. Echo had all the two-ways in their chargers, but the police scanner was making so much noise I had to turn it off. "Man, I don't know how the cops keep track of all that shit." Echo tried to tell me that was the best he could do, but I stopped him by handing him a $100 bill.

"Good lookin' out amigo! Chico, thanks man, as always you came through for us. Look, I'm taking this one now, and I'll be back for those in the morning."

"Okay, no problem my friend. If you need anything just call and we'll come to you," Chico said.

"I will," I replied.

Echo gathered up his tools and faded back into the shadows.

YELLOW BIRD

I followed Black back to the hood, when we got to the house the Lexus was gone, so Black parked the Jetta next to the other one. Candy came out to greet me like I just got in from a long day's work.

"Hi baby, did you miss me?" She asked.

"What if I said no?"

"I wouldn't advise that if I was you, cause I'm feelin' kinda' horny," Candy said."

"If that's the case, hell yeah I missed you. Hey, where did Toni disappear to?"

"She wanted to see Daishawn before we left."

"Anybody you wanna' see before we leave?" I asked her.

"Yeah, you naked."

"I heard that," Black said, grinning at us on his way into the house. We followed him inside.

"Damn homie, they actually cleaned up around here."

"I see, come here Florence and let me show you some love," Black said, heading straight towards Sandy.

When Black sat down next to Sandy and started kissing her neck, she picked up the control to the XBOX. "Oh you not fuckin' with me?" he asked.

"Black baby, I'll always fuck with you, but right now I feel like kickin' yo' butt in some football."

For the next couple of hours, the four of us battled back and forth. Toni and Voodoo showed up just about the same time. Within minutes of being inside the house, everyone wanted to know about the tranquilizer gun.

"Cuzz, you know you can't load that with too much or you might kill him," Black stated.

"Man it ain't like this shit came with instructions," Voodoo said.

"Yeah, but like I said, we want him sleep not dead," Black said.

"Where in the hell did you get that from anyway?" I asked.

"From an Animal Control office in Riverside. And the next person that ask me a question about this shit, I'mma' test it out on yo' ass."

"Check this out y'all, it's after eleven and we got a long day coming up. Candy, you coming with me?" I said.

"Do I have a choice?"

"Baby girl you always got choices fuckin' with me. Black, why don't you move the Escalade on the street and put that van in the drive way?"

"Why don't you do it?" Black shouted.

"Man I got other thangs to move and remove, like her clothes and her butt."

"Boy will you stop!" Candy said.

"I'll see y'all in the morning, and before I forget, Toni, since you skipped out on helping them clean up around here, yo' ass is cookin' breakfast," I said.

"Fuck you nigga, I'm glad yo' ass is barkin' out orders," Toni said.

Chapter 20

VOODOO

After a while Black and Sandy went off to bed. So the Polynesian and Black beauty laid on the couch with me, and even though I had been up and running since early this morning, I still wanted to make love to her. I know she could feel how hard my shit was, but she had other plans, like talking. While I played in her curly hair, I said, "You know you never gave me an answer right?"

"What answer was that?"

"Are we gonna' get this money together or what?"

"Okay let's say I agree to do this, where do you suppose we find the money?"

"I don't know, can't we just find another DEA warehouse?"

"That's not a problem, I already know where they are. But after we get into this one, you can best believe they're gonna' make some serious changes at the other ones."

"Okay, what about the FBI?" I asked, "I'm sure they have facilities like that."

"Yeah, they probably do. But why can't we just use this money to start a business?" Toni said.

"No, if we drop all our money into something big and it doesn't work out, you and I will be havin' this conversation again."

"Okay I understand, so I'll tell you what, once we're done with this shit here, and things cool off, I'll look at some other buildings and see what I can find."

"I guess that's all I can ask." She reached up and gave me a soft kiss, got more comfortable and within no time she was sleep. I wrapped my arms around her and laid there thinking until I too fell asleep. The morning came way too quick. Somebody's cell phone was on the coffee table buzzing like crazy, I'll be damned if anybody heard it but me. I looked at my watch, it was 6:30 a.m. Damn, I rolled out from under Toni and snatched up the phone. Come to find out it was the crew from up North. "What's up, who's this, # One?"

"Yeah, we're over in Lynwood at the Day's Inn. I just wanted to let y'all know we're here," #One said.

"Alright cool, everybody here is still sleep, so kick back, get something to eat, and by 8:00 a.m. we should be ready to get on the road."

"Alright, we'll be waiting on you, later!" I went into the kitchen and put on some coffee. While that was brewing, I took my overnight bag and headed for the shower. Ten minutes later I was dressed and back in the kitchen trying to scrounge up something to cook for everybody. While I was looking in the fridge, Toni walked up and put her arms around me from behind.

"Why didn't you let me take a shower with you?" she said.

"Cause, for one, we would have been in there for hours. Second, we have to get on the road real soon. Now go wake them other fools up and tell them to get ready."

"Damn, you barkin' orders and I can't even get a good morning kiss."

"Halitosis baby, Halitosis," I said, laughing.

"Ha ha, very funny."

By 7:15, I had eggs, potatoes and bacon on the table. This time when she came in, lookin' freshly clean, I gave her a kiss that said, I'm really tryin' to love you.

"See now, you keep taking my breath away like that and you might have a problem on yo' hands," she said.

All I could do was smile at her. Here I am with a beautiful woman, cooking for her, feeling like I'm in love, then I thought about the person I was yesterday. The real me, the killer, the drug dealer. Maybe she can somehow change some of that. The killin' I don't know, I think I enjoy that too much I thought smiling to myself. I guess the smell of food finally got everyone else into the kitchen. No good morning, no nothing, they just took some plates and had at it. Now if I had put some rat poison in this shit they'd think I was wrong.

"Hey Black, I answered your phone earlier, them' boyz' from Sac are over in Lynwood at the Day's Inn."

"How long they been here?" Black asked me.

"Not sure, but I told them we should be ready to push by 8:00 a.m."

"Alright cool, all that's left is to go get the other vans. Voodoo you mind leaving your truck with Chico?"

"Nah, as long as my shit don't end up in their car crusher."

"Okay then, when we leave here, the four of us will take your truck and you and Toni can take the van. From there we'll take the other two vans and shoot over to Lynwood."

BLACK BIRD

"Toni, I know you didn't get to test your computer system last night, but it's all good, everything is ready for you and like I said, you can try to find that other info while we're on the road if you want, it's up to you."

"Shit," Sandy said, "y'all wanna' find some more shit in there, we might have to do the same."

"No!" Candy said, "we get what we know is there and no more. You want some more money, get a damn job."

"I got a job, and I plan to retire this weekend,"
Sandy said.

"I know that's right," Toni said, giving her a high five.

"We need to stick to the plan Sandy and you know it," Candy said.

"Sis will you relax, nothing has changed," said Sandy.

A short time later we were done eating. After cleaning everything up, the six of us grabbed our stuff and headed outside to our vehicles. While I locked up the house Yellow Bird let the dogs out of their kennels. He also put out enough dog food and water to last a long weekend. He went into the extra dog house and came out with our bag of weapons. If the police ever show up they would have to go through Black Jack and Friendly to find them. Candy and Toni must have heard them coming 'cause they hurried up and jumped in the vehicles. When we got to the junk yard, the vans were gassed up and waiting for us. I gave Chico a C-note and told him to keep the Ford F-150 safe.

Next we made the ten-minute drive to the Day's Inn and found our Hit Squad. The parking lot had two black Navigators sitting side by side. Seeing nothing else that looked like it would belong to them, I stopped and blew my horn. # One stuck his head out the door, waved and went back inside. Next he came back out followed by # Two. # One knocked on the next door as he passed on his way to check out, and the rest of the crew put their gear in their trucks.

One came back moments later and greeted us. "What's up everybody?" I didn't like the fact that it was 8:10 in the morning and I had twelve niggaz' standing out in the parking lot, but it needed to be done. I opened the door to the computer van and passed out five of the two-ways.

"# One, we're headed to San Diego, and basically you guys are extra security, your main focus will be to keep them safe. I'm not anticipating any problems, but you never know. Toni, do you have the address to the place?" I asked.

"No, but since I have to go back in, I'll have it by the time we get out there," Toni said.

"Black, are we working for our usual fifteen G's?" # One asked.

"Yeah, you'll get that, plus each of you will get a key of heroin, how does that sound?" They all looked at each other and nodded their heads.

"There's just one condition, none of you are to move that shit in G-Parkway."

"I'll make sure of it," # One said.

"Alright look, when we get there we'll find our target, the three of us will figure out what we need to get inside the building with. The six of you will divide up into twos and find out where and how you wanna' cover the building. There will be only one guard on duty tonight, it will be Voodoo's job to take care of him, but that might fall on one of you. I know I haven't told you what we're up to, but know this, if the police show up, they're comin' deep, so be ready."

YELLOW BIRD & CANDY

Everybody paired off in twos and got ready to leave. Black made a radio check and all the vehicles responded that they were ready to go. But before Black could move out, Voodoo called, saying he forgot something. He jumped out and ran to my window with the Pass Port, then he gave one to Black.

"How does this thing work?" Candy asked.

"You plug it in the lighter, set it on the dashboard and if the police get close it will beep," Voodoo said.

Black hit the radio once more. "Does anybody need gas?"

Everyone said they were good and we headed to the freeway.

"Keith tell me something."

"I love you!"

"That's not what I meant. Tell me about those guys back there."

"What's to tell, we move some good size shipments of dope and they make sure no one tries to jack us."

"They look pretty young for that."

"They are, but that was for a reason. They needed money and money will make a person move in ways they never thought they could. We got them guns, taught them how to use them, and told them if they learn what we know, they will stay outta' jail. So far everybody has been winning."

"Are you gonna' stop selling dope after this?"

"Maybe. Why, what are you gonna' do?"

"I don't know."

"You don't know. Okay why don't you buy us a nice home to live in?"

"You would wanna' live with me?"

"Sure I would."

"I don't know Keith, that might be a waste of money."

"Why would you say something like that?"

"Come on baby, you know no one can do what you're doing for ever. You said you loved me and that I could never let another man touch me. Well I'm tellin' yo ass now, I'm not reverting back into no virgin if you go to jail."

"You mean you wouldn't be there for me?"

"I didn't say that. Them' white folks ain't just giving out football numbers, they're giving you the lines on the field too." I had to laugh.

"Baby with the kind of money we stand to make this weekend there's all kind of things you can do."

"Even get married?"

"Will you stop playin'? I'm eighteen, what would I look like being married at my age?"

"Candy we would do real good together, and I love you more than anything." His words had me staring out the window thinking of what it would be like to be married to him. But I knew deep down, if he keeps selling dope I was gonna' get pulled into it.

"Keith, do you love me?"

"Ain't that what I just said?"

"Okay, you have to stop selling dope. Wasn't there a certain point in this game you was tryin' to reach?"

"I guess, I really wasn't trippin', we just been making money."

"Okay, let me ask you this. How much money do you have saved up?"

"I don't know, about eleven."

"You mean to tell me you have eleven million dollars and yo' ass can't find something else to do? Oh now I get it, yo' ass just like sellin' dope and fuckin' all the bitches that comes with it."

"You don't understand. First of all, I don't throw my dick around like it ain't shit. Second. Eleven million dollars ain't shit, and third, there are people depending on us and some of them we just can't walk away from. We might be able to buy our way out, but walking away is not an option."

"So why don't you buy your way out?"

"I guess you didn't hear the homie when he said we're trying to get out from under somebody?"

"Yeah I heard him, but what I didn't hear either of you say was, after this shipment is done, you're done."

Damn, she was really on one. She has never told me she loves me, but the way she's talkin' what else could it be? I wish she was just another hood rat and I would bang on her ass, but that's not the case, so I said, "Check this out, you want me to stop doing what I'm doing right?"

"Yeah."

"Okay no problem, but you got a job to do."

"What's that?"

"Every time I move a load of dope I make anywhere from sixty to eighty thousand."

"So!"

"So yo' pretty ass need to come up with a way for me to do that twice a month."

"How in the hell am I supposed to do that? I never even made a thousand dollars a month."

"I don't know, but you better come up with something." See now that got her ass to thinking. I had no intention of making her come up with that kind of money, but a lil' motivation never hurt anybody.

After about an hour and a half of traveling south on the fifteen freeway, Voodoo came over the radio. "Black we got a location, you need to get off on Navigation Blvd."

"How far is that from where we are now?" Black asked.

"Cuzz, how am I supposed to know? I got us these old ass vans and none of them have a GPS system."

"Black this is # One."

"Yeah, what's up?"

"We're about thirty miles out, it's an hour away if you keep this pace."

"Good looking out. # One, why don't you take point and I'll follow you."

"I got you boss." The radio went silent and I looked over at her.

"Candy, what's up? You over there mighty quiet. Yo' ass tryin' to come up with a way to make this money ain't you?"

"I already know how to do that."

"Yeah, and how is that?"

"You can have my portion of the money we get outta' this warehouse."

"See I knew sooner or later you would tell me you loved me."

"Nigga I didn't say that."

"Why else would you give me four million dollars? Cause you love me as much as I love you."

"I just don't want anything to happen to you."

"Yeah yeah, I love you too."

"I didn't say that."

"Whatever, you keep yo' money, 'cause in a few months I'mma' make sure both of us is straight. Now come over here and play with this," I said, grabbing her hand and placing it on my dick.

Chapter 21

BLACK & SANDY

My man Chico had new engines put into the Astros, but the Navigator was eating up the highway like it was nothing. I actually had to get on the radio and tell #One to slow down. "Sandy, you know we're almost there, so for the last time, you sure you wanna' go through with this shit?"

"I know yo' ass ain't over there getting cold feet?"

"Cold feet, I don't think so, hell I wish Toni could find us four or five more of these warehouses."

"What if she could, would you really go in them?"

"Why not? The only thing is, I don't want dope, only cash. If we were to keep doing this I'm not about to be double hustling."

"So what's up? You sayin' you're getting out the dope game?"

"If I could find something to take up the slack, then yeah I'll get out."

"Will I have a part in whatever you do next?"

"What kind of roll you looking to play?"

"Come on Black, I know you got bitches all over California, I just wanna' be the one that's on top, the one you come home to each night, and I do mean you coming home each night.

"First of all, I don't chase pussy you should know that, so if you wanna' be at the top, you're half way there."

"Okay what will it take to reach the top?"

"Money, like I told you before, I love what you came up with. Now the question becomes, what are you gonna' do with this money? Cause if you go to spending it on bullshit, you're gonna' be looking to do this shit again."

"Maybe I'll buy a few keys from you and double up my money."

"Shit baby girl, I'm tryin' to get out the dope game and you tryin' to get in."

"What else is there? I'm fuckin' eighteen with no job."

"Look, Toni will listen to you, after we make this money you'll need to convince her to find us one or two more places to hit like this one. Then the six of us can open a big ass night club or something."

"You think we can do that?"

"Why not? If each of us can put in two million we should be able to do something real major."

"What kind of club you wanna' open?"

"A strip club of course. I'm talking about the biggest strip club in all of L.A., and I might just put it right in the middle of Compton. Besides, that's the hottest thang movin' right now. And since marijuana is damn near legal in Cali now, we could push out two or three pounds in twenty sacks a night, we'd make a killin'.."

"I guess you got it all figured out?"

"What's to figure out? The three of y'all will be running the place, and if we do this right, by the time you're twenty five you should never have to worry about money again in life. I see you over there thinking, it sounds good don't it?"

"Yeah it does."

"So are you gonna' talk to Toni about finding another place to hit?"

"Why can't we just use this money?"

"Cause baby girl, me and Yellow Bird have too much going on, and if you use all your money now, you will be broke again if the club fails."

"What if we can't find another place with this kind of money?"

"Shit, there has to be something out there, if need be, we'll come back to this one, I don't think anyone would expect that."

"Black you gotta be crazy if you think we can go back in this place again," she started as I looked at her, then she went on, "Black can I ask you a question?"

"Yeah, what is it?"

"Do you love me?" I was shocked for a sec and I looked over at her again.

"You sure you wanna' know the truth?"

"I need to know."

"Okay, yeah I love you."

"Good 'cause I'm going back on my word. I just hope like hell I'm doing the right thing."

"Doing the right thing, I know you not about to call this shit off?"

"No baby, but you know what? We need to be able to drive these vans directly into that warehouse. I know I said no one could change up our plans again, but fuck that. You wanna' find other places to hit, but why put ourselves at risk again when there's over a billion dollars' worth of shit right where we're goin'? So I say we load these bitches up with everything we can get our hands on right here and right now."

"Are you serious?"

"Hell yeah I'm serious. You guys still get the van full of heroin, plus the extra fifty bricks and we still get our fourteen million."

"Everything else we get into these vans the six of us will divide up evenly."

"I know two things, yo' ass is turning out to be a true gangsta, and I knew loving you was a good idea."

All I could do was smile and hope he was telling the truth. So I just looked out the window for a while and hoped all this shit would work out. A lot of the shit Black was saying made sense, we would be trying to do this shit over and over if we blew through this money. I never even thought of starting some type of business, and now that I think about it, I was about to hit them streets and hit 'em hard spending money. He also made another good point. Four million really ain't shit. So why not load these bitches up now and get it over with?

If we do happen to go to jail, it's not gonna' matter how much we stole, but who we had the audacity to steal it from. So I'm coming outta' there with as much as I can get my hands on. This was my plan and I'm callin' the shots, if the others don't like it, too bad. The lead car called Black over the radio. "We're coming up on Navigation Blvd."

"Alright," Black said, "when you get off the freeway head West and we should be able to find some place to stay for the weekend."

"I got you boss."

"Baby are you going to check out the warehouse today?"

"Yeah, the sooner the better. It's a quarter after one and we need to buy some tools to get in there with."

"Okay, when you come back I'll take the girls to do that. Besides, we left without any clothes and since you love me so much, you feel like sharing?"

"What, you need some money?"

"Yeah."

"Okay, you share with me, I'll share with you."

"Damn nigga, didn't I share enough with you last night?"

"It ain't my fault you keep making a nigga come back for more."

"Stop looking at me like that. You need to pay attention to the road before you hit somebody. Black will you stop playin', look he's about to get off the freeway."

"I don't know why you think I'm not paying attention? You could have been riding my dick all the way here and I would have been alright."

"Sometimes I swear you're a Freakaholic."

"And you see a problem with that because?"

"Man how we went from talkin' about money to fuckin' is beyond me. Black will you leave my pussy alone!"

I followed the Navigator off the freeway and everyone else followed me. Right away I liked what I saw. This was not a white area so the twelve of us would not stand out. The closer we got to Pacific Coast Highway, the more motels there was. When I spotted a Taco Bell I got on the radio and told # One to pull in there. I got all the drivers together and ran down to them how I wanted to do this. "Check this out. # One I want you guys to check in over there," I said, pointing to the South side of the street. "Since there are six of you, take three rooms if you need to, How are you on cash?"

"Don't trip, we're cool."

"Alright, we'll meet up in a bit."

"Once we all get checked in we're gonna' go have a look at this warehouse. Right now it's like 1:30 p.m. and if at all possible I wanna' get this job done tonight. Look, before we go, I know the homie told you a lil' bit earlier, and like I said, I don't expect any trouble, but we're on our way to fuck over the Feds, so I'm telling you now, if you wanna' opt out, now's the time to do it."

"We're good," #One said, "you called us for a reason. Besides, you three niggaz' pay good." We all laughed.

"Yellow Bird, get ready my nigga there's been another change," I said.

"Cuzz, you know Sandy ain't going for that shit."

"Don't look at me, it was her idea this time. Before we go, get your radios so I can charged them."

After I took care of that I told them to be ready to move in thirty minutes. We all checked into our rooms, then I called everyone to my room to let them know about Sandy's new plans.

"Why the change all of a sudden?" Candy asked.

"Because fat head, the six of us are going into business together," Sandy said.

"Let me guess", Toni said, "y'all wanna' open a strip club?"

"Yeah that's right, strippers, strippers and more strippers. Shit, we're gonna' have the baddest bitches and best weed Cali's ever known. Shit, I might have nothing but Brazilian bitches in our club," Sandy said.

"Oh you's a pimp now?" Toni asked. "And what's this about some weed?"

"Look, y'all can talk about that later," I said, getting back on track, "we got work to do. We wanna' load these vans up, get as much shit into them as we can and not have to worry about doing this shit again. So the only question left is, are y'all in or out?" I asked.

"You know this was the same shit me and Voodoo was talking about. I guess that's why they say great minds think alike," Toni said, as she shook her head.

"Keith, what do you two think?"

"Look, whatever we're going to do, can we just get it over with?"

"Alright y'all, everything is a go," Sandy said.

"Sandy, you can take them and go get y'all something to wear, have lunch or whatever. I'll get the tools myself and we'll meet back here in a couple of hours. Here's three hundred dollars, if you can't get what you need with that, you better steal it. Toni I need the address to the warehouse." After making sure they were good I took the fella'z and left the room, and went to make sure the computer van was locked up tight.

We then went across the street and I got the hit squad outside. "Look I want one of you guys to stay behind and keep an eye on that van. You can see it from here so there's no need to go over there, just keep checking on it. The girls are going to take the other one for a while." # Six said he would stay. "Alright, we should only be gone an hour or two. Go get yo'self a pistol, if anybody fucks with it don't shoot 'em, just scare them off, we don't need the attention."

"The rest of you load up, the warehouse should be just east of here. Two of y'all come ride with us and the three of you can follow. # One, since we don't have the radios, if you need me just use your cell phone. While we check out this building you figure out where you wanna' set up. Everybody good?" They all nodded. "Cool, let's move."

The warehouse turned out to be three miles away. Talk about hiding in plain sight. There was a cluster of buildings on each of the four corners. I found the one we were looking for, and I liked what I saw. I had three bay doors and one of them had a ramp, which meant we could drive into the building. I drove down the alley that separated the four buildings. One of the bay doors were open and I actually saw the van I think contained the fifty bricks of heroin. "Did y'all see that van sitting in there?"

"Yeah," Yellow Bird said, "you think that's the one we're after?"

"It could be." I drove to the end of the alley and turned around. I motioned for # One to stop. "Look, this is where we wanna' be, go back out and find somewhere for y'all to set up. Where that door is open, that's our target, call me when you're done."

"I got you, later." I waited a moment then drove back down the alley way. I was looking for mainly two types of cars, a Crown Victoria or a big body Caprice. Those are the car models the Feds love to use. Towards the office portion of the building there was only two vehicles that said police. One was a Crown Vic with an antenna on its trunk and the other was a blue and white truck that said security on its doors. A fork lift drove out the building carrying a trash bin, he dumped its load in a larger bin and went back inside. "Black, I know how we're going to get in there," Voodoo said, "You see that closed door?"

"Yeah, what's up?" Black said.

"It's aluminum, that means all we have to do is cut a hole big enough for one of us to go through. There will be a slide lock down in the corner, and we can take some Bolt cutters if there's a lock on the pull chain. We can pull the door open, let a van in and close the door behind it."

"Okay I like that, we can do that until all the vans are full. Yellow, we got a good plan, did we miss anything?"

"Not that I can see."

"So basically, all we need is something to cut our way in and some bolt cutters?"

"Yeah," Voodoo said, "we can get some shears. They're sharp and good for cutting aluminum."

"Shit I thought we would need to spend a lot of money on this. Voo, you think you can get that door open?"

"Yeah, it should only take a couple of minutes."

"Ricky, you see anything we might have missed."

"You talking to me?"

"You the only Ricky in this van ain't you?"

"Yeah, y'all just never use our names, so I forgot. But nah, everything looks good. I did see some cameras on that building over there. But don't trip, I can get rid of them with my Bush Master."

"I like that."

I backed the van to the end of the alley once more, as if I were looking for a certain address. I just wanted to make sure I wasn't missing anything. This time when I reached the street I turned out and kept going. I called # One. "What's up boss?" he said.

"Hey we're done, and now were headed back to the motel," I said.

"Alright, we'll be there soon." On the way back I found a Subway and sent Ricky in to get everyone something to eat. "Yellow Bird, it's time to offer up your opinion."

"It looks good, as long as that alarm doesn't go off when cuzz opens that door. We should be good to go through," Yellow Bird said.

Five minutes later Ricky came out of Subway's and I got everybody back to the motel. I told them to get some rest, at midnight we're heading back out. "I'll be back. I'm going to find a hardware store. I see the girls are still gone, but I should be back before them. So y'all lay low until I get back."

Chapter 22

CANDY

We were on our way to the Fashion Valley Mall and I was trying to get a grip on what we were doing. As it turned out everybody has been discussing ways to make more money. I thought four million would last me for years, but Keith told me that wouldn't be the case, and from the looks of things, Black and Voodoo told these two the same thing.

"Sandy, do we really need to do this?"

"What? Yes we do and we are. We're here and it's too late to turn back now. Toni will you talk to her?"

"Look girl, I know 'It's Hard Being The Same' for ya'll, but you two came at me with this shit and we agreed to follow Sandy's lead. And like she said, it's too late to back out now," Toni said.

"Candy, Black told me if we open this club and do things right, by the time we're twenty-five we would never have to worry about money again."

"Well the way you and everybody else keep changing shit, I'm just worried about making it through this weekend," I said.

"Stop trippin' Candy, nothing is gonna' happen to any of us. Toni, will you tell her everything will be good?" Sandy said.

"I just did that shit a minute ago. Candy I agree with her, we're gonna' be rich as fuck by tomorrow."

As Sandy pulled into the mall I still wasn't convinced. I kept feeling something was going to go horribly wrong.

"Look y'all I don't feel like going in there, just get me a pair of black jeans and a sweat shirt," I said.

"Man will you come on, we're not gonna' be in there that long," Toni said.

"Yeah, and to make sure, I'm stayin' here. Y'all not going to no club either, so get what we need and get outta' there." Sandy finally found somewhere to park the van, then she said, "You know what sis, sometimes I think you not right in the head."

"That might be so, but right now you think yo' ass in and outta' there in twenty minutes."

They just shook their heads and got out. To my surprise they actually came out in under an hour, which was a good thang 'cause it was hot as hell sitting in the van. "Girl you should have come in, it was some cute guys all over the place."

"Toni I got a cute guy and I'm tryin' to get back to him, so let's go."

"What's with the attitude?" She asked.

"I don't have an attitude, I'm scared as hell and y'all acting like what we're about to do ain't shit."

"Man," Sandy said, "you really need to stop it, for the last time we're gonna' be alright."

"How do you know?"

"I just do!"

"Don't look at me, she's yo' sister. She'll be alright, let's just get her back to the motel, she can take a nap and maybe calm down," said Toni.

"It's already after 5:00 p.m., and Black said we'll be leaving at midnight. Yeah a nap will be good for her. Sis we'll be alright, trust me," Sandy said.

It took another half hour to get back to the motel, Sandy just had to stop and get something to eat. The smell of Burger King made me have to go lay down on the floor of the van, lucky for me there was carpet. I just don't know how people can do this shit every night. "Sandy," I yelled, "if I go to jail tonight I'mma' kick yo' ass."

"Damn it Candy, will you stop it no one is going to jail. We got six trained killers watching over us, and if anybody so much as walk down that street I feel sorry for them," said Sandy.

"I know you're not sayin' somebody is gonna' get killed?"

"I don't think you should have told her that," Toni said.

"Look Candy, we're going to drive this van in there, fill it up with as much money as we can, then you and I are going to drive back to Compton like we just came from a weekend filled with lots of sex and fun."

"Well so far I haven't had either. Yo' ass dragged us into this so..."

"So nothing...You know what? Why don't you lay yo' ass back down and be quiet," Sandy said.

"Now I know you better hurry up and get her back to Keith before she has a nervous breakdown or something," Toni said.

"Man it ain't nothing wrong with her ass. I bet she don't have no nervous breakdown spending this fuckin' money."

"Stop!" I said, when she threw a handful of French fries at me. I ate one and moments later I realized I was starving. I crawled up to the front and stole Sandy's hamburger.

"Man yo ass lucky I'm driving. I don't know why you didn't order you something."

"I know huh. Toni let me have some of your fries."

"Hell nah, don't you owe me $20 from the last time we went out to eat?"

"I told you I got something for Daishawn."

"Man you got that shit like two days later."

"Ah, but I got it and he loved it," I said, snatching some fries from her lap.

"Don't eat all my burger Candy."

"I'm not, here." I gave it back and went to lay back down. "Thanks y'all I needed that."

Laying there I thought to myself, I'mma' fuck the shit outta' Keith when we get back, I'm not going to jail without getting me some of that dick. A short while later we pulled into the motel parking lot and Keith was standing outside our room naked and holding his dick, at least that's how I saw him. I opened the side door before Sandy came to a stop, I jumped out and ran up the stairs and took him by the hand.

"Come here I got you something at the mall."

"What's that?" He asked when I closed and locked the door.

"This," I said, taking off my pants and shirt. He followed suit and started unbuttoning his pants. I went down and pulled off his boots. He stepped out of his pants and before I could get back up his dick made its way into my mouth. As I sucked it I could taste the salt on him. I stopped for a moment, pumped on him a few times and just admired how perfect his dick was. The way he was throbbing in my hand I could tell he wanted back in my mouth, so I gave him what he wanted. He was jabbing at the back of my throat like a punching bag. Before he could cum I got up and took off the rest of my clothes. Next I walked him over to a small table and pulled out the chair and pushed him down. "You ready for this?"

"You know it."

I wanted him nice and hard so I sucked his dick a lil' more, when I came up this time his dick was already leaking pre cum. I turned around, pulled myself open and sat down on a dick that was so hard at first I couldn't go all the way down. When he forced himself all the way in I had no choice but to scream out. You would think as much as I wanted him I would have been nice and wet, but I wasn't. However, there was no way I was going to pass this up. At first he just held me there, and I reached back and gave him a hot kiss. "Baby I want you to fuck the shit outta' me." When he nodded his head I bent over, pulled my ass and pussy open as much as I could and gave him all the pussy he could handle. His hard ass dick was rubbing against my clit so much I came in a matter of minutes.

He was hitting me so good now you could hear how wet my pussy was. Moments later I got up and turned around and you could see all the cum I left on his dick. I got back on and started riding him like I was losing my fuckin' mind. I took both my titties, squeezed them together and made him suck them. Instead of selling dope, this nigga should have been a professional tittie sucker. I was riding him so hard every time I came down on him he hit the bottom of my pussy. Damn, I didn't know how he hadn't came yet. At one point he pushed into me so hard I bit down on his neck.

"What has gotten into you?"

"I just needed you to love me, now less talkin' and more fuckin'." He complied by picking me up and slamming my back to the floor. He pushed my legs up until they were almost behind my head and dug out my pussy like he was digging for gold. He had me moaning and hollering so loud somebody started knocking on the wall. He raised up and I could clearly see his dick going in and out of me. The shit was so sexy I got turned on all over again.

He started moving real slow, each time he came out I saw all the veins in his dick. "Yeah you love that shit don't you?"

"Of course I love it, but it feels like I'm getting a cramp." He was about to let my legs down but I said don't, and even though he had me bent in half I started fucking him to make him fuck me harder just so he could cum for me. "Come on baby fuck me." He started hitting it harder and harder. "That's right baby, who's pussy is this?"

"Mine."

"Then fuck it, that's it, fuck me harder." After a few more times of hearing that, and another knock on the wall from me screaming he pulled his dick out, started jacking off over me and he came so much some of it actually reached my neck. I could feel how hot it was.

"Did you like that?" He asked out of breath.

"Yeah, now come here and let me lick the rest of that." He let my legs down and came to put his dick back in my mouth. It never fails, you talk to any nigga while he's fuckin' you and he will cum in no time. To my surprise I think he's had enough. He was no longer hard and his dick was just like a big ass piece of meat in my mouth. I pulled him out for the last time, gave it a kiss and said, "Thanks big boy." I got up and went to the small bathroom to clean myself up. On my way I ran my finger through some of the cum covering my chest and stuck it in my mouth. I looked back at him with a smile. "Love you Keith," I said, closing the door.

YELLOW BIRD

I didn't want to think about what just happened so I got up from the floor and gathered up my clothes. Although it was over quick, she acted as if that would be the last time we would ever make love. I heard the shower running so I went in and washed up in the sink. I wanted to join her but something told me that wouldn't be a good idea. By the time she came out I was dressed again, and with a towel wrapped around her she walked up and put her arms around me. "I'm sorry Keith, it wasn't supposed to be like that."

"What's wrong?"

"We are supposed to enjoy making love to each other."

"Yeah I know, but you still need to tell me what's wrong."

"Hell the same thing that's been wrong since we started this shit, I'm scared to death. And just so you know, there was no way I was going to jail without having some more of this," she said, rubbing the front of my pants.

"I thought we talked about this? None of us are going to jail. Look, we've planned for everything we could, we got Toni on the computers, we got the six man security team and you're gonna' be armed."

"No, no, and hell no! I'm not carrying no gun," Candy said.

"Okay baby, if that's how you want it. But you have to stop worrying, the more you worry the more likely you are to make a mistake. Are you good? Look at me. Are you good?"

"Yes I'm good. I can do this," said Candy

"What?"

"I can do this!"

"Alright then, go get dressed before we end up doing some more fuckin'."

She smiled, gave me a kiss and went back into the bathroom with her clothes. Fuck that, if we pull this shit off I'm asking her to marry me. I walked out to the balcony to get some fresh air and saw Toni down in the van listening to the police scanner. When Candy came out we went down to check on her.

"What's up, you having any luck with that thing?"

"Not really, there is so much going on it's hard to keep track of what's what," Toni said.

"Well all I can say is, for tonight you need to listen for the words B&E and the address of the warehouse. If you hear that we need to get outta' there and fast," I said.

"Baby what's B&E?" Candy asked.

"Breaking and Entering. They may use a code but they can't get around using the address, so make sure you listen for that."

"Keith, it's after 7:00, can't we leave before midnight?" Candy asked.

"It's still too early and we still need to check things out with Black and Sandy. Toni you ready for this?"

"Hell yeah I'm ready. Listen, did you hear that?" Toni questioned, pausing, and holding one finger in the air.

"What?" I asked, now listening intently too.

"Four million dollars just called my name." We all laughed.

"So Yellow, did you work the kinks outta' her?" Toni asked.

"Yeah, she's ready to go."

"Good 'cause she had us worried as hell earlier."

"I'm alright. I just wish we could get this shit over with. Is it midnight yet?" Candy said.

"Sorry baby girl, we got a few more hours to go. Toni did you hear that? The scanner announced there was a B&E."

"Baby that's not boosting my confidence."

"Come on Candy, that's probably some junky doing some dumb shit." Toni hurried up and changed the subject.

"Hey Yellow, you know either you or Black needs to make the first move into this building," Toni said.

"Why is that? We want to make sure the twins get in and out alright."

"I know, but I assume you also want them to go right to the freeway too. Where are they gonna' go? They can't go to your house, what if you don't make it? Them monsters will eat they ass alive if they try to get in the yard. Then there's the problem of where are they gonna' park that van full of drugs."

"Yeah baby, them' niggaz' in yo' hood would have a field day if somebody happens to look inside the van," Candy said.

"Hold up, what I do know is this, y'all need to slow down with all these questions. Come on, lock up the van it's time for another meeting." A few minutes later I had everyone together and I told them of our small problem, which quickly turned into two problems.

"Shit," Black said, "we planned to move one van full of drugs and cash. Now were gonna' have three vans full of shit and nowhere to put it. See what happens when too many scenarios come into play?"

"Black this is what we'll do. You go in first, pack up that van in there. Voodoo will be there to help you, then you head home. You can take everybody's car keys and move any cars in yo' way," I said.

"Then you can just start unloading the van into the house. We'll send the twins in next. Again Voodoo will be there to help them out, and then they'll be on their way to the house. Once they're out, I'm on my way in. When the two of us are done, Toni can come pick up Voodoo and follow me home. This is the only way I can see this shit working in our favor," I said.

"One more thing," Toni said, "can any of y'all hot wire a car?"

"What made you ask that?" Black said.

"Cause, what if you can't find the keys?"

"Well since Black is gonna' be driving the van that's inside the building already, we need to figure out how he's gonna' get that started. Other than that, I can't see anything we might have forgotten. Hell if all goes well, we might have Toni drive her van in there and load it up."

"Shit, I'm down Yellow. If we have time, let's do it," Toni said.

"We'll see. Voodoo, have you loaded that dart gun yet?"

"Nah not yet."

"Do you even know how much to use?"

"No, but we can always test it out on you."

"Nigga is you crazy? Ain't no way I'd let you shoot me with that shit."

"Don't trip, about three CC's should do the job."

"Fool," Toni said, "do you even know what CC stands for?"

"For your information, every blue moon I showed up at school. It stands for Cubic Centimeter. I figure any more than that he might not wake up."

"We don't need that, so make sure you don't give him too much," I told him.

"Yeah, I feel you," Voodoo replied, half-heartedly.

VOODOO

But lil', did they know I had no intentions of letting the man wake up ever again. Killing is euphoric to me. I don't know whether I like killin' more or making money. And when I kill to make money, that's better than any drug high. I told them I would give the guard three CC's but I planned on giving his ass half the bottle. If his ass wakes up from that, I'mma' sue the people that makes the shit.

YELLOW BIRD

"Cuzz, what the hell are you laughing at?"

"Nothing, I was just thinking to myself." Man I swear, whenever there's a mention of someone getting killed, this nigga gets this far off look in his eyes.

"Voodoo, you said you got that from an Animal Control Center in Riverside, right?"

"Yeah why?"

"Nothing, I was just wondering." I need to check that shit out, I thought, if this nigga is killing people and I really think he is, I'mma' dust his ass off myself before he brings us all down.

Chapter 23

BLACK BIRD

"So is ya'll ready for this?" They all said yeah. "Sandy, did you guys get something to wear?"

"Yeah. I got us black jeans and hoodies."

"Alright cool. It's time for y'all to get changed. When you come back I got something for you."

"Ooh ooh, what is it?" Sandy said, getting excited.

"Ooh ooh nothing, now take them next door and change clothes," I told her.

"Alright dang, come on y'all."

When they left the room I went to the smallest closet and got our bag of weapons. "Is that what I think it is?" Voodoo asked.

"For sure."

"Goody, Voodoo like guns. Let's see what you workin' with."

"Since there are six of us, I got three Techs and the three 9mm's. Each of us will have two clips, we'll take these and the girls can have the hand guns."

"Sorry homie, Candy won't carry a gun," Yellow said.

"Of course she will," I stated.

"We already talked and she doesn't want to carry a gun."

"Well what she doesn't want to do and what she's gonna' do are two different thangs."

"Cuzz, I'm tellin' you she won't do it," Yellow said, confidently.

"Okay, I said, reaching into my pocket. I got this right here that says she will."

"Shit, you ain't said nothin', how much is that?"

"I don't know, the question is, can I get a bet?"

"Hell yeah, you got that," Yellow said.

"Voodoo you want some of this?" I asked.

"Alright, here's two G's, I got my money on Yellow Bird," Voodoo said. I took the cash and threw it on the small table next to the bed. While we waited on them to come back, I took one of the Techs and acted like I was inspecting it for any flaws. I took a clip, put it in and took it out. After a few more times of that, my last time removing the clip I put it in my back pocket. The trio finally came back.

Sandy spotted the guns and came to pick up one of the Tech Nines from the bed. "Baby is this for me?"

"I'm afraid not, but I do have one of these for you," I told her. Reluctantly she put down the Tech and took up the 9mm. "Hey look at it this way, they both shoot the same type of rounds and can almost do the same type of damage."

"I know, but I like this one better." I reached in the bag and got her two full clips. Next I did the same for Toni. She took the gun drew back and locked the slide. She looked down the barrel, making sure it was clear, then released it. "You know you're a natural with a gun in your hand," I said, respecting her gangsta.

"Thanks", she said, sticking the gun behind her back, "that's what crippin' will do for you." I had to laugh at that. Next came Candy. "Come here, the homie already told me how you feel and I can see it in your eyes, but here's the thing, either you take this weapon, load and unload it like we taught you or the whole thing is off."

"Hold up", Yellow Bird said, "ain't no way you callin' this shit off."

"Check this out cuzz, I'm not callin' nothing off, she is! We fuckin' with the United States Government, do y'all understand that shit? Each one of you niggaz' is taking something that shoots, and if some bull shit goes down tonight, y'all asses better try to stop whoever is standing in our way."

"So again, Candy pick up that pistol and load it." This time she did as ordered. I snatched up their money from the table, walked over and whispered in her ear, "Are you callin' this shit off or not?" She shook her head no and I handed her damn near seven thousand dollars. "I love you and you're gonna' make it home just fine." Then I gave her a kiss on her cheek and told Yellow Bird and Voodoo, "it was nice doing business with y'all. Always bet on Black."

I had no intentions of shooting anybody, especially not Yellow Bird, but you always need a backup plan and scaring them with a gun was gonna' be mine. Lucky for me I was able to talk Candy into taking the weapon. I know she's scared but I want everybody armed, I also know she's a follower and not a leader. If it had been her that came up with this plan, then I would be trying to convince Sandy to carry the weapon.

"Hey you two got any more cash on you?"

"I stay with a pocket full of money," Voodoo said.

"I'm busted", Yellow Bird said, "but give me a couple of hours, I'll have so much money I might have to buy bigger pants cause they got bigger pockets."

"Alright funny man. Candy give this fool $200 for me, I'll make sure you get it back."

"Hey what was this for anyway?"

"These two fools bet me I couldn't talk you into carrying a gun."

"Y'all up in here betting on me like it's a game?"

"That's the point, it's not a game and I needed you to know that."

"But what about the bet?"

"What about it, you the only one that came out on top."

"Sandy, Toni, how much money do you have on you?" I asked.

"I'm pretty much tapped out," Toni said.

"Sandy?"

"I got like $400 on me," Sandy replied.

"Hold the fuck up, how in the hell you got $400 when I gave you $300 to buy clothes for the three of ya'll?" I asked.

"Um, you told me to steal it," Sandy said, with a sly grin.

"That's what I'm talkin' about", Voodoo said, "why buy shit when you can steal it?"

"You know what, I can't even be mad at yo' ass, but y'all could've gone to jail for some bullshit shop lifting charge."

"I stayed in the van," Candy said.

"Stop telling," Toni told her, "you ain't in court."

"Alright, what's done is done. Give Toni half of that $400."

"Do I have to?"

"Bitch you better kick the fuck in," I said, getting agitated. Reluctantly she did.

"Look, it's after 9:30 p.m., Yellow Bird I want you to call across the street and tell them niggaz' to pack up, we leave here in twenty minutes." Before anyone could go to asking questions I told Sandy to come here. I took her in my arms and told her, "Sandy, you know I meant what I said right?"

"What's that?"

"That I love you." She looked up at me and I saw pure joy in her eyes. She kissed and held me so tight, it was like she had been waiting to hear that all her life.

"I love you too Black."

"Ain't that so sweet," Toni said, laughing.

"Man why are y'all still here? Go make the call cuzz, and ya'll clean out your rooms, 'cause I don't think we'll be coming back. You two go do the same," I said, motioning my hand towards Toni and Voodoo.

"Why we leaving so early?" Voodoo said.

"Actually we're not, by the time we get everyone in place it will be midnight or very close to it, and we still need to see what's gonna' happen when Toni turns that alarm off." As everyone left the room I grabbed Sandy by the ass and kissed her once more. "You ready for this baby girl?"

"You know it, we're about to get paid in a major way."

"Look you need to gather our few things together so we can get outta' here." But instead of listening to me, she held my hands to her ass and kissed me once more. When she came up for air I told her,

"You know you making my dick hard as fuck?"

"Good, I love it when yo' dick gets hard, now go lock the door real quick."

"Sandy we don't have the time for this right now."

"There's always time, now go lock the damn door." I did what I was told, and when I came back to her she said, "Now show me how much you love me." Before I knew it my pants were down, she pushed me on the bed and showed me her amazing head game. I'm telling you she sucked on my dick like it was her last meal. Sometimes it's hard to believe someone so young knows how to get down like this. Her hand and mouth found a cool rhythm and my shit seem to grow bigger by the second. She was going so fast and it felt so good I started talking to her.

"That's right girl, you better suck that shit." I took her hand away so she could take it all the way into her mouth. She then took her tongue and just licked around the tip of my dick and I almost lost it. She was jacking me off now. I wanted to cum bad as fuck and I think she knew it 'cause she went back to deep throating my shit. "Baby you need to stop, I'm telling you, you need to stop." But she ignored me and kept pumping away. She tried to come up for some air but I held her head and nutted deep in her mouth. With my shit still throbbing in her mouth I finally let her go so she could take a much needed breathe.

After I told her to go clean herself up I laid there a few more minutes thinking about what we were about to do and what it would mean if we pulled this shit off. We definitely needed to get out the dope game, or not so much as get out, but get out from under this Mexican Drug Cartel we've been fuckin' with for the last four years. They've been supplying us cocaine dirt cheap and I know they have gotten use to our money.

So, for us to stop buying our product from would be a major problem. There's only one or two ways to end this. Plan A, I offer them five hundred thousand dollars in cash, and if that doesn't work I'll go to Plan B. Which is, I'll take Yellow Bird, Voodoo and our six-man team and go on a killin' spree. We'll figure out how to get as many of them around that fool Oscar as possible, and then dust they asses off.

I jumped up and fixed my pants, moments later Sandy came out in all black. Looking at her, all I noticed was hips and ass in her black jeans. After that cold head game she put down, I really could have gone for some pussy too. My shit got hard again and I was on my way to her when someone knocked at the door. "Yo' ass lucky," I said, making a U-turn.

"Nah nigga you the lucky one, I know you was coming for what's in these jeans. But right now you work for me and you got a job to do."

"So I can't have none?"

"Nope, but you can open the door." She turned around and bent over to tie her shoes. Voodoo was standing in the doorway when I opened it, and as soon as he got a glimpse of Sandy bent over tying her shoe his eyes got wide and he said, "cuzz look at all that ass!" She looked over her shoulder and smiled at us.

"Homie if you want my opinion, I'd put that shit on a postcard and sell it all over the world, you'd make a killin'."

"Thanks Voo, that's so sweet of you," Sandy said, sarcastically

"Yeah yeah. Is y'all ready to go?" he asked.

"Yeah, we're on our way. Sandy will you stop teasing me with yo ass and come on, let's go."

SANDY

What I did to Black was just to take the edge off, now I was in beast mode. Everyone was down in the parking lot.

"Alright y'all it's time for business. Black give Candy her gun and ammo. Toni get the two-ways and head sets. As for the six of you, I already know you guys picked out spots to cover us from, but here's the deal. If a police car comes near our building you are not to do anything. But if they so much as turn a light on and shines it in our direction you let his ass have it."

"Sandy!" Candy yelled.

"Sandy nothing, this is our life here and it's either put his ass down in a major way or we're going to prison for a long ass time. And guess what Sis'. I'm not going to jail for shit, feel me?" There was nothing she could really say. "Black we'll follow you so we'll know where this warehouse is, from there we can find somewhere to park and wait on our turn to go in."

"Alright cool," Black said, "# Five remember that you need to get rid of those cameras."

"I'll take care of it, don't trip."

"Alright look y'all," I said, "we need to move as fast as we can. Black, don't you and Voodoo go looking for shit, the van is right there, open it up and start throwing shit in there. When Candy and I go in we'll get our initial target, then with Voodoo's help we'll start loading up the van and we're out."

"Is everybody good on all that?" There was no complaints so I said, "Let's move out." Candy and I followed the guys in the first van and Toni was behind us.

"What the hell has gotten into you?" Candy asked me.

"What?"

"The way you was laying out everyone's movements."

"I don't know, I'm the one that came up with this shit, and I wanted to show that I was in charge. Black do you read me?" I called over the radio.

"Yeah I got you, what's up?"

"I want you to do a radio check with everybody." Within moments all of us checked in.

"Sandy we're all good."

"Come in Voodoo."

"Yeah go ahead."

"You know you have to make the first move, you ready?"

"I've been ready, I just loaded the dart gun."

"How are you gonna' get to him?"

"I have no idea, we'll have to play it by ear. But the one good thing we have on our side is, no man can resist a beautiful woman in distress."

"Yeah, and we have three," Yellow Bird chimed in.

"Okay, I see what you're saying. If need be, I'll get him out in the street by saying my car broke down."

"Voodoo you just make sure yo' ass hit the right target with that thing."

"Don't worry I got you. Besides, I don't wanna have to kick Black's ass."

"Nigga please, it wasn't that much ass kickin' in Roots."

"Sandy, don't worry I'll hit him dead in the ass."

"Okay, then we need you to go to work on that door."

"I'm on it."

"Black, before you do anything make sure you get that van running."

"Baby girl, you're starting to sound nervous. Everyone knows what to do."

"I don't do nervous. I just want this shit done right."

"It looks like we've created a monster," Toni said.

"Yo' ass just make sure that alarm system is off."

"Don't worry about me I know what I'm doing. Shit if I had two more hands I would have turned it off while I was driving."

"Whatever. Black how much further?"

"About a mile and a half, we're almost there. Now get yo' ass off the radio before you run every one's batteries down."

Someone thought that was funny, it was probably one of the hit squad. "I just wanted to make sure everyone is on their toes."

"We are, now relax. We'll be there in a few minutes." For the next five minutes the radios were silent.

"Candy, you know we're gonna' pull this off, right?"

"You keep saying that so I have to believe it. But what I do wanna' do once we're home is put some protection on ourselves."

"I'm not following you."

"When we unload this van we stop at our money, then we go rent a storage unit and park our money in there until we get it divided up between the three of us."

"What, you don't trust them?" I asked.

"That has nothing to do with it. You never know what can happen. We agreed to split everything else with them, and while we're doing that I want our money somewhere they're not."

"Okay I feel you sis, and even if they ask we can tell them we are going to stash our money like we had planned. You know we can't leave it there long."

"Sandy I told you I'm putting mine in the bank. I'll rent as many safety deposit boxes as it takes to stash four million dollars. I'm telling you Sandy, you and Toni should do the same thing."

"I hear you, I may be the bold one, but your logical ways will pay off in the long run."

"Well I hope you really believe that, 'cause I don't want you to spend any money for at least a year."

"What! A year, why in the hell are we doing this shit if we can't enjoy it?"

"Yo ass can enjoy it all you want this time next year."

"Girl you trippin'," I said, nonchalantly.

"No you trippin', didn't you just call me logical?"

"Yeah."

"Okay then, you need to listen to me. These white folks are gonna' come looking for this money and all that other stuff, and if yo big head ass start popping up with shit you know niggaz' in Compton can't afford, you're going to jail, and you're gonna' take the rest of us with you. Didn't we have this conversation already?"

"Yeah, but nobody said anything about waiting a whole year to spend some money."

"Shit, do what you been doing."

"Yeah, what's that?"

"Spend Black's money." Smiling I gave her a high five.

Black's voice broke up our laughter. "Alright y'all here we go, here we go." As he spoke the two Lincolns sped by and broke off in two different directions. The forward van slowed almost to a stop.

"Sandy you read me?"

"I'm here."

"The building on the right is our target. The warehouse portion is down this alley way."

"Okay I got you."

"Toni, you see that?"

"I got you Black."

"Okay, from what I can see there's no one around, not even the security guard. Just so everybody knows, he drives a blue and white truck."

"Where do you suppose he is?" I asked.

"Don't know, but we might have to let someone else take care of him."

"Come in # One," Black called.

"Go ahead boss."

"Hey, did you plan to put anyone in that alley way?"

"No, we have long range weapons. But if you think I should I'll reposition some of my men."

"Yeah, there's two dumpsters in there, I think one man on each side would be good. One of them can take out the guard with the tranquilizer gun if he shows up. It's 11:10 p.m. so get them into position fast. Sandy, Toni follow me."

Black drove two blocks and turned left, we made a very big circle giving the others time to get ready. "Toni you read me?"

"Yes."

"Do you know the address?"

"Yes, it's posted on my computer screen."

"Good, you see this parking lot coming up on your right? I want you to park in there, back the van in so you can see the direction we just came from and go to work."

"I understand."

"Sandy. I want you to go back down this street to where we first made that left turn and find somewhere to park. When we get the word from Toni that she was able to turn that alarm off we're going in."

"What about the guard?" I asked him.

"We can't worry about him, if he shows up he'll be dealt with. Remember everyone, blue and white truck. Now go kick back until you're up."

"Okay baby, be careful."

"I will."

Chapter 24

BLACK BIRD

"# One you there?"

"Yeah boss."

"You got your guys in place?"

"Everyone is where they need to be."

"Good, we're gonna' make one more trip around then we're going in. Who do you have in the alley?"

"# Three and # Four."

"Alright. # Five you ready?"

"Ready boss."

"Alright do yo' thang." Moments later he came back.

"Boss, we have two shots two kills. Both of the cameras are disabled," #Five said.

"Good work baby boy."

"Listen up everybody, we'll be back in about five minutes. Toni, how you doing?"

"We're almost ready, I just need a couple more minutes, and you rushing me ain't helping."

"Sorry about that. Voo you ready?"

"Man let's do this shit."

"Okay you take the tools and I'll take the dart gun to the trash bin." I stopped the van and Yellow Bird and I changed places. "Keith, since you're going in after the girls I want you to find somewhere further away to park."

"Black come in, come in Black."

"Go ahead Toni."

"It won't work, I can't turn the shit off," Toni said, sounding frantic.

"What the hell you mean you can't turn it off? You've done this shit three or four times already."

"Ahh nigga I'm just fuckin' with yo' ass. Actually it's been off for a few minutes now and nothing has come over the scanner. You can go in when you're ready."

"Yo' ass need to stop playin'," Sandy broke in, "you damn near made me pee myself."

"Candy give her ass a cup, I'm out, I got work to do," Toni said.

"Boss you got some cold chicks on yo' team," #One said, over the radio.

"Tell me about it."

"Toni, are you sure we're good to go?" I asked, double checking.

"Yeah, but if I was you I'd make one more trip around to make sure no one shows up."

"Alright." But this time when we passed the warehouse and made it to the corner we went right instead of left. About four minutes later we was passing Toni's van again, and there was a slight glow from her computer screen. "Alright # Three, # Four, we're coming into the alley way now." I told Yellow to go down to the end and turn around. "Voo this is it." When the van stopped we jumped out, I ran to the dumpster and Voodoo ran up the ramp full speed and slammed into the bay door. He hit it so hard it sounded like a gun shot. Then I realized what he did. He jammed the shears into the lower portion of the door making a hole.

In under two minutes he had a hole large enough for us to crawl through. Once we were inside I had to hold him still, and I did a radio check. Everyone was good and all was quiet. "Alright baby boy, let's get to work." I looked around in amazement, the inside looked three times bigger than it did from outside. "Voo, get the back doors to the van open." I went to the driver's side and opened the door. From the inside of the van the fifty kilo's we expected to get, looked more like eighty. There were no keys in the ignition, so I checked the visor, no luck. But right under the front seat there they were. After about three tries I was able to get it started. I could tell it had a strong engine under the hood, and after a few more revs I shut it down.

When I jumped out the van I noticed the big ass hole in the bay door. At that moment, I wish I had some duct tape, but I just went over and pushed it closed as much as I could.

"Black you there?"

"What's up Toni?"

"When I first got into their inventory, I found a bunch of cocaine sitting on the floor, and from the looks of it, it's still there."

"Alright I'll take a quick look around." The first row of inventory was only a few feet away from the van and Voodoo had already thrown several large boxes inside the van. About twenty feet away was a pallet of cocaine sitting there. I could see around a corner, and sitting there was a 63 Chevy Low Rider so clean, I wished I could have put that in the back of the van, but I stuck to the script. I took six at a time and started throwing them in the van.

"Hey my nigga, how come you didn't come up with this shit?"

"Cause fool, I don't sit around watching T.V. all day." Once I was done I told him to keep working.

"I'm going to help the twins out."

"Alright just hurry up."

"Come in Toni."

"I'm here, talk to me."

"Look, I see a fork lift in here and I wanna' make things a lil' easier for the twins. Where's their target located?"

"Just a moment...Here it is. I have it on row six which should be "F" on the third shelf. The number on the container should be 489010, do you see it?"

"Nah, you know how much shit is in here?"

"From what I can tell it should be on the left side of the aisle."

"Okay I got it, this is a pretty big box."

Sandy chimed in once again, "Baby will it fit in the van?"

"Yeah, you'll have plenty of room."

"Okay." When I went back to get the fort lift I saw that Voodoo had put in major work. "Man," he said, "this place got all kind of shit in here. I've already thrown five boxes of cash in here."

"Cool, keep it up, as soon as I get this box down I'll come help you."

"Do yo' thang my nigga."

The forklift was electric so the only noise was the beep-beep-beep backing-up warning. Within minutes, I was able to get the box down and moved out to the front. The twins can take it from there, I thought. Next I went to start taking boxes and other stuff from the racks. The first box I took said Hand Guns on the label, there were thirty of them in all. My first thought was Sandman and the other lil' homies out there protecting the hood. We took another ten minutes of filling the van. "What do you think, we got enough?" I asked Voodoo.

"Yeah. Call the twins and get them ready to move."

"Toni, how does things look out there?"

"You're all good, there's nothing on the scanner and no vehicles has come down this street."

"Alright good. Sandy y'all get ready to move. I'm on my way out."

As I went to the bay door, Voodoo had thrown a few more things in the van. At the door there was indeed a lock on the pull chain. I took the bolt cutters he dropped on the floor and made short work of the Master lock. When I came back to the van I threw the cutters on the floor board. "You're good to go," Voodoo said, "but check this out, I'm layin' claim to this." He handed me what looked like a plastic wrapped cinder block.

"Nigga you know this ain't nothing but some Stress from Mexico?"

"I don't care, some of that shit be pretty good, and I won't have to buy no weed for at least a year."

"Alright," I said, throwing it over to the passenger seat. "Go get the door. I'm out! See you back at the house." I hit the two-way. "Sandy get moving, I'm leaving the building now. Has anyone out there noticed how long that took?" I asked.

"Twenty minutes." # One said.

"Nigga sometimes I swear yo' ass been in the military."

"Just doing my job."

"Alright, try to make sure everyone else doesn't spend longer than twenty minutes in there."

"I got you boss." I flashed my lights and Voodoo pulled the door up. By the time I reached the streets, Sandy was turning into the alley way. I waved to her and got in the wind.

VOODOO

Sandy was able to get the van in and turned around. The three of us got their box of cash in the van. After that everything went smoothly. It seemed like in no time at all # One came over the radio. "Sandy, y'all at twenty-five minutes, it's time to move out."

"Alright we're done," she replied.

"Yellow Bird you're up." The twins made their way out the building, they passed Keith a block away. Candy made sure he seen her waving at him. Over the radio he told her to be careful. My boy came in and turned around, and just like everyone else he was taken aback by what he saw. So I had to move him into action.

I had already loaded two vans so he was doing most of the work. Him being no stranger to hard work, he had the van full in fifteen minutes. Also being the street nigga he was, the last box he took off the shelf was full of hundred dollar bills, and he filled all four of his pockets and threw the rest in the van. "Voodoo I'm ready to get out of here, get the door. Come in Mad Scientist."

"I'm here Yellow."

"Look, can you move your van without turning off your computer?"

"I don't know, why?"

I was trying to decide whether to bring you in."

"There's only one way to find out, I'm on my way."

Yellow Bird had another thought. He went and got the last box he threw in the van. He started up and signaled for me to open the door, then hit the two-way. "# Three you there?"

"Right here boss, what's up?"

"When I come out come over to the van." As he pulled out # Three was there to meet him, and cuzz handed him the box of cash. "Here you go, this is just a lil' something extra for y'all. I don't know how much it is, but it's a lot."

"Man good lookin' out."

"We still got you guys on your other payment, see you in a few hours."

"Alright bet."

As he drove off # Three sat the box behind the dumpster and jumped back in. Toni came racing into the alley way like she was in the Long Beach Grand Prix. "Girl," Yellow Bird yelled into the radio, "will you slow the hell down."

"Sorry about that, the van acted like it didn't wanna' start."

"Just take it easy. I'll see you back at the house." Before he got too far away he asked if anyone seen the guard.

One said, "The only movement on the street was our own."

"Alright, keep your eyes open, his ass will have to show up sooner or later, we're on the last van, so we might have missed him."

"We got you boss." Toni was safely inside with the door closed.

"Baby look at all this stuff, where do we start?"

"We pretty much cleared this first row, so go over there and get started."

The first ten minutes went smoothly, then out of nowhere she heard laughter. When she turned the corner a man and woman was standing there. She had no shirt or bra on, and he was holding a bottle of Jack Daniels. It was the security guard; he's been in the building the whole time. Toni was the first to react, she dropped the four brief cases she was holding and went for her gun. I was at the other end of the aisle, something down there had caught my attention. But without the slightest hesitation she jacked off a round and started to fire.

The guard, although under the influence saw what was coming and reacted in two ways. He pulled the woman in front of him as he dropped the bottle, then he went for his gun. Toni put two hot slugs in the woman's upper body. Surprised by not hitting who she was aiming at, it almost cost her, her life. But the guard being shook up like he was, fired too low and too fast. Toni screamed bloody murder when the hot slug hit her just above the knee. I reacted when I heard her drop the brief cases. On the run I took the Tech Nine from around my neck and when I reached Toni I just stuck the gun around the comer and emptied the clip, then I reached down and pulled her outta' sight of whoever was out there.

I keyed my mic and told # Three and Four to get in here, fast! There was no movement or sound other than Toni, so I reached down and took her gun and eased out. There was two bodies about thirty feet away. They finally made it to us. "What happen?" # Three asked.

"She took a hit. Toni can you hear me?"

"Hell yeah I hear you, now stop yellin' and do something."

"Move," # Four said. He took off his belt and made a tourniquet around her leg. When he pulled and tied it she screamed again. She was sweating like crazy, but a moment later she held out her hands to be helped up. # One came over the radio.

"Everything alright in there?"

"Yeah, we got two dead and one of ours is wounded."

"Where in the hell did they come from?" # One came back. I hit my mic.

"It look like the guard was with a hooker, they came from the offices. I don't know how they didn't hear us."

"Voodoo, get outta' there."

"We will, but first we need to find a First Aid Kit. Did you hear any of that shooting out there?"

"No, and hopefully no one else did either," he replied.

"Alright look, y'all stay put and as soon as we look after her we'll be out."

"# One this is Three."

"What's up?"

"There's a box of money out behind that dumpster I was in, make sure someone goes to get it."

"I'm on it."

We got her over to the van. "Look one of y'all go over to that office and look for a First Aid Kit"

"I'm alright Voodoo."

"I'mma' act like I didn't hear that." # Four came back with the kit.

"I got this," he said, "look out."

"Voodoo."

"What is it baby?"

"I didn't mean to shoot that woman. He pulled her right in front of him."

"It's okay, you did what you had to do. Cuzz, you make sure she's alright, we need to go collect them empty shells in case somebody's prints are on them."

When we got back to Toni, it turned out the bullet basically tore a chunk of flesh from her leg. So # Four cleaned her wound and wrapped it up. She had already stopped bleeding. "See I told you I was alright."

"Thanks homie, you did a good job, now let's get the fuck outta' here."

"Hold up," Toni said. She hit her mic. "# One, is there any movement out there?"

"No it's all quiet."

"Alright we'll be out in a few minutes."

"What the hell are you doing?" I asked her.

"I ain't doing shit, but the three of you are gonna' finish loading this van up. Just make sure you don't hit any of the computer equipment."

"Man I like yo' girl," # Three said.

"You sure you didn't get hit in the head?"

"No but give me my gun back in case someone else shows up."

"Yeah she got heart alright," # Three said.

"Cool, y'all heard her, let's move." About ten minutes later # One told us it was time to get out.

"We're on our way." The two of them helped Toni up and into the van as I started it up. "Hey, give me the First Aid Kit, we might need it again."

"We're all good," # Four said.

"Alright open the door and we're out."

Chapter 25

VOODOO

I made it to the freeway and about ten minutes into our trip home Toni gave up a small moan. "How you doing over there?"

"I'm okay, it just hurts a little bit."

"Why don't you see if there is any pain pills in that kit?"

"No I'm cool."

"Yes you are, the way you handled yo'self was like a true gangsta."

"Maybe, but I'm still fucked up in the head about that lady, what if she has kids?"

"Look you can't do that to yo'self, if that white boy wasn't a coward, he would have pushed her out the way, but his punk ass did just the opposite. He got her killed not you."

"You know what I'm worried about more than anything?"

"What's that?"

"Tellin' my mama I got shot!"

We laughed and she gave up another moan. After a while she fell asleep. It was coming up on four in the morning and I had to make myself slow down. Now she was on the passenger's side moaning more and more, and I was starting to get worried. At 5:20 a.m. Atlantic Blvd. was right there. I got off the freeway and was making the few minute drive to

Black's house then it hit me. I had six armed killers following me. Instead of turning into their hood I kept going across Long Beach Blvd.

and went into South Side hood. I pulled into Winchell's Donuts and got # One out to talk.

"Check this out, y'all did a smooth job tonight but look, find somewhere to stay. Another motel or something. This coming afternoon we'll call you and have your full payment. You cool with that?"

"Not a problem. We'll see you in a few hours." After they left I took my cell phone and called Black. There was no answer. His ass must be sleep. I hung up, waited a few seconds and tried again. This time he answered on the third ring.

"What's up nigga, where you at?"

"Here in Compton, we're at Winchell's."

"Is everything alright?"

"Look, I sent # One and his boyz' to find a motel and told them we'll be at them this afternoon."

"Alright cool, but it still sounds like something is wrong. Where's Toni?"

"She's right here but she's hurt, I'll explain when we get there. You got room for the shit in this van?"

"Yeah, we should be alright."

"Cool, I'll be there in a few minutes."

"Alright bet."

We made it to the house in just a few minutes. The yard was clear so I backed the van into the drive way. When Toni woke up and saw where we were, all she wanted to know was where her Lexus was. I would have thought they were all sleep but as soon as I parked the van all four of them rushed Toni's window.

I went to try and take her from the van.

"Move nigga damn, you act like I'm half dead."

"I'm just tryin' to help." Seeing her leg bandage up, the twins said, in unison.

"What happen?"

"She got shot."

"Oh my god!" Candy cried, "move Voodoo, I told you something like this would happen. Sandy help me get her in the house." She tried to push them away, but when she moved her leg the pain almost made her start to cry.

"Fuck that," Yellow Bird said, moving past the twins to pick her up. This time without complaint she allowed it and he took her towards the house, but again all she wanted to know was where her car was. "It's a couple of houses down with the twins' Jetta's. Don't worry, it's safe." He got her inside and the twins immediately started nursing her and asking questions. I gave them the rundown of how they came from somewhere inside and about the shooting.

"Y'all should have seen her, she went right into beast mode."

"Fuck that," Candy cried, "we need to get her to a hospital."

"That's what we can't do, you left two people dead back in that warehouse, and the first thing that will happen when they're found, is see Toni's blood and check hospitals for anyone with a gunshot wound."

"Why you say me? I didn't kill anyone."

"It was rhetorical, you, them, all of us was involved and they're not gonna' care who pulled the trigger, you got two white people dead, and just because it's 2016, they still give out the death penalty for murder/robbery."

"God damn you Sandy, I told you this shit would happen."

"Candy stop worrying I'm alright, in a few days it will start to heal."

"In a few days, how in the hell are you gonna' explain this shit to Stacy?"

"I have no idea, but I do know this, it's almost six in the morning and I'm hungry as hell, so who's cooking breakfast?"

"I got you," Black said, "one bowl of Cap n' Crunch coming right up."

"Damn, you can't cook?"

"Not right now, you said you're okay and we need to get this last van unloaded."

"Speaking of vans, why is it only one out there?"

"Well for right now our two are on Greenleaf in the field, we'll take them back to the junk yard later.

"The twins said you guys are taking your money with you when you leave here," Black said.

"And you're okay with that?" I asked.

"Hey it's their money."

"Where in the hell are you gonna' stash fourteen million bucks?" I couldn't help but ask.

"Candy tell him."

"Why under my mattress of course." They all thought that shit was funny. "Don't trip we got a safe spot."

BLACK BIRD

"Come on y'all let's go unload this van, I'm tired as hell." But before I went outside I bent down and kissed Toni on top of her head. "I'm proud of you, you took care of business."

She managed to give me a smile. The cargo from the other three vans filled both bedrooms and a good portion of the garage. Our task took us just over an hour. When we were done, we took a moment to stand back and marvel at our handy work.

"Will you look at all this shit," Voodoo said, "Black it's gonna' take us a week to sort all this out."

"So, you got somewhere to be?"

"What about my Sacramento run Tuesday?"

"We might not make that run."

"Are you serious?"

"Yeah, we got so much cocaine and heroin, and no tellin' what else, we can cut these dudes loose once and for all."

"Nah Black," Yellow Bird shot back, "it would be good to make this last run."

"Alright, when that time comes we'll see what's up, but right now I don't see a reason to."

"Look y'all, tell me what you think. I was thinking of offering them a half million dollars in cash, then we can dump this shit until it's gone. Then it's like Sandy said, strippers, strippers and more Strippers."

"Shit," Yellow Bird said, "I like the sound of that. But do you think they will take the money?"

"We're not gonna' give them much of a choice," I said.

"It sounds like some killin' needs to be done," Voodoo said.

"Hopefully it won't come to that, but if it does, we'll take our hit squad and go on one, feel me?" I said.

YELLOW BIRD

See what I mean? This nigga is almost foaming at the mouth and we're only saying we might have to do some dirty work. I don't know what it is, but something is not right about cuzz. We've been fuckin' with him for some years and I'm surprised I haven't noticed this shit before. Then again I might just be trippin'.

VOODOO

This is the second time cuzz has looked at me like this. His ass keep on thinking what I know he's thinking, and I'mma' stop his thinking right along with his fuckin' breathing.

BLACK

For some reason they was looking at each other strangely. I started to say something but something caught my eye. It was four brown brief cases. It was something about them that got my attention. I told Yellow Bird to close the garage. "We'll get all the vans over to Chico in a lil' while." Then I took the cases into the house. When I walked in the living room Toni was still laying on the couch.

"I see those got your attention too. I was carrying those when the shooting started," Toni said. Then she added, "Not sure what's in them, but out of all the shit we brought home I wanted to see what was inside."

"Well don't talk about it, be about it," Voodoo said.

"Black, open them up and let's see if I made a wise choice," Toni said. I put the cases down on the coffee table and looked at her.

"Since you found them, you do the honors," I told her. When Toni opened the first case, everyone was filled with amazement.

"Oh shit, look at this," Toni said, in astonishment. The case was full of diamonds. Sandy grabbed the next case and it too was full of diamonds.

"Toni you didn't know what was in these?" I asked.

"No."

"Then I see why. All the cases we're tagged, but for some reason the tags were inside the brief cases.

"Shit," I said, "we can take all this other shit back, these four cases alone has made us millionaires. Just like the previous two, the next two cases were full of diamonds as well. Each tag told how many each case held, but the numbers were all different. "Candy this job belongs to you and you alone. You're gonna' split these up into six."

"Why her?" Sandy shouted.

"Cause, outta' everyone in this room yo' sister is about the only one that doesn't have sticky fingers, that's why. Now take these, go in the kitchen, get six of the largest mixing bowls you can find and get crackin'."

"But I'm sleepy," Candy cried.

"Girl you know rich people don't sleep," Sandy said.

"Here," Toni said, handing Candy the cereal bowl she was eating out of, "I like my diamonds with milk."

"Ah shut up nigga." We all laughed as she walked off.

TONI

While Candy was doing that, everybody else tried to stay busy. Black took the guys and drove the vans back to the junk yard. But before he left he asked me about the computer equipment. "Get rid of it, I'm going high tech. The twins already got me a new lap top."

"Alright cool, we'll be back in about an hour, you need anything?" Black asked.

"No I'm good."

Voodoo walked over and asked, "You still love me right?"

"I wouldn't go that far, but if you're asking am I mad at you, the answer is no, and here's a big kiss to prove it. Now get outta' here."

"Alright see you later."

Candy was over at the dining room table sorting the diamonds. Sandy went to take a shower, and I was already sick of laying on the couch. So, moving as carefully as I could, I went to sit next to Candy. When she looked up, she was surprised to see me sitting there.

"What are you doing?"

"I'm tired of lying there. I told you it's not that bad."

"I hope so," Sandy said, with concern in her voice.

She had medical supplies.

"Alright you, it's time to clean your leg."

"I thought you were taking a shower?"

"I did."

"That was quick," I told her.

"Girl you know her and water don't get along."

"Fuck you bitch."

"Whatever," Candy said, laughing.

"Sandy I sure hope you know what you're doing."

"Just be still, I got this. Where did the fellaz go?"

"To get rid of the vans."

"Good. Candy you need to hurry up, I wanna' leave before they come back. By 8:00 a.m. some self-storage places should be open."

"Where you wanna' find one?" I asked.

"I don't know, Paramount, Lakewood, South Gate, anywhere but Compton or Watts."

"I say Lakewood."

"Okay. Lakewood it is," she replied.

Candy was down to the last briefcase, taking a handful at a time and dropping one piece in each bowl. Sandy was finishing up with my leg. She cut the gauze and as she began to tie the knot she said, "See, that didn't hurt a bit." But just for spite she pulled way tighter on the knot than she needed to.

"Ouch, what kind of doctor are you?" I half yelled. Smiling, she wrapped up everything and took it to the trash.

"Toni will you help me with this please?"

"Alright, but yo' big head sister bet not come in here talkin' shit."

"Does your leg feel better?"

"Yeah, she actually did a good job."

"You know that shit could have been a lot worse?"

"Yeah, but it wasn't, so stop worrying, we got away with this shit and we're rich as fuck."

"Yeah let's hope so."

The two of us were able to finish before Sandy could bother us. Sandy brought Candy some sliced apples and buttered toast. "Here you go sis, I can't remember the last time I seen you eat."

"Thanks, did you eat something?"

"Yeah. Y'all almost done?"

"Yeah. You know this is some beautiful shit, but I wouldn't wanna' do this again. Sandy go in there and see if you can find some zip lock bags." Moments later she yelled she couldn't find any.

"Girl these niggaz' sell drugs for a living," I yelled back, "it's some in there somewhere." Finally she came back with an unopened box.

"These were over the refrigerator along with like ten other boxes."

"See what I told you. I bet if you look hard enough you'll find a lot of Baking Soda too." In the end there was four diamonds left. Candy took one and dropped it in a bowl and slide it to me.

"Here you go baby girl, since you took one for the team, you get this one."

"What about those?" Sandy asked.

"These three my mini me, I'm going to take and have identical necklaces made for us."

Next she took the bowls and dumped them into bags. We each took a bag and left the other three on the table. Right next to the front door Sandy found our car keys. "Y'all ready to go?"

"Yeah, who's driving?" I asked.

"Sandy you take the van, Toni and I will go in my car."

"Wait, before we go will one of y'all go bring my car down here and put it in the drive way?"

"Man ain't nobody thinkin' about that damn Lexus."

"Hey, what about me takin' one for the team and all that?"

"Candy, go get her car please."

"Give me the keys."

"Sandy, do you think one of us should stay here? I mean it's not like we can lock the place up.

"You wanna' stay?"

"I don't care. I just want my car."

Candy shook her head and took off down the street. We heard the engine of the Lexus rev, then she took off so quick the tires gave up a slight squeal. Moments later she was pulling into the drive way. When she got out she said, "I see why you so hyped over this thang, that short trip was almost sexual."

"See, that bitch is bad ain't it?"

"Yeah, I might have to get Sandy to buy me one of these."

"You can have one of these if you want, I got my sights set a little higher. Benz baby sis."

"Well as long as you remember our agreement," Candy told her.

"What agreement?"

"We spend no major money for one year."

"Let me guess, you're scared we'll go to jail?"

"Hell yeah, somebody is gonna' come lookin' for all this shit, you both know it, especially with what we left behind. So the same goes for you, no buying lavish ass shit, agree?"

Reluctantly I nodded my head. The twins hugged and gave me a kiss then headed to the van, "Candy, you know what? We haven't even looked at our money yet."

"We can do that once we get it outta' the van and into the storage unit." I watched them as they left the house. I rubbed my hand across my Lexus and limped back inside. With nothing to do but wait, I went into one of the rooms and found a pair of sweats and a tee-shirt. Next I made sure the house was locked up and went to take a bath. There was nothing in here built for a woman. I guess these niggaz' don't believe in taking baths.

Running the hot water I looked around. I found some clean towels and some Vo5 Shampoo, which I squeezed into the tub. Then I found something really good. On the sink under a towel there was a cigar box full of weed. Hell, maybe they do relax in the tub every now and then. I rolled a nice joint, undressed and eased down into the hot water. I put my leg up in the corner and closed my eyes for a moment. I fired up my joint and in almost no time at all it went from a joint to a roach. They always seem to have some good ass weed around here. I started thinking about Daishawn and wondered if he will like Voodoo. Or better yet, will Voodoo like him. I've been taking birth control pills since I had the baby, but I know every man wants his own son.

Damn, we been so caught up in this lick, I haven't even asked him if he has any kids of his own. Hell we haven't talked about much of anything besides fuckin' and making money. The sex was almost too good to be true, and now that we have all the money we could possibly need, I guess it's time to see if he wants to know who I am. Or was he just trying to jump up and down in my pussy.

THE CONCLUSION-TONI

Like an hour later I was still high but my bath water had turned cold. I got out, dried off and got dressed. I cleaned the tub as best as I could, fighting through the pain, then I was tempted to roll me another joint, but passed. To my surprise the guys were back. Yellow Bird was sitting at the table playing with his bag of diamonds. "You know Toni," he said, when he saw me, "I don't know who's prettier, you or this bag of ice."

"You bet not let Candy hear you say that." Laughing I limped over to Voodoo. He was sitting on the couch and he had a big ass block of wrapped plastic on his lap.

"What's that?" I asked.

"This here beautiful is all weed."

"Damn, you playin'."

"Nope, and if you want to, you and I can go shack up somewhere and have sex two or three times a day, and smoke this until it's all gone."

"Shit," Black said, sitting across from us, "I like the sound of that."

"Nigga the only part of that that sounds good to you is the sex part."

Before he could say something smart, the twins walked in. When Keith saw Candy he said, "You're just in time."

"In time for what?" She asked.

"We were just talking about very secluded places, having lots and lots of sex, and smoking all of that until it's gone."

"What's that?" Candy asked

"About twenty pounds of weed."

"Sandy, how does that sound to you?" Black asked her smiling and showing his pearly white teeth.

"Baby you know I'm down for whatever."

"Candy what do you think?"

"You know I don't let my sister get too far away from me."

"And you know I need a vacation so my leg can heal up," I added.

"Okay then look, you ladies figure out where you wanna' go, Candy you can find us a good Travel Agent and on the first of July, we're outta' here. So you guys have a little over a week to get y'all shit together. Right now I'm going to go pay off our hit squad and send them home," Black said.

"When I come back I'll get some sleep. But when we come back from our vacation, ya'll know what we're gonna' do.?"

"What's that?" Candy asked.

"We're gonna' take over Compton like Pinky and the Brain tried to take over the world. I'm out!" Black said, as he exited the house.

IT'S HARD <u>STAYING</u> THE SAME

****

ERIC "TURK" CURTIS

Chapter 1

CANDY

The dream was so vivid, I kept hearing Toni scream, then I heard gunshots. They were so close that I sat up in bed trying to catch my breath and wiping my eyes. Looking around, I realized where I was. Keith was sound asleep, but then the sounds came again. Gunshots rang out and I looked towards the open window across the room. I guess he was so used to it, because he didn't move at all.

It was Monday morning and I knew we had to be getting home soon. Sandy, Toni and I knew we were already in hot water with Promise and Stacy, so we decided to just spend the whole week where we were. Late Saturday, Black, Yellow Bird and Voodoo took the vans back that we came home with, then our day turned into two days of hard labor.

It was crazy, everyone staked out a spot for themselves in the house and we started dividing up our loot, as Voodoo kept calling it. Sandy, Toni and I ended with another six million dollars. It took Black three hours to divide it six ways. There were so many kilos of drugs that after the guys got their initial 50 kilos, we started a human chain from Black's bedroom to the living room. It didn't matter whether it was coke or heroin, we just threw bricks into each pile.

Once that was done, we moved into Keith's room and started over. I gotta' tell you, I didn't like what I was seeing. We were only half way through the second room and each pile had no less than forty bricks. I couldn't tell one kilo from another, some had markings, others had writing, a few even had spider's stamps, yet each were about the same in size.

"Anybody wanna' buy a few keys?" Sandy asked, looking around the room at everybody.

"Keith, what are we going to do with all this stuff?" I asked before anyone answered her.

"I know huh," Sandy cut in, "Black said I didn't wanna' be in the dope game, but we ended up in it anyway."

"First of all," Keith said, "we can sit on this shit as long as we need to. There's really no need to move any of it, we have plenty of cash. So y'all don't trip, we'll figure out something later, now we need to finish this shit because we haven't even started on the garage yet."

When it was all said and done, each of us had about two hundred kilos each. There wasn't much weed, and I didn't want none anyway. We did each get a box of jewelry. It was so much still left-over that we just started taking handfuls. Hell, how do you divide up jewelry anyway? Not to mention we had our diamonds. Voodoo told us we should have kept at least one of the vans, because we had so much stuff it would take us days to move it all using our Jetta's and Toni's Lexus. But we needed to get this stuff to the storage unit with our other cash.

Keith ended up letting us use his Escalade, and after two trips we were all done. Even though she tried, we were giving Toni a pass because of her leg, and it was definitely a lot of work for the three of us. Still breathing hard, I waited to hear more gunshots but there was only silence, so I eased outta' bed to get dressed.

Monday morning came way too quickly and I didn't wanna' leave Keith, but it was already passed 9:00 am, so I went to get Sandy and Toni. Thankfully we managed to get outta' the house without Black, Keith or Voodoo knowing we left. As I was hoping, Promise was gone to work by the time Sandy and I got home. I wasted no time. After a hot shower I told Sandy it was time for her to do the same so we could go.

"Go! Go where? We just got home," she cried. "Sandy, we have two weeks to get ready for our trip and I wanna' get as much money into the bank as I can before we leave."

"Damn Candy, we just got here."

"I know," I told her, "and now we're just leaving, so go get ready." Being that this was Sandy I was talking to, she complained some more, but she finally agreed that it wouldn't be a good idea to leave all that money in the storage unit. The drugs and other stuff I really didn't care about.

I brought one thing home with me from the robbery, so before leaving the room to go downstairs I fed the fish some fish food and diamonds.

"Girl what the hell you doin'?" Sandy said, from her bed.

"Shit, I have no idea what to do with them. I damn sure don't know who to sell them to. Besides, who's gonna' notice them in there? As long as no one comes in here and steal the fish tank, they're safe."

"I guess!" Sandy said, as I mixed them around, then left the room.

SANDY

Yeah, all them niggaz' thought I was crazy, now look - I'm the baddest bitch in Compton. I got close to twelve million dollars in cash, a bag full of diamonds, some other jewelry, and so many kilos I could afford to sell them for nine thousand each and still make a killin'. Now all I have to do is figure out - 'sell them to who'? I hate that two people were killed, and that Toni got shot. But the shit still worked out way better than I could have ever dreamed.

And to put icing on the cake, I put the pussy on Black so good, put so much money in his pockets, that the nigga done fell in love with me. You know how we said, 'IT'S HARD STAYING THE SAME?' Well that was especially true for me. Candy wanted us to put all our money in the bank and not touch it for a whole year. Well I just couldn't see it going down like that.

As far as I was concerned, I was still the boss. So while she went to find safety deposit boxes to put her money in, I was in Westwood, buying my first house. I was able to find a don't ask - don't tell sista at a Real Estate Office. With the cash I showed her, she was more than willing to help me...

About the Author

I was raised in Compton, California. I have been incarcerated for just over twenty years. About four years ago, I began to dabble in urban street writing. "It's Hard Being the Same" made me fall in love with writing. From other novels to short stories, I continue to try and come up with new ideas to write about. I hope you enjoy reading "It's Hard Being the Same" as I did writing it.

Photograph by Peter Merts

ERIC 'TURK' CURTIS

Eric 'Turk' Curtis is a creative writer from Compton, California, also known as Hub city. Compton is notorious for it's urban street life, so during his 20 + years of incarceration, Eric discovered a love for the pen in writing classes with instructors like Zoe Mullery. Now he is using his innate and developed skills to tell tales about the city he was raised in. He has completed a trilogy about three young ladies who have dared to take on the streets, love, and even the government - in "It's Hard Being The Same"; "It's Hard Staying The Same"; and "Black Magic". Now he hopes to bring these and other completed, but unpublished works to the world

Available Now...
@www.amazon.com

It's Hard Being The Same. By Eric Curtis

Roxxy. By A.C. Bellard

Ideas More Powerful Than Force. By Ricky Gaines II

Neologic Thought. By Ah'Khemu

Coming Soon...

Street Karma by Leo Fountila IV

Only A Chosen Few by Mack Malik

✻ ✻

For ordering info please visit our website or call
www.capgainesllc.com −302-433-6777

CAPITAL GAINES LLC
4023 Kennett Pike #2082
Wilmington, Delaware 19807
www.capgainesllc.com
Telephone: (415-857-5433)
Email: cg@capgainesllc.com

MAIL PAYMENT TO:

CAPITAL GAINES LLC
4023 Kennett Pike #2082   ORDER YOUR BOOKS AND HAVE THEM DELIVERED QUICKLY
Wilmington, Delaware 19807

TITLE OF BOOK	QUANTITY EACH	TOTAL QUANTITY	METHOD OF PAYMENT	PRICE EACH	TOTAL PRICE
IDEAS MORE POWERFUL THAN FORCE				$15.00	
IT'S HARD BEING THE SAME				$15.00	
ROXXY				$15.00	
TRIUMPH				$10.00	
NEOLOGIC THOUGHT				$10.00	
STREET KARMA				$15.00	
ONLY A CHOOSEN FEW				$15.00	
TOTAL					

SHIP TO:

NAME:
ADDRESS:
CITY/STATE/ZIP CODE:
PHONE:
EMAIL:

FROM:

NAME:
ADDRESS:
CITY/STATE/ZIP CODE:

Made in the USA
Middletown, DE
27 September 2022

11160510R00136